THE T

First published in 2011 as a Kindle edition

Cover Design by James Sadlier: jamessadlier@me.com

This is a romantic thriller, including some mathematical themes, centred on Iran's nuclear ambitions. It features a team of students from the University of Edinburgh and a designer of clocks from near Arbroath, his wife and their dog. The action takes place in Tehran, the Arabian Nights Hotel, a disused betaspodumene mine in the south of Iran, the British Embassy in Muscat, Oman, and in parts of Afghanistan, on Ben Lawers overlooking Loch Tay in Scotland, in London in Number 10 Downing Street and the Foreign Office and on the London Eye.

Enjoy.

Prologue

April 1998

Anheim Mossada gingerly opened the front door of his house and looked outside. It was a clear night and the moon was almost full. That did not matter. The street was so well lit that he would be noticed immediately, moon or no moon, if anyone were about. The moonlight added piquancy, letting him see all the way north-eastwards to the hulking buildings in the city centre where policy was made and justice was meted out. These distant seats of power were framed in his view by two minarets, sombrely silent at this hour. It was 3.30 a.m. Anheim took a deep breath to muster courage. The cool night air in his lungs and the strong aromas from his garden flowers dispelled any sleepiness. He scanned the street. It was deserted, as it had been on the previous two nights, except for the same three cars, two on his left and one farther down on the right at a lamp-post. All three cars looked empty. There was virtually no wind. So the door would not slam shut. He decided to go for it. He fetched a step ladder from the laundry room and tiptoed with it back along the passage to the front door. No sound came from his mother's room downstairs and all was quiet upstairs. He manoeuvred the step ladder through the door, leaving it ajar. Then he ran with the ladder down the short path by the flower bed and crossed the street to the bus stop opposite. He erected the ladder, climbed it, pulled a screwdriver and an adjustable spanner from his hip pocket and began to loosen the nuts and bolts that held the left and right facing plates of the bus sign to the frame. When the plates were about a centimetre apart he reached inside his jerkin and lifted out a black plastic sheath that held his meticulously hand-copied sheets of notes and diagrams. He inserted the sheath between the plates and tightened the nuts with trembling hands. Then he jumped off the ladder and ran with it back into the house.

Safely inside he replaced the step ladder, hoping his heavy breathing would not awaken the household. He was committed now. The insurance policy was in place, almost. He crept into the family room and began to carve his initials and the date-like numbers on the inside of the lid of the window seat. Black ink in the grooves would age the carving, making it look as if it had been done when he was a boy.

Chapter 1

June 1999

On most days Tehran's Square of Righteousness is an oasis of aloof respectability. Overlooked by the Courts of Justice and encircled by six minarets, all within earshot, it demands circumspect behaviour from all who enter. Provided you do not break into a run or gesticulate wildly, but walk with appropriate decorum, you may traverse the square under the watchful eyes of the Fedayin-e Islam, and they will leave you alone. Today is different. For one thing it is exceptionally hot: the thermometer by the doors registers 48 degrees. By now the respectable oasis will be transformed into a crucible of formidable solemnity. The crowds lining it will feel uncomfortable, wishing they were somewhere else, yet fearful of having their absence noted. He almost smiles. That is one fear that need not concern him. For him, of course, it will be the ultimate release. Be dignified, he was warned. Be meek and accepting. Do not shout, wave or try to communicate in any way. Otherwise, he knows, they will drag him back ignominiously to an unspeakable horror in the dreadful dungeons of Death Row, and the next in line will be quickly prepared to undergo the more merciful public execution.

Paradoxically, he realizes, the very pathos of his situation is his last chance at immortality and victory. If by his demeanour he can inspire someone in that crowd to follow the trail and research his story then at least the memory of him will not be consigned to heartless oblivion. If that person is sufficiently brave and clever, he or she may survive to thwart the insane intention of the theocracy. Then the full triumphant story will be passed on from generation to generation. He clings to that hope, rehearsing it again and again throughout the remaining moments of his life.

The glare off the paving stones was intense. Sweltering in her burqa, standing between her parents among the families of other officials on the steps at the top side, Soraya looked down. The police must have the worst of it, she thought, seeing them fan out from the courthouse. They would be facing the sun during the execution. She shuddered, not sure yet whether she could face the ordeal of watching it. It would be her first time. She tried to avoid looking at the heavy brown doors through which the condemned man would be led.

She glanced to each side, trying to gain calmness from her parents' faces. That had always worked in moments of stress. Today their countenances were phlegmatic rather than calm: expressionless, staring straight ahead. She went over what they had told her to prepare her. Only treasonable offences receive the traditional form of execution, her father had said. Culprits of dissent are simply hanged without ceremony: the Fedayin-e Islam sees to that. When she asked what treason had been committed her father said he was not sure. Her mother suggested it went back to the war with Iraq, but that seemed unlikely since a full decade had passed.

She looked at the crowds lining the two sides in front of the shops and cafés. Most of them were shielding their eyes like sailors saluting on deck as their ships left port. She found that by tilting her head she could bring in a seeming patch of blue, reinforcing the impression that the crowds were on battleships. Not everyone down there was silent but voices were subdued. The result, to Soraya's ears, was a low warble, more menacing than the traditional hullabaloo that women made on sending their men off to war.

You are becoming fanciful, she told herself, a sure sign of nerves. Her anxiety was now accompanied by increased physical discomfort. She became aware of heat rising through the soles of her shoes, of sweat trickling between her breasts and around her waist. It was almost a relief when the double doors were opened and all conversation ceased. The prisoner emerged, dressed in a sky-blue shell suit. He was flanked by a policeman on each side and followed two paces behind by the Ayatollah in his white ceremonial robes. The prisoner seemed remarkably calm. As he walked, his shaven head glinted as if to emphasize that this was his moment. Soraya felt faint. The four shimmering figures moving towards her seemed to be walking on water. Sternly she shut her eyes, took a deep breath, and then adjusted her gaze to the new angle as they came closer. The mirage vanished. Everything now happened with awful clarity.

As the prisoner reached the centre of the square the Ministers of State who were present rose from their chairs and the Attorney General stepped forward to the microphones.

'Anheim Mossada, you have been found guilty of treason against the sovereign state of Iran. May Allah, the All-compassionate, show you mercy.'

The prisoner looked towards where she was standing. Had he made eye contact or was that just part of a sweeping motion as he took a last look at the sky? She could not be sure. Then he simply knelt over the block. Soraya froze, vainly willing the execution to be stopped, hoping against hope for a last second reprieve. She shut her eyes at the crucial instant. Since the microphones remained on everyone around the square must have heard, as she did, the swish of the scimitar and the thud as Anheim Mossada's head was severed from his body. Her eyelids flicked open. Horrified, she saw the immediate gush of blood. It did not quite reach the line of ministers. A trivial thought flashed through her brain as automatic as the spurt of blood. They would know how far back to sit, she registered, from much experience. Then a state of numbness took over. She watched as the police quickly moved forward to encircle the body. The ministers and the darkly clad executioner walked up the steps, duty done, to their limousines. A white van was driven on to the square. The body and head were wrapped together in a sheet and bundled into the van. Cleaners in green uniforms mopped up the blood with disinfectant. Then they folded the ministers' chairs and placed them also in the van. All this she saw in a stupor, mercifully out of touch with her emotions.

She was roused by the strong scent of antiseptic vapours rising up the steps. She observed her father's nodding from time to time as he recognized colleagues from the Department. No one smiled. The crowd, now thoroughly silent, began to disperse. Just when the dullness was wearing off and her critical faculties were returning to their accustomed sharpness the silence was broken by the harsh shrieks of unoiled shutters as shopkeepers prepared to resume business. She took in a swift breath and felt her fists clench and her shoulders tighten in reflex action. She noticed that others experienced the same involuntary reaction and for the first time that day sensed a kind of comradeship, however spurious and fleeting. Like her, the sensitive ones in the crowd looked elsewhere as the van was driven off towards the State cemetery.

Soraya and her parents remained silent until they were safely in their car, a Renault some five years old. The upholstery was blisteringly hot. They opened all the windows, for the air conditioning would take too long to become effective.

'Father, that was dreadful.'

'Hush, child, people will hear,' warned her mother.

Her father started the engine. 'I know, Soraya. I'm sorry you had to see it.'

They drove slowly at first through a warren of narrow streets, edging their way past barrows laden with sweetly smelling fruit stacked invitingly in an inverted V-shape. Soraya barely noticed. Her mind was on the execution. Who was Anheim Mossada? What act of treason had he committed? Facing imminent death and not merely observing it, how could he have been so much calmer than she? Was he a hero and not a villain at all?

Eventually they reached the wide boulevard that led to their suburban home. As they picked up speed, leaving the high-rise buildings behind and gaining an unimpeded view of the mountains to the north of the city, Soraya was still wrestling with questions. There was so much to find out. Her parents clearly did not have all the answers. Maybe they knew a little. 'Had he no relatives to comfort him?' she asked.

'I believe they had all fled to Iraq ... Look, I'll have to return to work. Help your mother prepare lunch and go back to school in the afternoon. It's important to get back to normal right away. I shall see you this evening with news to cheer you ... This evening, Soraya ... Are you all right, Aisha?'

'Ah yes. He took it so calmly. May Allah be merciful.'

As she walked with her mother up the short driveway to their house Soraya asked again about Anheim Mossada. 'Do we know who he was, what he did?'

'Soraya, dear, sometimes it is better not to know. Your father has told us there seems to be a connection with Iraq. That must be all the Governing Council has chosen to say on the subject. We can only trust their judgement ... Now cheer up. Your father was right. Put that execution behind you.'

'All right.' She said this with a smile that lit up her eyes. It was the first time she had lied to her mother.

Air conditioning made it blessedly cool inside. Mother and daughter wasted no time in changing. Aisha walked quickly into the master bedroom suite at the back, saying, 'Race you,' as she closed the door. Soraya went straight to the drying green and hung up her burqa. She dashed into the laundry room, removed her soaking clothes and put them in a basket for the maid. Then she ran naked upstairs to her bedroom and through it to the adjoining bathroom to indulge in a cool bath. There's another race going on here, she reflected grimly as she hurriedly sponged herself: time to grow up, to get away from this over-protectiveness. Within two minutes she was out again, refreshed, and drying herself with her favourite bath towel, orange with blue and yellow desert flowers embossed. She slipped on underclothes, a shirt and a fresh pair of trousers, found a band for her hair and threaded it to form a long black ponytail. Then she tripped downstairs and called through the door to her mother who was stil dressing.

'Beat you. Shall I start cutting the peppers?'

'Yes, thank you, Soraya. I shall be right out. Have you hung up that burqa?'

'Yes, Mother.'

Soraya's father, Nasher al-Jerad, remained standing with the other senior civil servants as the Governing Council filed in. He kept disparagement off his face as they took their places. One or two, he conceded, might be in the secret inner circle of those who initiated major policy with the Ayatollah and planned how to present it. When this was done skilfully the idiots in the Governing Council thought they were taking the lead, coming up with the bright ideas. Not that Nasher claimed to be innovation personified. He had no illusions about his own importance. His role was to implement, to manage, to take care of details; never to initiate. So far he had been content: there had been no conflict. As far as the economy was concerned the leadership had been sound, even though he could see through the tactics. It would be interesting to observe how the pantomime would unfold this afternoon.

The Ayatollah entered. The Governing Council rose and stood like the civil servants behind them until he sat.

'Gentlemen, I thought that went rather well, didn't you?'

The Ayatollah leaned back in his ornately cushioned chair, hands folded over his stomach. He still wore the ceremonial white aba and turban. His voice was loud and confident in the high-ceilinged chamber that had seen better days as the throne room of the Shah's palace. The throne had been ripped out and replaced with the Ayatollah's chair which was only a little less grand. There were now cracks on the green walls extending to blotches of white, and subsidence had made the marble floor uneven and treacherous. Only last week an elder statesman had taken a tumble as he shuffled to his chair on the semicircle for the Governing Council below the raised dais from which the Ayatollah chaired the proceedings.

There were murmurs of assent from the Governing Council. Yes men. Well, maybe they had just witnessed the consequence of saying no. Probably only three or four people in the assembly knew what that execution was about, Nasher guessed. He certainly didn't; and that was fine by him: least said, soonest mended. The problem was Soraya. She had clearly been affected by the execution. Once that girl got the bit between her teeth ... Thanks be, she'd be leaving soon. He'd miss her terribly, and Aisha would be devastated, but it was all for the good. He realized he had begun to shake his head, imperceptibly he hoped. Around him and in a row behind him sat the leading civil servants armed with briefcases loaded with reports that might prove to be relevant. There was no reaction from them, thank Allah. He hadn't started a negative wave.

'The cleansing phase is over for the present, may Allah be praised.' The Ayatollah did not pause this time. Sycophantic sounds could be overdone; there was no opposition to rile, after all. 'Today I want us to consider the future. Our problem is in principle no different from that of any other nation. We want to maximize our economy subject to constraints.'

Nasher allowed himself the fleeting observation that his daughter would have loved this. Lagrange's method for finding such maxima was a recent addition to her mathematical weaponry. He forced himself to concentrate as the Ayatollah continued.

'What makes us unique is the nature of our constraints and, on the positive side, our particular assets. Definitions of our constraints and assets will inform our policies. Get these definitions right and we shall be on the righteous path: getting them wrong or exaggerated will lead to disaster ... So, gentlemen, who will define our constraints?'

There was an embarrassing silence in the chamber as the echoes aints, aints, aints faded. Then, from the second arc of the Governing Council, a young cleric stood up. His beard was unusually long and his sombre garments contrasted with the pristine whiteness of the Ayatollah's.

'May it please your Eminence, we have but two constraints. They are fundamental and, as your Eminence said, they must define our purpose. First, we hate Israel with a passion for all the wrongs against us and against our Arab brothers. Second, we despise the Western powers for their disproportionate support of Israel and for their infidel decadence.'

Again there was silence. In previous years, Nasher reflected, there might have been a chorus of approval, even a standing ovation, but this committee knew its chairman and had been caught too often in his traps.

The Foreign Minister, Saban Kandar, to whom Nasher reported, got to his feet with an expressive exhaling of breath. He was a big man, somewhat rotund and inclined to perspire, dressed in a pinstripe suit over a tieless shirt. 'With your Eminence's permission.'

The formal nod and open-handed gesture were given.

'We all appreciate the sentiments expressed by our colleague, the Mullah Ahmed. If these are absolutely to define our policies, however, it is difficult to see how we can trade at all, never mind successfully, except with Arab and other Islamic nations; and not all of these are on the best of terms with us.' This produced a knowing rumble of agreement. 'As your Foreign Minister I would urge a more pragmatic approach stemming from, if I may say, more careful definitions of our constraints.'

'Thank you, Foreign Minister.' The Ayatollah smiled. 'The task I have set you all is not so easy, is it? Our Islamic beliefs have always contained political considerations. Let us come back to that question of constraints another time. Now, what about our assets?'

The Mullah Ahmed immediately stood up a second time. This induced a broader smile from the Ayatollah. 'My young friend, you are being most helpful today.'

'Thank you, your Eminence. Our assets are oil and agriculture, especially fruit ... And we have water but would like more.'

Encouraged by the Ayatollah's smile the entire Governing Council began to laugh. The cleric glared at them, sweeping his eyes from right to left and back again before resuming his seat.

'Come, my young friend, do not be angry. You have stated our assets succinctly. We do need more water. This implies buying the latest technology. So we must sell more oil. How can we do this?'

The Energy Minister caught his cue. 'By reducing our own consumption, your Eminence.' This was one of the few ministers for whom Nasher had any respect. He was a bespectacled intellectual with a glorious head of white hair who had considerable difficulty rising to his feet and stood clutching his walking stick for support as he continued to speak. 'We could do this without hardship if we had nuclear power.'

'Good. Then, gentlemen, that is what we must do: develop nuclear power.' The Ayatollah paused to make eye contact with senior members of the Governing Council. 'Now think hard about our constraints, how our actions will be perceived, how to proceed to best advantage, step by step ... Come prepared to discuss this in seven days' time.'

The Mullah Ahmed drove himself back to his mosque. As he strode along the main corridor he was followed wordlessly by six men who had been awaiting him at the entrance. They took their places on the carpeted floor in the mullah's private room.

'My friends, we must be strong.' The mullah looked keenly into the faces of his henchmen. What he saw seemed to please him, for he went on, 'By the grace of Allah a huge opportunity is arriving for us: nuclear power.'

The tough faces around him tightened and the eyes lit up with excitement.

'But, Mullah, we are not nuclear technicians. We can make bombs, sure, but a nuclear bomb ...'

'I do not ask you to make a nuclear bomb, Ali. Others will do that. Our job is to persuade ... forcibly ... for I regret to report that the Governing Council would let this magnificent opportunity slip by. This is what we must do ...'

In the maths class they had been studying conic sections. They had done the circle and the ellipse. Today it was the turn of the parabola.

'Who can define a parabola?' boomed the teacher.

Soraya knew but kept silent: there were boys in the class. Eventually one of them answered.

'A parabola is the locus of a point that moves such that its distance from a fixed point, the focus, is always the same as its distance from a fixed line, the directrix.' The young man hesitated, thinking furiously, for the teacher seemed to be expecting more. 'A-a-and the directrix does not pass through the focus.' He rushed these words out, breathing quickly.

'Good. Now, keeping that definition in mind, I want you all to write down the polar equation. Then see if you can calculate the arc length from the apse to the point above the focus on a line parallel to the directrix. It is one of the prettiest calculations you will discover in mathematics: trigonometry and calculus mixed together. You will have to use integration by parts. I have a box of turkish delight for anyone who can solve this before tomorrow's lesson.'

Soraya loved this style of teaching: a few hints and then letting her get on with it. She also approved of the bribery and corruption from which she had frequently benefited. "The basis of all good education," her father had quipped. Mind you, she was careful to share the spoils of war and not to win too often. This time, however, she was torn. On one hand she really wanted to win, to race home and have the derivation written out before her father arrived for dinner; but on the other hand she had to find out if her teacher knew anything about Anheim Mossada. She waited until all the pupils had left the classroom.

'Sir, I must apologize for missing school this morning.'

A smile. 'No need, Soraya. I know you had to attend the execution. Are you all right?'

'Yes, thank you, sir ... Did you happen to know the condemned man, Anheim Mossada?'

The teacher did not hesitate. 'No, Soraya. It's an unusual name. I would have remembered if he had attended this school.'

Too much to hope for, she accepted. That just left the library and the internet. The former would likely be a wild goose chase through old newspapers, and the internet was too dangerous: left a trail. Besides, postings on the internet could be altered, history rewritten ...

Her teacher cut through her thoughts. 'You seem terribly interested in this man.'

'Oh no, sir. Just a little curious. I've never witnessed an execution before.'

Soraya thanked him and left. The library would have to wait or her mother would wonder what she was up to. There had to be a better way ... Of course: the phone book. She smiled, hearing in her mind her maths teacher's familiar words: the simplest solutions are usually the best. Outside, it was still almost as hot as it had been at the execution. She walked as quickly as she could without perspiring too much. That should get her home at the usual time. On turning into her street she looked appreciatively at the substantial stone-built houses where upper-middle-class Iranians had lived for generations.

They had left the exteriors unaltered except for the addition, in some cases, of satellite dishes. The houses were detached and set back to provide space for neat front lawns. The grass was uniformly brown in high summer because watering was forbidden but in spite of this the street presented an impression of quiet prosperity, a haven. It would be a wrench to leave her lovely home but it had to be done. She stepped inside, called out to her mother and gave her a hug which was warmly reciprocated. She must not upset her. Surely she could check the phone book unobserved.

Soraya busied herself with the parabola problem at the kitchen table while her mother finished washing and drying china cups and saucers. Eventually her mother left, carrying a tray of china to the display cabinet in the drawing room at the other end of the house. When she could no longer hear her mother's footsteps Soraya tiptoed into the hall, opened the cupboard in the hallstand and took out the phone book. It was a rare name: there were only eleven Mossadas listed but none had A as the first initial. No luck there. On the other hand, the book was less than six weeks old. If he had been in jail on death row the listing would have expired. She knew that as a rule her father kept the previous issue of the phone book for a month or two before disposing of it in case any extension or reference numbers he had scribbled in it were still important. But it was not there; had been thrown out already. This must have happened recently. Perhaps it was in the bin outside. She opened the back door quietly and rummaged in the bin. There it was. No time to read it properly. She flipped the pages and tore out the list of Mossadas, replacing the book in the bin and making sure it was covered with rubbish much as before. She crept back into the kitchen and examined the page. Yes there was an A. Mossada. Great. It had to be him.

Now she had an address. Well, a district at least. So he had lived in Tehran, in the southwest sector. There was a fact at last. But it was hardly a surprise. He must have been close to the seat of power; and not just geographically, she realized, but intellectually as well. To be entrusted with a major secret he must have been an educated man with a special skill, almost certainly in politics or science.

She heard her mother returning from the drawing room and hid the page underneath her exercise book. She refocused on the parabola problem. It seemed far removed from the matter at hand. But was it? She paused to reconsider. Perhaps it did have a certain relevance. Maybe Anheim Mossada had had to solve it too when he was her age. Maybe she was following in his footsteps. Maybe this was the best way to learn about him: maybe the only way.

'Anyone who thinks decisions are made in formal sessions of the Governing Council is naïve,' said Nasher. He knew he had to win this, to be at his persuasive best, for Soraya's sake and, indeed, for the good of the State. His voice, his gestures - reinforced by his thick eyebrows and trim moustache - would have to be at their most compelling. He was standing at one end of a conference table, dominating his departmental colleagues who were seated around it. 'It is up to us in the Department to flesh out the policies for our Minister to present to the Governing Council for ratification. In other words, the buck starts here, is reared here and grows mature here before it is let loose.'

They were in the Department's conference room on the ground floor. The throaty sounds of lorries climbing the hill outside made it necessary to keep the windows shut. So a large fan wafted a downdraft of air, rustling the papers on the conference table.

'Let me give an outline. Oil is going up in price and will continue to do so for the next several decades as it begins to run out, for that is a property of all obsolescent commodities. It would be criminal to miss out on the oil bonanza. So we must sell it rather than use it. The Energy Minister was right. We must develop nuclear energy.'

One particular sheaf of papers was making too much noise. Nasher looked at it pointedly and immediately an embarrassed colleague lifted the papers and held them tightly on his lap.

'Now here is the difficulty,' Nasher continued. 'The very nations to whom we would sell will be deeply suspicious of our motive in developing a nuclear capability. They may, in fact, implement sanctions and boycott all our products, yes, even our oil. Look at how they are restricting oil production in Iraq through sanctions. So we must not be isolationist. On the contrary, we must begin to interact with the West ...'

There were intakes of breath around the table. Here we go, thought Nasher. He raised his right hand. 'This does not mean surrendering our principles, our grievances, our constraints. But as an act of salesmanship these must be put on a backburner. The best hope of resolving them is through co-operation, and that will not happen until there is mutual trust. Wooing the West must start immediately.'

He out-stared his colleagues one by one around the table. He was rewarded eventually with thoughtful nods. Only then did he deliver his punch line.

'While we are adjusting our international posture we should send the best of our young people to their universities, for these students on both sides will likely be the leaders when it really matters.'

The parabola problem had proved to be more tricky than expected but Soraya finally solved it, and clenched her fists with delight. The first of many fences, she thought, as she finished dressing for dinner. They always had dinner formally in the dining room. Next to her own room, it was her favourite. She remembered how enormous the room had seemed when she was a little girl for then the polished oak table was usually compressed for just the three of them seated around it. Now that she had grown up she was often present at dinner parties. On these occasions the table was extended by inserting up to four leaves, and at its maximum it almost met the walls, leaving just enough room for the dining room chairs at each end. There was a mirror over the tiled fireplace. Soraya caught her reflection as she helped her mother to set the table. Good, she thought. The blue ribbon goes well with the shawl Father brought from Portugal. Shame about the face: healthy looking; not at all sophisticated like Mother's. It needs make-up; and those eyebrows are far too full. Still everything seems to be in the right place and there are no blemishes. Now where's the Lisbon painting? There, the small one behind Mother's chair, a dark perspective of an alley; not very enticing.

She scanned the walls, reminiscing. What a lot of pictures, each evoking a tender moment. Such a miscellany of oils, water colours and framed photographs of the numerous cities Father had visited. She could almost feel his hands under her armpits as he picked her up to let her examine each newly acquired painting or photograph. The British cities were the most interesting, such strange buildings, all angles and sharp edges. The castles were best, and the skyline of Edinburgh was the best of all. Wouldn't it be marvellous to go there to study?

After dinner, as she had expected, her father presented her with the list of European universities that would accept her as a student of mathematics. 'I wrote to the British ones,' he said, giving her a knowing smile, 'informing them that you had received extra tutoring in English for the past eighteen months. So they had no excuse to reject you on language grounds.'

Hooray. The University of Edinburgh was offering a place. Just the one note of caution: they would decide after the first year whether she might enter the course for an honours degree. Not a problem. She hugged her parents and kissed them.

'Will I have to wear the burqa?'

Her father raised his hand as her mother was about to speak. 'From now on, Soraya, you will have to make many decisions and live with the consequences. Your mother and I are confident of your integrity. You will find that integrity is not enough, however. Suicide bombers have integrity. You must work out for yourself what is right, and you must be right in all the important decisions. Strive for perfection, Soraya.'

'And may Allah protect you,' said her mother.

Chapter 2

Her first view of Edinburgh was from the air. It was a clear evening in early October. As they began to descend Soraya immediately recognized Arthur's Seat and the Salisbury Crags. Then she made out the castle and the distinctive canopy of St Giles Cathedral. Having seen pictures of no more than the central area she was surprised by the extent of the city stretching towards the setting sun. Later in the descent she admired the golden reflections from the river Forth with its islands and the boats ploughing up and down, and during the final approach she marvelled at the functional beauty of the rail and road bridges over to Fife. She strained to see as far as Kinross. Would Loch Leven come into view? No, there were hills in the way. As the plane landed she wondered if she could be as brave as her heroine, Mary Queen of Scots, escaping from the castle on the island in the loch. Would she ever be cool enough under pressure to perform a trick like Mary's with the keys and the napkin?

An airport bus brought her to Waverley station. She had enjoyed the drive, especially the last part when she was in the city centre looking up to the castle, but she was beginning to feel tired. It was crowded and noisy at the station with continual announcements. She made out the word Leuchars. At least that was easy to pronounce. Encouraged, she joined a queue for taxis. She was pleased that the looks she got from passers-by were of curiosity, not hostility. Exactly like mine, if you could see them, she thought. Eventually it was her turn. If the driver was surprised to be confronted with a burqa he gave no sign. My father would approve of this man, she acknowledged, a true diplomat. As he drove through the Old Town he pointed out the Old Quad. of the university and intimated that in the years immediately following the Second World War the walls used to be lined with policemen's helmets every

Saturday night following "encounters" between the students home from war and the

police.

'Things have been quiet since then. Maybe you can jildy them up a bit,' he said with a wink as he carried her bags into the Hall of Residence where she would spend her first two years.

As she walked towards her first class in the James Clerk Maxwell building Soraya felt all the excitement of an eager student on the first day of a university career. She looked up to the heavens. It was windy under a pale blue sky with just a few scudding clouds. Her burqa made a flapping noise, like applause when the soloist first appears. Well, here she was, all set to give a great performance. A group of girls walking ahead of her wore navy blue duffle coats with the hoods up. She smiled to herself: it's as if they're trying to make me feel at home. She extended the thought. Metaphorically at least she was on the trail of Anheim Mossada. He must have felt similar emotions on his first day. Perhaps for him it was not a maths class, and certainly it was not at this university: he would not have been permitted to study outside Iran back then; but in principle she was reliving his experience. Where would it lead? Back to Tehran eventually, that was certain. But first she must gain the best marks in all her courses. Her father's exhortation was ringing in her ears: strive for perfection, Soraya.

It was a shock to see how undisciplined her fellow maths students were. When the lecturer entered no one stood up. Most of them continued to converse.

'Stop talking,' he had to say. When there was silence he wrote on the blackboard the single word, Limits. Soraya thought he was going to lay down ground rules of behaviour but instead he wrote the less than or equal to symbol.

'It means just what it says,' he said. 'For example, 2 is less than or equal to 3. That is a true statement.'

Soraya wondered if she was in the wrong class. Surely this was too elementary. But suddenly the lecturer began to write at speed, filling the blackboard with lemmas, theorems and proofs, and rubbing out to leave space for more furious writing. She just managed to keep up as she copied everything into her notebook.

At the end of the lecture the lecturer walked out of the room without comment, as remote as ministers leaving the scene of an execution, she thought. She finished copying what he had left on the blackboard.

'Too much like hard work,' a voice sounded to her right. With a start she realized that she was being addressed by a boy with tousled fair hair and a huge grin. To emphasize his point he wiped his brow mockingly.

Soraya laughed. He held out his hand. 'John Russell,' he said.

'I am pleased to meet you, Mr Russell.' She bowed but did not take his hand. 'My name is Soraya al-Jerad.'

'Please call me John. And may I call you Soraya? We're fellow students, after all.'

Soraya nodded and said, 'Of course you may.'

'Let me guess. You're from Morocco, Soraya?'

'No. Tehran. I'm Iranian.'

'Ah. Such a long way to come. I hope you'll be happy here. See you later.'

As he got to his feet and departed she noticed his physique. He was tall and broader in the shoulder than the boys at her school in Tehran. But he was rather chunky and the backs of his shoes were unpolished. He was far from dapper. On the other hand she was sure he was one of the few who had stopped talking when the lecturer arrived. Maybe he would turn out all right.

As the weeks went by Soraya got to know John better for they were taking exactly the same subjects: maths, physics and mathematical physics. He was the most likeable person, she decided, but terribly slipshod. When working he did not pile his books neatly as she did. He seemed to have a generally carefree attitude. As if to confirm this, she learnt that he was an all-rounder at sports without having any special aptitude. He described himself as B-team material. She wanted to shake him.

They often went together to the Student Union for what John teasingly called "a guilty cup of coffee". On these occasions they were usually joined by three others. The first was Elspeth Johnston who had been at school with John. Elspeth, small and cheerful, a staunch Presbyterian, had been good at geography, John said, and was now enrolled to study social anthropology. Then there was a gangly, red-headed boy from Inverness called Nicol Anderson doing theology but with no intention of becoming a minister. Were all Scottish men inherent drifters? The third was Nicol's girlfriend since the Freshers' Ball, Betty Black (with appropriately dark hair), who, spoilt for choice with a fistful of Highers, had opted for physics to please her parents. Betty had no religious affiliation as far as Soraya could make out. Well, it takes all types, she was finding.

John, Betty and she had just attended a physics lecture in which the lecturer, deriving a correction factor for the period of a simple pendulum, had written a "d" instead of a "delta" before the angle of tilt in his diagram. At this, most of the maths students, having had the rigorous way of approaching a limit drummed into them, began to hiss and stamp their feet. Understandably, the lecturer was annoyed. But he did not expel them. He won Soraya's respect by simply pointing out that neglecting the mass of the string was a far more significant point; and he finished, somewhat exasperated, with the killer punch, 'Mathematics is a substitute for thought.'

Following that lecture, Soraya, John and Betty took a bus uptown to meet Elspeth and Nicol outside the Geography Department where Elspeth's Social Anthropology lecture had just finished. They headed for the Student Union. Although Soraya knew she was far from unique in wearing the burqa she was disturbed to find as they walked along the cobbles of Drummond Street that she was still making heads turn. The possibility that this was due to the animated body language of her friends demonstrating that she was clearly the centre of attraction in the group did not occur to her. It had to be the burqa. They crossed the busy South Bridge road, entered the Old Quad., crossed it and mounted the steps to the Union at the far end and found a table by a window. John and Nicol brought the coffee on trays and immediately the girls handed them the exact coins to pay their share.

'So, Soraya and John,' Betty began, speaking loudly against the din of conversations around them, 'maths is just a substitute for thought, eh?'

'Very funny ... I suppose there's some truth in it at this level, but wait till next year.' John eased back in his chair and glanced at Soraya. 'What do you think?'

Soraya took a sip, considered her answer, and decided to be diplomatic. Her vocabulary was improving daily and with it her confidence. She knew that she had standard English pronunciation of all vowels. It was just the heavy accent on the h consonant that proclaimed her as a Middle Easterner and she did not mind that at all.

'I think all subjects have a bit of autopilot in them: following the rules, referring to points made by previous workers or doing something similar to what has already been done. It would be terribly hard work if they didn't. Maybe maths has more than most. Maybe that's why I like it.'

Elspeth joined in. 'All this rivalry is a bit stupid, don't you think? A bit tribal?'

'Absolutely,' said Nicol. 'If we wanted to, we could divide the entire population into tribes or mutual admiration societies. Each of us, no doubt, would generate his or her distinctive list. I'll make a start. There are the aristocrats; that's one tribe. Then people who recognize fellow members by their rigorous use of English; they all come from Inverness, by the way.'

'And people with a great sense of humour,' chimed in Betty. 'Never to be found in Inverness.'

'And beautiful people,' said John, 'which let's all of us out.'

'Speak for yourself,' said Betty with an exaggerated patting of her hair which made Elspeth laugh.

'Anyway,' said Soraya, 'before we exhaust the possibilities I'm getting back to work. Anyone coming to the library?'

In the library Soraya stared at her lecture notes on vector analysis and thought about the burqa and the reasons for veiling. She had been ready tacitly to criticize the Western compulsion to reveal all, or at least to show off, to vaunt class and privilege. Some insecure students did indeed demonstrate these failings. But her friends were not like that. Certainly John was not. For a well set-up, rather handsome (his clear blue eyes were ... were ... terrific) and clever young man he was amazingly modest; and if Nicol was a bit more full-of-himself he was fundamentally decent, and so were Betty and Elspeth. Anyway, the burqa was doing the opposite of what it was supposed to do. It was attracting attention. Soraya decided to wear it no longer in Edinburgh and she would not compromise with a simple veil. She would hang up the outer shells and dress like the rest of them.

The next day, when Elspeth asked her why she had abandoned the burqa, Soraya explained simply that she felt it was counterproductive. This was accepted with equanimity by her friends. The standard jeans and sweater fitted in perfectly with the others' attire but could not hide the loveliness of the full figure underneath. As John said to Nicol later, 'She is in a no-win situation.'

Soraya wrote to her parents explaining why she had given up wearing the burqa. Within a week there was a letter back full of support and encouragement. The main news, her father had added, was that his esteemed colleague, Dr Abdul Hanser, the Energy Minister, had died. He had been found in his house at the foot of a flight of stairs. One slip too many. No one had yet been appointed to succeed him.

The mathematics course had a section on base systems of numbers. Soraya wondered if Anheim Mossada had studied this too. Maybe not, for she learnt that this part of the course was an Edinburgh speciality in honour of the late Professor A.C. Aitken who had been the leading proponent of the duodecimal system. In his own experiments, the lecturer informed them, the Prof. had proved that 100 man-hours of work in the decimal system could be accomplished by only 60 in the duodecimal because round numbers occurred so much more often, 12 having twice as many factors as 10. 'If only we had learnt to count using our knuckles instead of our fingers,' Professor Aitken had said, 'how much easier life would be.'

That's all very well, thought Soraya, but far too late. The damage is done. You missed the boat, Professor. Maybe there was a lesson there: she vowed to make her mathematics relevant, to apply it when it would make a difference.

Back in the Union for coffee, Soraya was surprised to be confronted by Nicol urgently asking her to explain about tribes.

'We were all talking like experts the other day, but you are the real expert ... heaven sent, if you'll pardon the expression. And I have an essay to write. So give.'

'Have a heart, Nicol. I'm not a lecturer.'

'I really want to know, Soraya. It's desperation time. Please.'

She relented. 'Well, funnily enough, as John and Betty have just heard in a maths lecture, the number 12 is the key. You'll have heard of the twelve tribes of Israel ...'

'Just a minute, Soraya,' Nicol interrupted, 'if you don't mind my saying, you mentioned Israel just now without emotion, not that I was expecting you to spit on the ground or whatever, but surely you, as a Muslim, hate the Israelis.'

'We're not over-fond of them, it's true; but it was not always so. Up to 1948 we were perfectly at peace ... No, let me rephrase that. There was an unavoidable battle against three of their tribes in the time of the Prophet Muhammad, blessings be upon him, but apart from that no animosity until 100,000 Palestinians had to evacuate their homes so that the State of Israel could be formed.' Soraya found her voice rising and quickly adjusted. 'Anyway, let's not get into that hot topic just now.'

'Right,' said John. 'You were talking about 12, Soraya.'

'Yes,' she said, glad to be put back on track, 'it crops up a lot. For instance, where I come from, in Iran, we are all Shi'as, not Sunnis which is what most Muslims are outside Iran, Iraq, Azerbaijan and Bahrain. In particular, as Dr Fischer would say,' - she smiled at John and Betty – 'many Shi'as, myself included, are Twelver Shi'as, meaning that we recognize the succession of the 12 imams. In a way, we're rather like the Roman Catholics who recognize a succession of popes, except that the imams were all blood relatives of Muhammad, blessings be upon him.'

'And are the Sunnis a bit like the Protestants?' asked Elspeth.

'I suppose you could say that. They give greatest importance to the Qur'an.'

'Just as Protestants concentrate on the bible, you mean?' said Nicol.

'Yes ... There's another group called the Ismailites. They hold that there were six great prophets: Adam, Noah, Abraham, Moses, Jesus and Muhammad. And each of these had an interpreter who taught his prophet's secret meaning to those who were capable of understanding it. So again the number 12 comes into it. Of course there were many more than 12 tribes. They all started as sets of blood relatives but it's hard to keep track of them due to alliances and reformations as religious sects ... But, Nicol, you'll know all this, surely, from your courses.'

Nicol coloured. 'Some of it sounds vaguely familiar. You're easier to understand. Ever thought of lecturing in theology?'

'No thanks. Maths is enough for me ... But I'll tell you one thing you may not have heard. It's about the next number, thirteen. In your culture the superstition is that 13 is unlucky. In China it's used as a derogatory term: if you're described as "13 points" then you are regarded as thick; not that that could possibly apply to any of us.'

'Of course not,' said Betty ... 'Although some theologists ...'

'Quite,' said John, a restraining hand on Nicol's shoulder, 'but what does 13 mean in your culture?'

'Mortal danger.'

'Wow, that's heavy. I'll use that,' said Nicol. 'Bet I get an A.'

'You'll never ever get an A,' said Betty.

'Never ever? Betty, with such a flair for language you should take up politics. But I give you advance warning that unless you want to revert back to natural philosophy I actually think that you'll have to make forward plans to check up on your subject matter and put in 110% for a relatively long period of time until you are further exacerbated and become a complete stranger as an investment for the future so that you can potentially predict ahead of time broken promises that people don't keep, make a vast fortune, rusticate in the countryside and wear imports from abroad using more especially the latest contemporary ...'

'Okay, I get the message.'

Soraya laughed. It was good to see Nicol back on form. But it had not been entirely a solo effort. She gave John her warmest smile. She felt he had earned it.

Soraya flew back to Tehran for the long summer break, having achieved first class merit certificates in all her subjects. All maths students accepted for the honours course had been advised to study two books to prepare them for the second year: Aitken's Determinants and Matrices, and Differential Equations by Piaggio and Ince. So she had good reason and full parental encouragement to spend many hours in the library. Not all of these were devoted to honing her mathematical skills.

Anheim Mossada was about forty at the time of his execution, she gauged. If he had graduated from university when he was twenty-two, that would have been in 1981. So she asked for newspapers published in June of 1980, 1981 and 1982.

At last she found him. He was listed among the top graduates in physics from the University of Tehran in 1982. So he probably did not reach his fortieth birthday. What a waste. What a shame.

Don't get all emotional, she told herself. Think ...

The library did not keep back issues of telephone directories, but census data were available. So much the better. She ploughed through the census forms and discovered that Anheim Mossada was the second son in a family of five; he had two younger sisters and another brother. They had lived in southwest Tehran since 1971. The full address was given and the profession of the head of the household, Anheim's father, was stated as "purchasing manager". The elder brother had married and left home in 1975 and the father had died in 1979. That made Anheim the new head of the household. So where were his mother and younger siblings now, Soraya wondered. What had Anheim done after university? These questions were more sensitive politically. She knew she would have to tread carefully.

The next day, armed with a clipboard, she went to the library as usual, consulted a street map of the southwest sector and left early to catch a bus that would take her there. The house, number 29, was in an avenue of identically structured dwellings but stood out from the rest by virtue of having an excellently tended front garden. In general, the avenue was respectable if a little run down. It was the sort of place where she supposed a purchasing manager might have lived. She doubted that the family would still be there.

She rang the bell. A middle-aged woman came to the door.

'Government census,' Soraya said, producing the clipboard from under her burqa. 'Just two questions: what is your name and how long have you lived at this address?'

The woman, who had been nervous at first, seemed relieved to be getting off so lightly. 'We are the Hakeem family. Let me think. We moved here about eighteen months ago.'

'So you bought the house from the previous family, did you?'

'No. The house was empty. We purchased it from the council.'

'Thank you,' said Soraya, making a show of noting this on her sheet. 'That's all we need for the present.'

The great thing about the burqa was that it made you anonymous. She decided to risk one more visit. She rang the bell of the next door house to her right, number 27. No one answered. Why couldn't things go smoothly? She knew she should continue down the street in case anyone was watching but the best bet was now with the neighbour to the left. She pretended to check the house numbers, changed direction and rang the bell of the Hakeem's other neighbour, number 31. It was an old man this time.

She tried a gentler approach. 'Good morning, sir, I'm here to check a detail for the census bureau, the CENSUS BUREAU, sir.' Allah, please don't make this so difficult, she pleaded. 'They just want to know if you lived here at the same time as the previous owners next door.' She indicated Number 29.

'Oh yes. Nice family, the Mossadas. And the Hakeems are nice too.'

And everything's as right as right can be. 'I'm sure they are, sir. Do you know where the Mossadas went?'

The old man shook his head sadly. 'They just disappeared, well over a year ago, without saying goodbye. A few days later the removal vans arrived.' He leaned towards her. 'One of the sons was executed, you know.'

'Oh really. How awful. Do you know why?'

He looked up and down the deserted street before answering. 'All I know is that he had a good job in the Defence Ministry, but I expect the - what d'you call them - census people know that already.'

'I'll make sure they do, sir. Thank you for your co-operation. Goodbye.'

Soraya walked unhurriedly to the bus stop and waited for a number 52. Not everything was going her way: the first bus to arrive was a 17 which she waved on. She saw inquisitive faces at windows across the street but was not alarmed. She was virtually invisible, after all.

Nasher rarely talked about his work to his family, but on Soraya's last evening of the summer holidays he had evidently decided to break this rule. Over coffee after dinner he brought up the subject of Iran's nuclear policy.

'Construction of our first facility is well underway,' he said, a hint of pride in his voice. 'Eventually we'll have many more. We'll be like France, generating nearly all of our energy at nuclear plants. That's where the future lies, Soraya.'

And probably the recent past, she thought.

On the flight back to Heathrow Soraya considered what she had learnt. Anheim Mossada was a physicist who had worked at the Defence Ministry. If he went there straight from university then he had worked for them throughout most of the war with Iraq and for many years subsequently. It was therefore possible, she conceded, that the treasonable offence had occurred during the Iraq war and had only come to light more recently. That was the received wisdom. Most pragmatic people, like her parents, would accept that explanation and put it from their minds. But to her it still seemed improbable. So what other explanation was there?

She went into a toilet to change out of her burqa. By the time she emerged she had the alternative explanation worked out. What if Anheim Mossada had been a member of a team performing a feasibility study on the nuclear issue? The timing fitted much better. What if he discovered that the real policy was to develop nuclear weapons; and he broke ranks, tried to contact journalists? He was caught in the act. The other members of the team, probably not all Iranians, had to be kept in line. As a terrifying warning to them Anheim was publicly executed. No doubt his family was seized one night, taken far away – perhaps to an orchard in the South – and hanged. It all fitted.

She realized she could not discuss this with anyone, certainly not with her parents, nor even with her friends at university: you never knew how far loose talk might travel. She had no real proof yet. It was simply a theory. But she was right. She knew it. Iran was not just planning the deployment of peaceful, domestic nuclear energy. The secret agenda was much more terrifying. She would prove it. More to the point, she would do everything in her power to prevent it.

Chapter 3

At the start of the second year John was elected Amusements Convener of the Physical Society. He proposed the youth hostel at Loch Ossian for just after New Year and twenty people signed up. In darkness they got off the train bound for Fort William and points west at Corrour Siding on the edge of Rannoch Moor. They shivered at first and sweated later as they walked a strenuous mile by torchlight with their heavy rucksacks and cases to the hostel, wondering if they had made an awful mistake. But morale improved the next morning as they looked through the windows of the upstairs dormitories down the loch to the mountains beyond. The five friends loved the whole experience, walking round the loch, climbing the snowy peak of Ben Alder one day, and for a dare John even took a dip the day before the loch froze.

'It wasn't that big a deal,' he said to cut short the cheers as Soraya handed him his towel. 'William Wallace – now that was a really tough guy – probably went for a swim every morning before breakfast. If my teeth would stop chattering, Soraya, I'd tell you all about him.'

They took turns in cooking porridge and smoky bacon and eggs for breakfast and usually a pasta dish for dinner. They joined in songs and Scottish Country Dancing in the evenings. John marvelled at the slimness of Soraya's legs as she whirled and turned in Strip the Willow. How could such thin legs support such a well-endowed body? Yet she went up Ben Alder like a mountain goat. Amazing girl.

Throughout the week they composed new verses to Rickety Tickety Tin and at the end John awarded Betty the prize of a free ticket to The Gamma Function for the most bloodthirsty one:-

Her only uncle died in bed
Sing Rickety Tickety Tin
Her only uncle died in bed

Where she used an axe to chop off his head
He screamed and gurgled while it ble-e-ed
But a radio drow-owned the din, the din
A radio drow-owned the din.

Back at university John was falling in love with Soraya. Wherever he was, walking past the Meadows on his way to the first lecture of the day, half listening to a sermon in St Cuthbert's, out for a run towards Penicuik, he could not get her out of his mind. She did not seem to realize how beautiful and desirable she was: that lovely oval face with the perfect skin; and that voluptuous figure, those legs. Her innocence and modesty were driving him to distraction. No good can come of it, he told himself. Just stay friends, nothing more or you'll spoil everything. He decided to take up athletics and joined the Cross-country Club. To get fit enough to compete he began to attend circuit-training sessions in the gym. He felt his body was of an awkward size, too much of it for long distance running but not enough for field events. Maybe if he worked at it he could become a creditable miler and fifteen-hundred-metre man in the summer term. Maybe that would keep his mind off Soraya.

Soraya's parents, Nasher and Aisha, took turns in writing. Nasher's latest one was brief because he was inundated with work. Rather than appoint a successor to the Energy Minister the Ayatollah had chosen to amalgamate the Energy and Foreign Affairs departments because both were intimately involved with the nuclear policy. The Foreign Minister was now head of the new Department of Energy and Foreign Affairs. So for me, Nasher wrote, it is like suddenly taking on development and production as well as marketing and sales. But I expect you are working just as hard as I am.

As Amusements Convener, having organized The Gamma Function, John felt obliged to attend. No, let's be honest, he corrected himself: it was a golden opportunity to ask Soraya. How to handle it, though. Nicol and Betty would certainly be going; lucky Nicol, profiting from Betty's free ticket. Elspeth did not seem to have a boyfriend unless she was being tremendously secretive. There was nothing wrong with Elspeth. She had always been a good sport and she was not unattractive; just one of those popular girls who did not immediately attract men sexually. Surely her time would come. In the meantime what could be more natural than all five of them going together? He caught up with Soraya and Elspeth as they were heading for the gymnasium.

'Listen, you two. The only dance I'm any good at is The Dashing White Sergeant and you need two partners for that; so would you both come to The Gamma Function with me?'

As the girls looked at each other John stuttered on, 'Nicol and Betty will be there. We could all go together. So you wouldn't have to dance with me all night.'

'We'd love to.'

Everybody said the Ball was a great success. John and other committee members had seen to it that the hall was well decorated with shapes of crepe paper and garish posters on the walls. The band was really good, playing alternately Scottish Country dances and disco for which it had supplied its own lighting. And the food was great, both the turkey dinner at 10 p.m. and the full breakfast at 2 a.m. to bring the evening to an end.

John had given equal time to Soraya and Elspeth, and Nicol had danced with them too although he spent most of the evening with Betty who looked sensational in a low-cut red dress. For a girl so self-possessed Betty seemed nervous that evening, John thought, her laughter a little too shrill. He asked her up. She was a very good dancer and could handle conversation easily while performing her complicated moves. She almost made him stop in his tracks when she told him that she had decided to give up physics.

'Such Paschen is not Fermi,' she giggled.

'Gosh. What are you going to do instead? Not politics, surely. That was just a joke, wasn't it?'

'It started that way. But the more I thought about it the more I realized that politics was what I wanted to do.'

'Well, it's a big, brave decision ... You know that very few politicians took politics at uni.?'

He twirled her twice as the music came to its climactic end. Her dress billowed out, rising high to show shapely legs. She hugged him, kissed him quickly on the cheek and thanked him for the dance. John temporarily lost the thread of the conversation. Girls at close quarters were extremely disconcerting.

As they walked back to their table Betty continued as if the hug and kiss had been part of the dance. 'But I don't want to become a politician: a civil servant, maybe. I fancy living in London for a while. What about you? Where will your mathematics take you?'

'Right now I haven't a clue,' said John.

He handed her back to Nicol. As the evening advanced John noticed that she clung to Nicol in the slow dances. They truly were an item, those two. But whether she realized it or not she had delivered a wake-up call. John looked at and considered his two partners with renewed interest.

Soraya and Elspeth had gone shopping together that afternoon. Elspeth had chosen a short velvet dress of crimson and black. Killer heels made her much taller but she had to remove them for the reels and jigs. Soraya's dress was a deceptively simple dark blue evening gown, modest but very sexy on her. Her slim bare arms were in view for the first time. She was truly lovely. What had started for John as interested observation now turned into full-scale love and desire. He could not wait to be alone with her.

Elspeth lived at home, close to the hall at King's Buildings where the Ball had been held. So John and Soraya dropped her off first with kisses all round. As the taxi continued, the driver having considerately closed the window between him and the passengers' section, John took Soraya's hand and told her that he loved her.

'Oh, John,' she said, turning to him, 'I have known that for a long time. But it is wonderful to hear you say it at last, for I love you too.'

They kissed, very gently. Then John led her to the door of her Hall of Residence and said goodnight.

They met again after the mathematical physics lecture on Monday morning. Soraya asked him if they could go somewhere else for a cup of coffee. 'Just you and I.'

They went to a coffee shop next to Blackwell's bookshop opposite the Old Quad. and found a small table in a corner. A song by Wet, Wet, Wet was blaring forth.

'Soraya, I'm crazy about you. You're gorgeous and beautiful and brave. How brave I thought you were the moment I saw you, coming alone to such a different culture.'

'Much easier than the other way round.'

'Well, maybe, but that's just it. We're so different.'

'No, John, we're very alike.'

'Right.'

They stopped talking for a bit, each enjoying the feeling of being in love. Then they both started to talk.

'After you, Soraya.'

'What will your parents think?'

'Right now they're six thousand miles away, in California, with the rest of my family, younger brother and sister. So it will be a while before they get to meet you, but when they do I expect they will be surprised, enchanted and delighted in that order. How will your parents react to me?'

'Same way, I'm sure. Maybe less surprise ... John, we can make a difference. We'll get our degrees and I'll go back to Iran and you'll do whatever comes next in your career, but we'll keep in touch all the time and help to keep our two nations on good terms. If we do this well we can overcome everything. Two perfect lives.'

John smiled at her. He looked much fitter these days and in the mornings you could just make out a parting in his hair. 'I want it to work. See, you've even got me cleaning my shoes. But perfection's a tall order and I'm not sure I'm up to it. You know I want you here and now.' John reached for her hand and squeezed it.

'"Now" I can understand, but "here"?' She glanced around the busy coffee shop and returned her gaze to his pleading blue eyes, a mischievous smile on her face.

John laughed. 'You're sounding more like Nicol every day. Hair splitter ... I'll try to be patient.'

'So shall I.'

In the third year, those doing physics or mathematical physics left the maths classes. Soraya and John, as committed mathematicians, now had to choose which advanced branches of mathematics to take. They rejected statistics and topology and opted for number theory and operations research largely because they liked the lecturers who would teach those subjects.

'To get you started on number theory, let me try you out on this puzzle from a charming book called A Mathematical Kaleidoscope by Brian Conolly and Steven Vajda. I hope you will all read it in your spare time, not that you will have any.'

Soraya could see that Dr Fischer was enjoying himself, no doubt fascinated to find out if any of "this lot" could solve it, but for once she was too involved with her own thoughts to rise to the challenge.

'It goes something like this ...'

It was too hard to concentrate. No further progress on the nuclear front had been made during the long summer back home. It was frustrating. The more Soraya thought about it the more she became convinced that Anheim Mossada had made eye contact with her just before his execution. It had not been a terrified look. He had been stern, resolute, extremely brave. His last free action had been to urge her to carry on the fight. For that she needed ammunition, something to go on. But her father had reverted to his customary discretion, had not been forthcoming with new information. The newspapers had been full of tirades against Western powers for threatening sanctions or worse unless Iran abandoned its commercial development of nuclear energy. All froth and no substance. She would have to get inside the system somehow to determine the true facts. For that, she needed this degree, and it had better be a good one. She forced herself to listen. It was something about finding two numbers with precious little information; not unlike her preoccupation, she thought. Maybe she could catch up, figure out what she had missed ...

'... well, Mr S looked at the number on his scrap of paper and said, "But that's impossible. I can't tell you the numbers and neither can he." Mr P, who had not bothered to unfold his piece of paper, seemed to wake up at this point. He took a notebook from his pocket and started to scribble. Not to be outdone, Mr S also took out a notebook and began to write. After a little while Mr P said, "I know what the two numbers are," and Mr S said, "So do I," and, would you believe it, both were right. So what were the two numbers?'

There were only nine in the class. Everyone looked nonplussed.

'The trick in all such puzzles is to find the starting point. After that it's plain sailing. "Autopilot" I believe you cheeky devils call it. What are the key words?'

Soraya would have volunteered: her diffidence in the presence of boys had long gone; but she could not find the start of the piece of string. She chastised herself for not listening at the beginning.

'I can see I'll have to tell you,' said Dr Fischer. The key words are "and neither can he." Suppose Mr P had been given a number like 6 or 10 or 14 or 15, the product of two different primes. He would have known immediately what the two numbers were. Mr S saw from his number that none of the possible combinations was the sum of two primes. Now work it out. Remember Goldbach's conjecture, certainly valid in this range of numbers, that every even number can be expressed as the sum of two primes. So Mr S had to have been given an odd number. But which one? Remember there's a unique answer.'

As usual, Soraya was there first. 'Four and thirteen,' she said.

'Brava. Now what does that suggest?'

John got it right away. 'Card games.'

'I might have guessed you'd get that, J. Russell. Misspent youth. Yes. Interesting, isn't it? We've stumbled on the perfect structure for a pack of cards by thinking, not too deeply, about the properties of prime and composite numbers. Now let's get down to serious work. I must make you all thoroughly at home with the singularities in power series of integers. Who knows? One of you may provide us one day with an elegant proof of Fermat's last theorem.'

And who knows, Soraya added quietly to herself, these numbers may become critically important one day.

A year later Soraya got her first class honours as expected but John just missed a first. In retrospect, he admitted to himself, he had probably spent too many hours on the running track and had little to show for it, one sub-five-minute mile as a second string runner against Glasgow University. Although offered a Research Assistantship to do a post-graduate degree in numerical analysis at Sheffield John decided to leave the field of mathematics and to try for the Foreign Office. It seemed the best way to keep in touch with Soraya. At his first interview they advised him to prove he had the ability to learn languages. 'Why not jump in the deep end and take a course in Arabic? There's a good fast one at Sheffield. You had been thinking of going there anyway. Come and see us again next year and we'll put you through the tests. And stay fit. That's important.'

'Soraya, my dear daughter, I am so proud of you. First class honours in mathematics. How many firsts were awarded?'

'Three, Father.'

'Well that shows what an achievement you have made.'

They were driving back from the airport in a nearly new BMW. Soraya was dutifully wearing her burqa, having put it on in a toilet about half an hour before landing. She was appreciating the air conditioning.

'I think we should now have a serious discussion. Don't worry. It's not about sex; I've always left that in your mother's capable hands. It's about something much less pleasant which you must now hear because soon, no doubt, you will be expected to play an important role in supporting the government.'

Soraya sat up straight. Surely now she could get closer to the truth. She waited for her father to continue.

'I'm sure you remember the execution you had to witness.'

'Yes, Father.'

'Did you ever wonder why the prisoner was so calm?'

'It puzzled me. But I was glad he did not add to the horror of it.'

'Quite.'

For a moment Soraya saw John's face saying that word in English, or the similar word, "right". Strange that the two men who meant most to her should both have that courteous way of showing that they understood and did not require further explanation.

Her father continued. 'They are always calm. The entire scene is staged to make a point for all to see. But care is taken not to revolt the crowd.'

It was difficult to think of such a distasteful matter on this beautiful day. The sun gleamed on the mountains and Soraya realized how much she had missed her homeland.

'Why do the prisoners co-operate?'

As she asked this Soraya perceived the answer, in essence at least. She began to feel sick.

'I see you have worked it out. They are threatened with something much worse than a clean, swift death. Soraya, you must know the details. One of the prisoners on death row is buried alive in a coffin in the presence of the others. Death can take up to two hours. The prisoners hear the cries, the desperate scratching, the forlorn coughing. Then the coffin lid is opened and all the prisoners are made to look inside. After such an experience they do exactly as ordered ... Recently it was decided that the process took too long. So now the unfortunate who is put in the coffin is given a revolver loaded with a single bullet in the firing position. They usually shoot themselves after five minutes. The brave ones hold out for ten. Claustrophobia is a terrible experience.'

Her father glanced in the rear-view mirror, indicated a move to the right and slowed, allowing the two cars behind to pass. Shortly afterwards he pulled into a lay-by and switched off the engine. Taking Soraya's hand and looking into her eyes he continued, 'After the bang is heard the coffin is opened and the prisoners see the gruesome body. So far the change in procedure has made no difference to the behaviour at executions.'

'So cruel. Why have you told me this, Father?'

'First, so that you are in no doubt about the consequences of betraying the State. Be very careful in all you do as you enter a new phase of your life. And second, because having heard this you have time to absorb it and recover from your reaction to it. Then, when some governmental official calls you in and tells you - as he thinks for the first time - your reaction can be more clinical and composed. Believe me, such reactions are noted and make or break careers ... Soraya, there is nothing you or I can do about these things ... Just keep your own integrity, my Daughter.'

Soraya hoped she was managing to conceal the impatience she felt, that the expression in her eyes was not giving her away. Dear Father, protective to a fault. Whatever happened to that speech "integrity is not enough"? Did that only apply outside Iran? Once the burqa was on again was she expected to suppress all indignation, to accept meekly the propaganda of the Governing Council?

Not on your life.

Chapter 4

January 2004

For some people, living dangerously means nothing more than pouring champagne recklessly towards the top of the glass. That was how it had been for many years for Roddy McKie and his wife, Margaret. They lived an idyllic lifestyle in a modest country house in Angus. Neither wealthy nor poor, they had sufficient to enjoy a simple, safe life. Both of them worked from home. Roddy was an engineer, not yet ready to retire, and Margaret a solicitor with a small farming practice. When they had a minor success to celebrate they would buy a bottle of cava or occasionally champagne.

All this changed when, to Roddy's surprise, one of his inventions hit the jackpot.

It was one of those unusual winters in Angus when there was more snow near the coast than in the glens. Winds from the arctic pummelled the snow down the Eastern side, most of it landing in the North Sea. So the coastal towns of Montrose and Arbroath got the worst of it; or the best of it if, like Roddy, you enjoy the snow.

'I'm taking Dougal for a run in Victoria Park, Darling. Do you want me to pick up anything in Arbroath on the way back?'

'We're dangerously low on brown sugar. Could you bring a salad too? Make it a Caesar. Let's live a little.'

Margaret was on a diet with the result that Roddy also was losing weight and making better times on his runs. It was invigorating running on the snow with a light snow falling. The tide was in and they could hear as well as see the breakers fighting against the wind. The coastline of East Lothian had disappeared but the tip of the Fife peninsula was just visible through the falling snow. Dougal ran ahead at first, sniffing at where other dogs had been, but there were no people or dogs out in this weather and Dougal soon returned to trot alongside his master. All Roddy could smell was the divine freshness of a winter morning. After a warm-up jog of a mile in the cross-wind they got down to serious training, doing sprints of about a hundred and sixty metres between a shelter and the end of a football pitch and trotting back to start again when two minutes were up. Thirty-five seconds was Roddy's ration for the sprints, and the last one had to be inside thirty seconds. Today's target was seven iterations. Once he could do fifteen, Roddy reckoned he'd be fit enough to run a mile in six and a half minutes, not exactly an Olympic qualifying time but not bad for a sixty-five-year-old with a dodgy knee. Then he'd be ready to take a group on the twenty-five mile circuit up Lochnagar in the summer.

Dougal was an excellent pace-setter: a loveable, beautiful, athletic form of chocolate labrador loping effortlessly just ahead in two inches of snow. On the seventh iteration Roddy concentrated on lengthening his stride over the first twenty strides. Then an acceleration over the next ten. Now he was going as quickly as he could. He relaxed his face and kept his form, lifting his knees, driving back his elbows and pushing hard at the ankles as he glided, palms slicing the air, over the last twenty-two left-rights. Under twenty-nine seconds, best yet. He thumped the air with his left hand and gave his dog a hug.

After a shower and a cup of coffee with Margaret, Roddy went to his computer, Dougal at his feet. The second clock was nearly ready. The quadratic one had been pretty enough with its spiral of the 24 primary squares adding to one large square but it moved too slowly. 'Like watching paint dry' had been the unkind remark at the presentation in Glasgow. Well, we learn from our mistakes. Roddy's second clock had five times as many lights, was three-dimensional, and if you put two of them together, one peaking at noon and the other at midnight, you had a busy spectacle that demanded attention and told the time at all hours with as much precision as you could want.

Three weeks later the clock was ready for a demonstration. Forget the Science Centres, Roddy decided. He got an appointment to give a boardroom presentation to Ove Arup, the construction company that had built the Scottish Parliament.

'Let me cut to the chase, ladies and gentlemen. What you see on the screen is a projection of a working clock. The sculptured version will be built with light emitting diodes in the two rotating chandeliers and on the carpets. As the lights go out in the chandeliers they go on in the carpets, and vice versa, extinguishing layers and completing squares every hour, and the two systems are in antiphase. You could have one at each end of a ballroom, in an airport concourse, in the foyer of a large hotel ...'

The chairman cut in. 'Mr McKie, are you willing to build this for us in Iran?'

Soraya was co-opted into the nuclear programme as a Junior Scientific Officer and signed Iran's Official Secrets Act. Any hope that this would quickly put her in a position to find out more about Anheim Mossada was effectively dashed. She was instructed to spend the first weeks reading text books on nuclear physics, a subject that had not been part of her university education. She was given no access to papers written by senior workers in the nuclear programme. Patience, she told herself. All that will come. After a month she was given a tour of Number Two Facility which was to the northeast of Tehran, close to foothills that looked to her like overgrown sand dunes. The facility was still under construction. Indeed, she learnt that construction had been halted and restarted many times while she had been in Edinburgh. The site covered about fifty acres. Soraya was struck by the contrast between the very dusty exteriors and the scrupulously clean working areas indoors. She had to put on clean-room clothing no fewer than seven times during the tour. The building where she would work was uninspiring, a concrete monstrosity about a hundred metres on a side. Offices and a small laboratory had been completed on two sides of the perimeter but the vast middle was a dusty open space.

'We're still in the design phase,' was the cryptic explanation.

Soraya was assigned to the Fuel Team. Their job was to manufacture enriched uranium.

John was thrilled to be accepted by the Foreign and Commonwealth Office. He needed to work on his Arabic, he was told, but his results in the numeracy, literacy and intelligence tests had been satisfactory and he had scored exceptionally well in physical fitness. That was due to the excellent sports facilities at Sheffield. Having signed the Official Secrets Act he was admitted as a Trainee Intelligence Officer and was assigned to Middle Eastern Affairs.

'John, we know all about you and Soraya al-Jerad from your screening. How is she, by the way?'

'Well, I think. All she was allowed to say was that she is involved in the science side of things. Her emails are censored, as you might expect.'

'So must yours be, I'm afraid. But we want you to keep in touch with her. And you should learn Farsi as well. We'll put you through a course.'

John sat among the new recruits at his first Departmental meeting. Everyone stood up as the Foreign Secretary entered. John's first impression confirmed what he had been quietly told by his Section Head, Peter Lipscombe: the man loved the glamour of the job. He was literally on stage. When given the standard tour John had learnt that the conference hall with raked seating was traditionally used for the In-house Review before the Christmas break and one of this Foreign Secretary's innovations had been to authorize the construction of a permanent stage with curtains and floodlights. What a tosser! The presence of recruits like me, John thought, gives him an excuse to go over old ground. Sure enough, the Foreign Secretary launched straight into a review of policy.

'Let me just repeat the position of the F.O. on Iraq. It was impossible to decide whether Saddam was strutting and bluffing or did indeed have weapons of mass destruction.'

Immediately, John noticed, the audience resolved into three groups: the senior ones kept studiously straight faces; those who had heard it all before but had still to master the niceties of F.O. behaviour were restive; one of them whispered, 'Scarlett was yellow,' and was rewarded with thumbs-up from his friends. Most of the new faces around him, oblivious of the remark and its reception, continued to give rapt attention.

'If he had such weapons,' the Foreign Secretary continued, 'it was not clear that the inspectors would be able to find them while he was in power. On the balance of probability our advice to Downing Street was that it was more likely than not that Saddam had WMD. That, as we now know, was incorrect.'

John had to suppress a smile. The recruits on both sides of him obligingly pursed their lips as if they held a share of corporate responsibility and were somehow to blame.

'Now we are faced with a similar situation regarding Iran but the key question is different. We know that there are hard-liners, not least the current President of Iran, although his blustering may be mainly for domestic consumption. The hard-liners want to develop nuclear weapons.'

This was serious. Soraya was living and working in a fearfully treacherous environment. He had to help her somehow. John was not even tempted to smile as he observed the Foreign Secretary briefly putting on his serious expression and then relaxing to present the face of a reasonable man.

'They may well be outnumbered by Iranians who just want nuclear power as part of an energy portfolio. Then again, why do they need nuclear energy when they are so rich in oil? Have they suddenly turned green?'

This produced smiles, and not just from the recruits. The Foreign Secretary was clearly delighted. At last he gave the specific order.

'What I want to know from definitive intelligence is which group in Iran actually rules the roost. If the hard-liners really do have executive authority then on no account may we allow Iran to develop or even have access to enriched uranium. On the other hand, if the hard-liners are essentially a fringe group that will never be allowed to manufacture nuclear weapons then a negotiated settlement is possible. It would require routine inspection by the West. The Nuclear Powers might offer in return a scaling down of their nuclear arsenals.'

'Israel would not like it, sir.' John recognized the senior analyst on Middle Eastern Affairs.

'Israel may have to lump it. Though serious, that is not the main point. The main point is that our intelligence must be good enough to give a definitive answer on the balance of power in Iran, and I don't just mean weight of numbers. I mean: which group, warlike or peaceful, would control the development of nuclear energy? Now put your minds to how we can gain this intelligence.'

After some weeks of intensive linguistic instruction John was summoned by Peter Lipscombe. 'There is someone I want you to meet - accidentally on purpose.'

As Roddy was doing his preparatory stretches, one leg at a time for a count of fifteen over the back of the bench where he had parked, he noticed a young man in a track suit running smoothly towards him. Roddy finished his stretching exercises and let Dougal out of the car as the young man passed. Dougal caught up with the young man and ran beside him for about twenty metres before returning to Roddy who had begun to trot farther back. They all met again towards the far end of the park as the young man was on his return leg. This time Dougal ran forward to meet him and jumped in the air around him. The young man stopped and patted Dougal who responded enthusiastically.

'Sorry about that,' said Roddy. 'I hope you weren't running against the clock.'

'Not at all. He's a wonderful-looking dog. You exercise him like this every morning?'

'When I can. I haven't seen you around here before. Just up for a holiday?'

'Yes. Thought I'd walk Jock's Road to Braemar and maybe the Lairig Ghru after that.'

They were beginning to cool down. 'Well ... Shall we run back? ... if you don't mind an old man's pace ... Jock's Road is fine but the Lairig is not what it was ... All cut up by too many mountain bikes ... even motor bikes ... lazy sods ... I'm taking Dougal up Lochnagar on Wednesday ... circular route from Glen Doll ... back by Jock's Road ... There'll be a few of us going ... Care to come along?'

'Absolutely,' said John. 'Sounds great.'

'There's a letter for you, special delivery from the Foreign Office,' said Margaret.

'I wonder what they want now. I filled in all their pesky forms.'

Roddy took the letter up to his study and opened it carefully. Then he came rushing back downstairs. 'They want me to visit them in London tomorrow morning. Something urgent has come up and they think I can help.'

'All right, James Bond, you'd better book your flights. Down and up from Dundee, I presume. Dougal will survive until you get back. I'll have dinner ready, with champagne.'

The appointment was not until 10.30 a.m. So Roddy treated himself to a leisurely breakfast at Prêt à Manger near Marble Arch before walking to the imposing building of the Foreign and Commonwealth Office. He mounted the steps to the revolving doors of shiny glass and polished brass. The pillared foyer was larger than he had expected. Portraits of previous Foreign Secretaries covered the walls but Roddy had barely time to take them in. Security was tight. He showed his letter of invitation, passport and driving licence to a guard just inside the doors who checked that his name was on a list. Then he advanced to one of the receptionists, signed in and received his Visitor's badge.

'I'll tell Mr Lipscombe you have arrived.'

In less than a minute a short, pink-faced man of about forty came out of the lift and introduced himself.

'I'm Lipscombe. Thank you for coming, Mr McKie. Let me take you up.'

They got out of the lift on the third floor and entered an open plan office space. About half of the twenty workers had headphones on. All were staring at computer screens. No one paid them attention as they walked round a side of the "bull pen" to Lipscombe's office. There were two mugs of steaming coffee on Lipscombe's desk.

'Milk and one brown sugar, right?'

'How did you know?'

'You'll see in a minute. Let me get right to it, Mr McKie. First, congratulations on your contract with Ove Arup for the Arabian Nights Hotel in Tehran.'

'Is something wrong with the export licence?'

'No, not at all. We're delighted ...'

'Then what's the problem?'

Lipscombe picked up his coffee and with a gesture encouraged Roddy to do the same. As he lifted his own mug Roddy noticed that Lipscombe's left pinkie was missing. Lipscombe caught his glance. 'Oh that. Ancient history ... Back to the present. There isn't a problem. We want you to do us a favour.'

'If I can, certainly.'

'We want you to take someone on, as an employee ... one of our people ... so it won't cost you anything.'

Roddy took a long sip. A spook on board. Margaret will be excited. 'Will he or she be any use technically, I mean in the installation?'

'I think you'll find him very useful. You've already met him. I understand he steered you through the clouds from Locknagar to Cairn Bannock.'

Roddy winced over the Englishman's pronunciation and immediately felt guilty for focusing on a minor point. After all, he, the over-confident leader of the mini-expedition, had committed the sin of venturing into the mountains without a compass. He hoped Lipscombe would interpret the wince as reaction to an embarrassment remembered.

Lipscombe pressed a button on his desk and a few seconds later John walked in.

'Prime Minister, the Foreign Secretary has arrived.'

'Show him in please, Janet, and bring us coffee when you get a chance.'

The Foreign Secretary had been invited to the Prime Minister's office many times. It was rectangular and of modest size given the importance of the PM's position. His desk was at the end farther from the door. The main part of the room had four comfortable armchairs around a coffee table. There were only two pictures on the walls, both impressionistic. One showed a deserted running track on a rainy day and the other, more to the Foreign Secretary's taste, was clearly a bird's eye view of a football match. You always knew if you were in trouble for then the PM would remain seated at his desk and no coffee would be served. On this occasion, however, the PM rose from one of the armchairs.

'Robert, good to see you. Take a pew. Coffee's on its way.'

'Thanks, Tom. Everything under control?'

'For the moment. All quiet on the Eastern front. You and I have to think long term, however.'

So it was going to be about Iran. On your mettle, Bob. Listen for clues. Which way is he veering?

'How good is our intelligence on Iran?'

A discreet knock and Janet appeared with a tray of coffee and biscuits. The Foreign Secretary knew not to touch the biscuits: made a bad impression on this fitness freak of a PM. He carefully poured them each a cup of coffee to show how steady his hand was before answering.

'Getting better but still poor. We're trying a new tack, latching on to bonafide construction and installation businesses ...'

'The thing is, Robert, no matter how hard you try you'll never be able to persuade me on the basis of intelligence. At best, it's never foolproof; and at worst ... Well, you saw what happened in Iraq.'

Show no emotion. But, my God, what a hypocrite!

'Are you saying, Tom, that this time – I mean as regards Iran – when you finally decide whether to go the military route or the diplomatic that that decision will not be based on intelligence?'

'Yes.' The uncompromising monosyllable was accentuated by a piercing look straight in the eye. The Foreign Secretary was forced to blink as the PM continued. 'But don't underestimate the role of intelligence. We need it to persuade others. Do you follow me, Robert? The intelligence that you divulge to me must support the major decision which you and a few others in Cabinet will make with me; and I know I can rely on you to join this process with full patriotic integrity.'

Just as well no one is listening. Wouldn't put it past him to be recording this, though. 'Of course you have my full support. I ...'

'Robert, Robert. Detente worked in the Cold War because both sides realized that setting off a nuclear bomb would be suicidal. We were dealing with rational people. That's not the case with certain factions in the Middle East. They can't wait to get their hands on the ultimate suicide bomb. Some of them even think they would survive a nuclear war. We cannot take risks with intelligence that suggests they only want nuclear power for peaceful purposes. So don't ever bring me reports in that vein. I'll tear them to shreds.'

'Understood, Prime Minister.'

Chapter 5

April 2005

The change in the political landscape looked more significant than it really was, Nasher reflected. The Ayatollah had not gone away. He was still the ultimate authority. But he had lost the Presidency. He was no longer the front man. If you were prepared to be a little cynical – Nasher's upper lip tightened a fraction in the glimmer of a smile - it was easy to analyse what had happened. The Presidential Election had come at the wrong time for the Ayatollah. He had had to raise taxes to pay for the investment in nuclear technology. His reasoned argument about future benefits was outweighed by the mood of current misery. The people voted with their stomachs. Nasher caught himself shaking his head again; he'd have to watch that. The paradox was that the man they chose to replace the Ayatollah was, if anything, even more pro-nuclear; but that was not why he got in. Oh no. He was elected on a promise of running the economy better. Just that. No proof. Any port in a storm.

It made for more lively meetings with the Governing Council. That was the good part but it had ramifications. The change in leadership suited the eruptive Mullah Ahmed down to the ground, and the new President, not shy about voicing his own anti-Israeli sentiments, welcomed Ahmed's outbursts. Faced with that double act, Saban Kandar, now the Minister for Energy and Foreign Affairs, had to use all his powers of tact and persuasion to minimize the damage from exacerbating Western opposition to the nuclear programme. It was a race against time: could facilities be up and running and demonstrably peaceful before Western fears rose to such a pitch that they were sabotaged or suffered strikes from the air?

Nasher sighed. The consequence for him was a huge increase in work load. He was directed to redouble his efforts to make the facilities operational. He spent hours every day pouring over flow charts with his engineers, determining critical paths, continually updating plans as daily targets were met or narrowly missed. So many things had to be done simultaneously. If all the effort were put into the manufacture of enriched uranium, clearly the first essential stage, no doubt that would succeed, but the design of the control rods would be the next stumbling block, and the steam tanks had to be installed, and the chimneys, and the electrical generators, and the pylons to link with the grid which itself had to be expanded. On top of all that, foreign workers had to be vetted, housed and fed. There was, in addition, the obvious requirement that all workers, himself included, should be monitored for radiation. Evacuation procedures had to be written, rehearsed, modified. Indeed every operation had to be planned and formal records had to be kept and reviewed. And perhaps the most important point of all was to keep morale high.

On that last point Nasher had support from his Minister. Huge progress had been made by the fuel team thanks largely to Soraya's mastery of operations research techniques. Her proposals for the number of centrifuges, their layout, the minimizing of operations handled remotely in what they referred to as "the glove box" (in reality a robot-controlled space surrounded by walls with large windows eighteen inches thick) had all been followed to the letter. The result was that at the beginning of April, three months ahead of schedule, the fuel team leader was able to report that a 3.5% enrichment of uranium had been achieved. With exaggerated optimism he predicted that it was all over bar the shouting. All they had to do now was scale up production, for the 3.5% level of enrichment was sufficient for the power stations.

Saban Kandar and the President decided to make a big play on this success. On April 11th they hosted a major press conference where the enthusiastic support of the assembled scientists and politicians was evident to the world. Later that day Kandar called Soraya to his office.

'Soraya, your valuable contribution has been noted. The efficiencies you instigated have reaped this early reward for the nation ... Now I want to talk to you further about efficiencies.' He pressed a bell and immediately a servant appeared with a tray of juices and an open box of turkish delight. 'Your favourite sweetmeat, I believe.'

Things are looking up at last, thought Soraya. 'Thank you very much, Minister.' She selected a glass of mango juice and a small square of turkish delight.

'Now, Soraya, all of us who are able must take on more than one job. Look at your father. Indispensable in so many areas. I'd be lost without him.' He picked a glass of papaya juice, drained it in a few gulps and reached for a large slice of turkish delight which he waved, spraying glucose over the low table and his trousers as he spoke. 'There are two more jobs I'd like you to take on.'

Soraya nodded politely. Finally her footsteps were hot on the trail of Anheim Mossada. He must have been groomed for advancement in a similar way.

'The first I think you will enjoy. By a happy coincidence it can be included in our current celebrations. Along with your parents I want you to attend a reception and ball at the Arabian Nights Hotel. The ballroom has had an interesting clock installed, all very mathematical, right up your street; and the party is to mark the completion of the installation. But it is really a diplomatic occasion, an opportunity to show Westerners that we are not savages. So dress up. Your father will give you the details.'

'Thank you, Minister. I shall look forward to that.' Was this a test? The man had probably read emails from John about the clocks. She quickly added, 'I know a little about the clock because a friend from university is employed by the company that designed and installed it. I hope he will be present at the party for it would be very pleasant to renew his acquaintance ... I am sure you also would enjoy meeting him, Minister.'

'I already have, Soraya. He's a fine young man. John Russell, isn't it? Yes. He particularly asked that you might be invited ... Now let us move on to the second task. It is much more serious. It cannot have escaped you that there are threats, especially from the Americans, to destroy our nuclear facilities. They are paranoid, these Americans, but we must be prepared in case they are foolish enough to carry out these threats.' Soraya put on a suitably serious expression as the Minister looked at her gravely and continued. 'We must assume that they know where all our facilities are located, for we have not been at pains to hide them, except in one case. You see, Soraya, were the Americans, or others, to destroy our facilities – and with them many of our scientists – it would put back our programme by many years. But if we had even one facility still in operation we could quickly get back on track. So it's very important that we keep one secret.'

'I understand, Minister. You would like me to work there too?'

'I knew you would understand, Soraya. Yes. You will be part of a small, carefully selected team to keep our nuclear ambitions alive. Just in case. Your father knows about this facility, of course, although even he has not seen it and does not know its location. I have spoken with him already. He understands that you cannot discuss this with anyone, not even with him.'

'And the other members?'

'They, like you, are being recruited over the next few weeks and months ... From now on, Soraya, this must remain an absolute secret. Do you understand the seriousness of that undertaking?'

'Yes, Minister, and thank you.'

The Arabian Nights Hotel was built on the highest plot of land within the city boundaries, about a mile from the centre in the embassy district of Tehran. The hotel had been completely revamped. From the outside, by day, external elevators were the most noticeable innovation: by night, the entire building was lit with a light show featuring all the colours in a succession of seemingly random patterns. Reflected light was caught in the lines of fountains within the rows of palm trees on either side of the promenade leading to the front entrance.

It was a cold night in late April and the ladies all wore thick shawls and veils as they walked from their limousines or taxis into the hotel, but once inside these were removed to reveal evening gowns as splendid as any seen at major occasions anywhere in the world. The Press had been invited. For the first hour they photographed arrivals and gained interviews with foreign diplomats, steering them to freshly upholstered sofas throughout the vast foyer. There was just one topic: international reaction to Iran's milestone of enriching uranium. The impression most journalists got was that the international community had been caught on the hop. It was too early to tell what form the reaction might take. Somewhat disappointed, the journalists and cameramen followed the glittering crowd into the ballroom.

The ballroom was in the shape of the letter D to give room for a full orchestra in the curved area. There was a bar at each end, for this was a designated international hotel. Broken rows of comfortable upright chairs filled the long side s facing the dance floor and the orchestra beyond. No one was sitting down, however. Everyone congregated on the dance floor with glass in hand. Finally they had something to talk about other than enriched uranium. The spectacle of the clocks took their breath away. Two chandeliers, slowly rotating in opposite directions at differing speeds, one over each end of the dance floor, were partially lit from the top in one and from the bottom in the other in alternating layers of red and yellow, the lights digitally increasing in one and decreasing in the other every few seconds. Underneath the chandeliers, on the dance floor itself, large square carpets of lights were attracting equal attention. At first, people stood around the two squares to watch as light seemed to fall from one chandelier to its carpet and to rise from the other carpet to its chandelier. Alternating borders of red and yellow lights increased from the centre or decreased from the perimeter of the carpets to form squares within each large square in response to the waxing or waning of the number of lights in the chandeliers. Gradually people were unafraid to walk over the inlaid glass across the carpets of lights.

'Don't you see, it's two giant clocks,' someone whispered. 'One builds up to the middle of the day and the other to the middle of the night. It's like rainfall and evaporation. See. There's more happening just now on that one over there. You can tell the time by looking at either chandelier or either carpet but depending on the time of day one set will give greater precision than the other. There must be tens of thousands of lights all told.'

'But why does it come out in perfect squares on the carpets and completed layers in the chandeliers at the end of each hour?'

'That's the beauty of it. You'd have to ask the designer. There he is, I think.'

The Minister for Energy and Foreign Affairs excused himself from the group surrounding Roddy and Margaret, climbed into the conductor's podium and raised both arms to hush the throng of invited guests. He spoke in English.

'Distinguished Guests, Ladies and Gentlemen,

'I am Saban Kandar, for my sins the Minister for Energy and Foreign Affairs, and it gives me great pleasure to welcome you all to the beautifully refurbished Arabian Nights Hotel and to this magnificent ballroom. The British companies led by Ove Arup performed the construction and installation work three months ahead of schedule.' There was a ripple of applause. 'We also achieved our milestone of enriching uranium three months ahead of schedule. Must be something in the air, don't you think?' More applause and some laughter. 'Like all of you I have been admiring the clock, or should I say the clocks, although I must admit that I do not fully appreciate the mathematical subtleties. But I am sure many of you gathered here have already worked out the mathematics behind the design. Like music, mathematics is a common language. For our two great countries, however, it is more than that. It is the purest ingredient of our cultures since ancient times and has become for both of us the true engine of our economies. I trust that this mathematical clock will herald many co-operative ventures between the United Kingdom and Iran and indeed between Iran and the West generally as bonds of friendship are strengthened ... Now I am going to ask Mrs McKie, the lovely wife of the inventor, if she will do me the honour of dancing with me, and I call on all of you to follow us.'

The crowd moved outwards to leave the central area vacant as the Minister led a forewarned and rehearsed Margaret to the dance floor. The orchestra struck up a jive. Immediately Kandar came to life, strutting his stuff. For a fat man he was amazingly energetic. Margaret quickly matched his movements and allowed herself to be flung, twirled and caught time and again. For fully two minutes the crowd watched and applauded until Kandar signalled that everyone should join in. Thereafter the standard of dancing fell considerably, as few Iranians were confident to let themselves go in an exuberant dance that was foreign to them. But some, encouraged by their cosmopolitan dance partners, did their best.

There was a short break and then the music changed to a waltz. Fresh partners were sought and those who had not risked the jive got up for the waltz.

John held Soraya close to him. She was wearing a long dress of shimmering green, low cut this time. White gloves covered her forearms. A bracelet of rubies over her right glove matched a high necklace. Her eyelashes seemed longer than he had remembered and her eyebrows were now pencil thin. She wore her hair up, woven into a beehive shape. As they glided across the dance floor her exotic perfume filled his nostrils. To John she looked as he imagined Sheherezade must have looked: utterly desirable.

'Alone at last, almost.'

'Almost,' she whispered back.

'Did you like the speech?'

'It was all right, I suppose.'

'Standard political stuff. Quite an operator. He's some dancer, though.'

'So are you. Much better than last time ... Been practising?'

'Day and night. All the better to sweep you off your feet.'

'John, we need to talk.'

He led her off the dance floor towards one of the bars, collected a glass of orange juice for each of them and guided her to the chairs. This was the moment he had been looking forward to and dreading in equal measure. For the first time, he could not be wholly open with her. She knew from his emails that he had been learning Arabic, but not that he was now proficient in Farsi as well. She knew that he had a job with the clock installation company but she could not know his real purpose in coming to Iran.

Soraya must have had much the same on her mind, for she said, 'John, in spite of that speech about developing friendship, you know, I'm sure, that we are being watched.'

'Sure, Soraya. That's only to be expected.'

'And John, there are now some things I may not talk about.'

'Right.'

They fell silent for a moment, sipping the orange juice.

'Is everything all right, Soraya? You're not in trouble?'

'Everything's fine. Really. It's just that we must have some secrets.'

'Soraya, I love you. I'll stay patient. Just promise that you will let me know if ever you are in danger.'

'I promise.'

'Right. Let's go back to the others.'

'We're so glad you could come, Mr and Mrs McKie, and thank you for allowing John to come too. Welcome to our house.'

'We're delighted to be here, Mrs al-Jerad. This is a real treat for us,' said Roddy. 'As for letting John come, I could not have stopped him. But he has earned a free evening.'

Nasher took their coats. Margaret handed Aisha a box covered in tartan wrapping paper. 'Just a flavour of Scotland,' she said.

'And these are from Belgium,' said John, handing over his present of chocolates.

'Well thank you all. My husband does not get abroad so much as he used to. So we really appreciate presents from other countries. Now do come through. Soraya is ready to pour refreshments.'

Aisha led the way. She wore a long skirt of floral print and a pale blue blouse that matched one of the flowers in the print. High heeled white sandals, a pearl necklace, just one ring. Terrifyingly understated elegance was Margaret's impression as she followed Aisha's graceful figure down the hall. Roddy and she had dressed conventionally in suits. She managed to resist uttering Cleopatra's famous line, "One is so limited when one travels."

But she need not have worried. Aisha and Soraya were charm itself. Aisha led Roddy and Margaret to the two most comfortable chairs in the beautifully carpeted drawing room and Soraya served them and her parents juices and dates from a trolley before summoning John to help her in the kitchen. A baby grand piano covered in family pictures dominated one end of the room. Margaret asked Aisha if she might get up to have a closer look. Among the framed photographs there was one showing Soraya receiving a copy of the Arabian Nights from a middle-aged man.

'That's her English tutor,' said Aisha in response to Margaret's enquiry. 'As a child Soraya loved the stories and it was clever of her tutor to teach her to read them in English. We gave her a pair of bookends when she went to university in Edinburgh and now she always has that book in pride of place along with her dictionaries and favourite text books wherever she works.'

Margaret then looked down the room. French doors at the other end opened out to a walled garden of fruit trees. The bulk of the room was lined with sofas and an assortment of chairs, some unashamedly low and comfortable, others elegantly upright. Margaret said how much she admired the room. Aisha thanked her, confessed to preferring the peacefulness of the fruit garden, led her to the French doors for a better look, and modestly changed the subject.

'Tell me, Mrs McKie, are you a mathematical wizard like your husband or are you like me? I sometimes feel like a fish out of water in the presence of my clever husband and daughter.'

Margaret smiled and wiped a stray curl of almost natural red hair out of her eyes. 'You and I must stick together, Mrs al-Jerad, for I am not at all mathematical.'

'If the clever husband might be allowed to butt in, I'm sure there are lots of other ways of being clever, Mrs McKie. What is your profession?'

'I'm a solicitor. Most of my clients are farmers.'

'Then we shall treat you with great respect, for lawyers can be terrifying. Don't you agree, Mr McKie?'

'Terrifying indeed.'

Aisha and Margaret exchanged grimaces. Aisha said, 'Now that cannot be true of your wife ... But tell me, Mr McKie, what gave you the idea for your clocks?'

'It was something my grandfather told me about sermons in the Church of Scotland many years ago. When the time came for the minister to deliver his sermon the senior member of the congregation, called the Session Clerk, would bolt the minister into the pulpit, start an hour glass on the ledge for everyone to see, and not let the minister out until he had preached for a full hour. The story goes of one particular minister who liked the sound of his own voice, or as we say in Scotland "fancied his barra" and felt he was just getting into his stride when the hour was up. He waved away the returning Session Clerk, turned the hour glass upside down, and kept going for another hour ... Fortunately we hang ministers now if their sermons last more than ten minutes. How long do sermons last in the mosques?'

'It varies,' said Nasher. 'Our local mullah manages to get his points across quite quickly. He never takes more than fifteen minutes. But others, I regret to say, resemble the minister in your grandfather's story ... But please continue about the clock. I'm fascinated.'

'Well that's really about all there is to it. I wanted to make a "twelve hour glass" clock that turns upside down, so to speak, for the second twelve hours, and drains light rather than sand. It was then just a case of finding the right mathematical series to make the patterns come out as squares.'

'Then, I suppose, it became an engineering problem?'

'Exactly. That's when the hard work started.'

'I know the feeling.' Nasher got up to offer refills. 'I don't think it will be long before Soraya calls us through for dinner, but there's time for another glass.'

'John and Soraya are clearly very fond of each other,' said Margaret as she accepted more grapefruit juice.

'Oh yes. And we are delighted,' said Aisha.

'Two excellent young people,' said Roddy.

Nasher returned to his seat. 'I know what must be on your minds,' he said. 'It's the religious difference, isn't it?' Nasher paused while Margaret and Roddy nodded. 'They are both committed to their respective religious beliefs and find much in common. But I'll not minimize the difficulties. We must leave it to them.'

Religion was the last thing on John's mind as he helped Soraya in the kitchen. They had spent the first minute in a tight embrace until Soraya whispered that they had better get on with the final preparations for the meal. Her hair was down this evening, shorter than it had been in her student days. Now it lay just short of her shoulders, framing her lovely face most beautifully. She must have had it cut and reshaped since last night at the reception and ball.

John picked up her apron which he had untied and let fall as soon as he had taken her in his arms. He helped her back into it and tied the strings as they had a final kiss. She made him put one on too and laughed at the picture he made in the sunflower pattern. Then she set him to carving the leg of lamb while she laid out the first dish, prawns in a spicy tomato sauce on a bed of couscous.

'When you have opened these bottles of wine we can ask them into the dining room, John ... How do I look? Not too dishevelled?'

'I've never seen you dishevelled, more's the pity. You're lovely, Soraya. Good enough to eat. And I'm very hungry.'

'Thank you, kind sir. Now behave.'

After the meal as they were drinking coffee, dark and strong, Roddy said, 'There's a big debate about nuclear energy in Scotland also. For us the issue is decommissioning: deep underground or on the surface. We're having a conference at the Gleneagles Hotel in the middle of June. I'd like to invite you all. I'm sure you and Soraya would find it interesting, Mr al-Jerad, and I know Margaret would love to take Mrs al-Jerad around the area.'

'That's very kind of you,' said Nasher, 'but unfortunately I shall not be able to get away.'

'And I must therefore stay also,' said Aisha.

'But Soraya should go,' said Nasher. 'Decommissioning is not an issue we have considered seriously yet, but we should definitely take the opportunity to learn about it.'

'Thank you, Father. And thank you, Mr McKie.'

Saban Kandar had thought hard about how to keep in touch with the Mullah Ahmed. No one suspected that they were working together, of that he was sure, and he had to keep it that way. In public they would continue to take opposite sides for that provided the best security. Keeping the momentum going, however, required one on one private meetings. No doubt he could arrange meetings in isolated spots, under cover of darkness if necessary, but sooner or later they would be caught and neither fancied the consequences. Much safer to visit openly, nothing to hide: he, a peace-loving man, trying vainly to win over the fanatical mullah. Saban Kandar, therefore, always made appointments through his secretary to meet the Mullah Ahmed, sometimes summoning him to the Department, more often arranging to meet in the mosque.

'Come back for me in one hour,' Kandar told his driver. Then he walked to the main gate and stood to one side to make way for those who were leaving after the late afternoon service. He was recognized and greeted respectfully by the departing crowd. After the last man had left he took his turn to shake hands solemnly with the Mullah Ahmed and they walked together into the compound. Anyone looking through the gate would have seen the Minister gesticulating and leaning persuasively towards the impassive mullah.

It was only about thirty metres to the mosque but the energetic body language had left Kandar perspiring.

'A cool drink, Ahmed, for the love of Allah, or I'll die.' Kandar removed the jacket of his suit and slumped to the floor, his back against a wall. There were damp stains on his pink shirt across his ample stomach and emanating from his armpits.

Ahmed brought a long drink of the juice of limes. He himself never drank at the mosque until the sun had set.

'Better?'

'Thank you, my friend.' Kandar roused himself. 'Progress is good but there's a lot to do. As you know, we have achieved the basic level of enriched uranium, good enough for power plants. All we have to do is put it through seventeen more steps of centrifuging. Then it will be 85% enriched. For a time we can pretend that the seventeen more sets of centrifuges are for seventeen different power plants. After all, the French have more than fifty.'

'What about just buying weapons grade uranium from the Russians?'

Kandar snorted. The sound from his large hooked nose could have come from a trombone. 'A non-starter. Too many strings. We couldn't control it.'

'And on the wider political front?'

'Politically it's not too bad. The West is threatening a surgical strike but that's a long way off and they don't know the real target. In fact, you and I – and your heavies of course - are the only ones who do.'

'So what's the'

'The problem is the bomb itself. We need a small, reliable design team. This must be recruited from the larger technical team. I have already made a start. Eventually we shall come to the point that the two teams must diverge and the major one must not know the real purpose of the minor one; and we'll keep that purpose secret even from the minor elite team for as long as possible. But you can leave all that to me. I'll just keep you informed ... How is progress on your side?'

'With respect, Minister, I think you will need me when it comes to "recruiting". They won't all come quietly. You'll certainly need me when they find out what they were recruited for.'

'Perhaps you're right, but as the Americans say, let's try diplomacy first. Anyway, your end of things. Is your team still motivated?'

It was becoming somewhat malodorous in the confined space of the mullah's office. Ahmed opened a window and peered out to ensure that no one was about.

'Well, they quite enjoyed the subtle despatch of the Energy Minister but they're not enjoying the hard slog of extending the underground chamber at the mine. It's having to work at night that gets them down. I tell them the work will be more in their line later when they have to enforce the building of the bomb ... In my official role I've done the usual fire and brimstone sermons but people are becoming inured. There's not much appetite for attacks against the Israelis. They are worried about reprisals.'

'Well, keep chipping away. You can't expect much support until the first bomb has exploded. Then you'll be amazed how suddenly patriotic everyone becomes ... By the way, history tells us that we need to set off two bombs to force surrender. So you'll need two different delivery strategies.'

Ahmed digested this new requirement. 'When must these be in place?'

'You have a year at least, maybe longer.'

'No problem then. Let me know if you need my help in recruiting the bomb team from your technocrats.' He said that disparagingly as only a hardened soldier could.

Chapter 6

'Keep him waiting, Janet. Two minutes should do it. No coffee.'

After precisely one hundred and twenty seconds there was a knock and the Foreign Secretary walked in. Was that a drop of sweat on his temple or just a vestige of rain? Seated at his desk the Prime Minister said, 'What's the latest from Iran?'

'Nothing good to report.'

'Take a stab at answering the question.' This said very softly.

'You told me not five months ago, Prime Minister, not to report intelligence that seemed to show their motive was peaceful.'

'Seemed to? Well does it or doesn't it?'

'Too early to ... All right, if you insist. It does.'

There was a long pause. The rain against the windows made a thrashing sound.

'My dear Robert, you must improve your listening skills. Part A, as you correctly stated, was "Don't report to me the wrong intelligence." But you have neglected part B.'

The Foreign Secretary looked genuinely puzzled.

'Don't you remember? Thou wert not wont to be so slow. "Never underestimate the value of intelligence. I need it to persuade others." Instead of pursuing that line you have very efficiently set in motion a recipe for disaster. I'm not the only one who says so. The US administration is furious. You yourself said, "The idea of invading Iran is inconceivable." Not the cleverest thing for a Foreign Secretary to shout from the rooftops just as negotiations are getting underway. And far from providing me part B you have virtually ensured that one of your underlings will announce to the world that Iran has nothing but peaceful motives.'

'I assure you, Prime Minister, that none of my people ...'

'Oh grow up. The risk of a leak is enormous ... Don't you get it yet? This is all about risk analysis: not F.O. Intelligence "risk analysis"', he made exaggerated quotation marks in the air, 'but big picture political risk analysis.' The P.M. stopped for breath. 'Let me spell it out. We cannot afford not to blow up their nuclear capability. Think of that as the new part A. Now you tell me the new part B.'

'You would find it rather helpful if I could provide you with confirmatory intelligence.'

'By George, he's got it. Almost.'

'Almost, Prime Minister?'

'So what else would I find "rather helpful"? For God's sake, man, what is absolutely required as a matter of urgency?'

It *had* been a drop of sweat, for it was now accompanied by at least five others.

'I must put a stop to the existing intelligence operation.'

'Finally ... In fact you must stop it stone dead. STONE DEAD, Robert. So get on with it or I'll find something less demanding for you to do.'

'Cinco de Mayo,' said Betty.

'Sink or what?' mumbled Nicol, his head still on a pillow.

It was Sunday, the seventh of May. They were having a long lie-in after a late party. A shaft of sunlight streamed through the bedroom window as Betty hauled open the curtains. This did not score a direct hit on Nicol's head. He continued to lie prone. Betty opened the window. That did it.

'What a godawful noise. It's Sunday, isn't it? No respect for us natives.' With a resigned grunt Nicol swept back the bedcovers, leapt out of bed, and lurched apelike towards Betty at the window. He picked her up and dumped her back on the bed.

'Oh no you don't,' she shouted. 'Cawfee. Your turn.'

'All right ... What was all that noisy sinking about? I was having a super dream about you.'

'I was musing.'

'About me?'

'No, you vain thing. It suddenly hit me that the bloodbath of a reshuffle was announced on the 5th of May.'

'So?'

'Go and make coffee, you ignoramus. You've heard of a tale of two cities?'

'Something to do with the French, wasn't it?'

'Droll. Well so is this, except it's a tale of two nations, Mexico and America. Listen and learn, you ape. The fifth of May is the anniversary of the Battle of Puebla in 1862 when 4,000 Mexicans smashed a French army twice its size.'

'Bully for the Mexicans, but how did the Americans come into it?'

'Cause and effect over and again. Very romantic. No, let me put it in language you can understand.' She gave him a despairing look. 'Never mind. The point is our esteemed Prime Minister has littered their parades with the corpses of his political ex-cronies. That glorious date is now contaminated.'

'Are you saying he should have waited until tomorrow morning?'

'It would have been the decent thing to do.'

Nicol smiled at her. 'I'll make the coffee,' he said.

They had been living together for over a year. After graduation, Nicol had followed the conventional route of "theologists gone bad" as Betty put it. He took a course in accountancy and was hired by a venture capital firm in Canary Wharf. As for Betty, having graduated a year after Nicol with an upper second in politics, she had done well in the Civil Service examinations and was now working in the Home Office. They had pooled their resources, or rather, having none, had dickered with their combined incomes to buy a one-bedroom flat in Wandsworth.

'So I can keep an eye on my clients in jail,' said Betty to the mortgage lender who laughed and waived the requirement for a deposit.

After graduating with a good degree in social anthropology Elspeth had remained in Edinburgh to do a course in photography at Napier University. She kept in touch with Betty who was the only other of the five friends still in Edinburgh. When Betty left to work in London where Nicol was now established Elspeth was on her own. She decided it was time to do something adventurous. She applied to join an expedition to Borneo sponsored by the National Geographic magazine and was accepted. The last Betty heard from her was a postcard sent on arrival in Borneo.

The new Foreign Secretary was the first woman to have acceded to that job. She was renowned for her loyalty but it was not clear to whom or to what she was loyal. Was it the Prime Minister or was it the Labour Party? Perhaps, in the end, it was her career. Time would tell.

Upon her return from a rushed visit to meet her opposite number in America she called Lipscombe for the second time to her office.

'Has anything happened during my trip?'

'No, Minister.'

'Is John Russell back yet?'

'Yes.'

'Let's have him in.'

John's first impressions of his new overall boss were favourable. She surprised him by getting up when he entered the room and even more by walking round her desk to shake his hand.

'Peter Lipscombe has told me all about you, John, but I've been looking forward to meeting you in person.'

She was below average height, could not be described as beautiful, but she could certainly be charming. She wore a bright orange pants suit with lipstick to match, making a startling gash across her pale face. When they were all seated she continued. 'I see that you are a mathematician by training, John. So without doubt you have a logical mind. Now, applying strict logic, what can you say about the situation in Iran?'

'I have no conclusions as yet, Minister.'

'Good. Neither have I. For example, I have just seen, in Washington, the full translation of the letter from the President of Iran to President Bush. Apart from an outburst of sabre rattling the letter states again and again that Iran has no intention of developing nuclear weapons. Fine. The letter proves nothing, of course ... Now let me probe into what you have done in Iran.'

Lipscombe gave John an encouraging smile as the interrogation began.

'Let me review the facts. First, you are in love with the daughter of the man in charge of Iran's nuclear programme. True?'

'No.'

'What?'

'He is not in charge. Saban Kandar, the Minister for Energy and Foreign Affairs, is in charge.'

Lipscombe butted in. 'But in practice Nasher al-Jerad, Soraya's father, runs the show. Right?'

'Yes.'

The Foreign Minister raised her hands above the desk top, signalling a pause for thought. 'This may not be a trivial point. In my experience, if you are running an organization, you may, you should, have complete control over the activities of people who report to you. But if you are, in effect, second in command like a Chief Executive Officer you cannot control the person in charge, the Chairman of the Board. He may be working to a different agenda ... So John, let's slow down. I'll ask just one question at a time, and I'm afraid they are personal. Are you in love with this girl Soraya?'

'Yes.'

'And she reciprocates?'

'Yes.'

'And her family welcomes you?'

'Yes.'

'Well that's good and bad from our point of view. We would not otherwise have this excellent contact but you must not let your feelings cloud your judgement.'

'Right.'

The Minister turned to Lipscombe. She bit her lower lip and rocked backwards and forwards in her chair, marshalling her thoughts. John imagined a cartoon of her as a long jumper egging herself on for a record breaking attempt. She said, 'I think we may be on to something here. What if this Saban Kandar, with or without the knowledge of his President, has a private agenda. He alone is in a position to make it happen secretly.'

She turned to face John again. 'I think you should try to find out more about this Minister for Energy and Foreign Affairs. He's my opposite number after all. Frankly, I take everything he says with a pinch of salt anyway, but it would be nice to know what he's really up to ... Now go, both of you, and work out your tactics.'

Betty had taken licence in claiming that her "clients" were in Wandsworth Prison. In fact they were all in Bellmarsh High Security Jail. Before the reshuffle, the team of which she was most definitely the junior member had been discouraged from arranging deportations. 'It's a question of priorities,' they had been told. For Nicol's benefit Betty translated this as 'We'll save the hassle, the legal costs and the airfares. They've done their time, after all.'

'There's no such word as "hassle"', said Nicol.

'Easy to see you don't work in the Home Office.'

Nicol started to play devil's advocate. 'Listen, you gorgeous crumpet, and learn from a superior intellect whose natural skills have been finely honed in matters of discourse. Suppose we have an al-Qaeda fanatic finishing his time in custody. Is it smart to deport him or better to release him under surveillance? Where is he likely to do us more harm, free to reorganize from within his own country or monitored here where we can keep tabs on him? Maybe he would lead us to hidden cells.' Warming to his subject Nicol continued, 'Of course, the monitoring is very expensive and unless it is done thoroughly a policy of releasing but not deporting could be disastrous. The worst of all options for national security is to release him and not to switch on surveillance at all. It is also the cheapest option and the easiest for a busy Home Office Department to adopt.'

'Which is just what I said to begin with,' said Betty.

The Cabinet reshuffle suddenly made Betty's life much busier. Now, with religious zeal, Betty's team set about negotiating and arranging deportations. The first step was to obtain a "statement of unintent", as Betty called it, from the destination country, promising not to imprison, torture or kill the deportee. Then the courts had to have their say, judging whether the crime had been great enough to justify deportation and whether the statement of unintent was credible. Finally arrangements had to be made with scheduled airlines, or a charter flight had to be organized, to whisk the unwelcome guest out of the country with a suitable armed escort. It was suddenly a lot of work.

Betty was given the case of Terias Shammon. Shammon, a Jordanian national, had been convicted of inciting religious hatred and his release date was only two months away. Jordan did not want him back. Under pressure from Betty's Section Head, citing UN protocol, Jordan reluctantly agreed to accept him and sent the formal letter of understanding regarding Shammon's human rights. Shammon's lawyers, however, successfully challenged the credibility of the letter of understanding. So another country had to be found. Betty proposed Iran and managed to negotiate the terms of deportation.

'My first success,' she told Nicol. 'You may take me out to dinner.'

From behind his desk Peter Lipscombe stared alternately at John and at the blank piece of paper in front of him.

'Let's take this as a working hypothesis,' he said. 'Soraya and her Ma and Pa are good, wonderful people. They are loyal to Iran. Soraya and her father are engaged in the development of nuclear power but only for peaceful purposes. They are against making nuclear bombs.'

'I'll go along with that,' said John. 'Soraya was straight with me in saying that there were some things she could not talk about. She'd hardly have said that if she were knowingly involved in developing bombs. In that case she'd have said nothing at all.'

'Unless she were bluffing ... Be fair, John, and icily logical. No offence.'

'None taken, Peter.'

Everyone in the Department had huge respect for Peter Lipscombe. He had earned his exalted position the hard way, in the field. Captured and tortured by the Fedayin-e Islam towards the end of the Iran-Iraq war, he had engineered a daring escape from Tehran, rescuing two of his MI6 colleagues in the process. Examples like that bring out the best.

John said, 'Look, we're not getting very far. Let's extend the hypothesis.' He got up and walked a couple of paces to the door and back, his hands in his pockets. 'Either everyone is to be taken at face value and there is nothing to fear or at least one of the players I've met has devious intent. The most likely candidate is Saban Kandar. Her ladyship back there identified him as a possible villain purely on a structural basis, and I think he's altogether too smooth.'

'All right. Now how can we find out?'

John sat down again and struggled to answer the question. 'I'll see Soraya next in June at the Gleneagles conference on nuclear decommissioning. Roddy McKie has invited us. But don't expect any state secrets to be transferred then ... I go back to Iran in July for the scheduled quarterly maintenance of the clocks. I'll keep my ear to the ground.'

'You're going to have to do more than that if we're to make progress.'

They stopped talking. The only slight sound came from the fan in Lipscombe's laptop. Eventually John said, 'There's only one way. If Roddy agrees, and with your permission, I'll take Soraya and her parents into my confidence. To them alone I will blow my cover. I'll tell Soraya the truth, that I work for the Foreign Office and that our only concern is that Iran should not develop nuclear weapons, that we recognize Iran's right to develop nuclear energy for peaceful purposes.'

'Won't that put Soraya and her parents in a compromising position?'

'Yes I'm afraid it will ... I'll give them the opportunity to cut me off and to divulge this information about me immediately to the Iranian authorities. I don't think they will. I think they will co-operate with me, with us, and watch Saban Kandar like

hawks. I'll stake my life on it.'

'You may have to,' said Lipscombe.

Chapter 7

June 2005

Soraya could hardly believe that she was in John's arms at last. The International Arrivals hall at Edinburgh Airport would hardly be her first choice for a romantic destination, but to feel his lips on hers however briefly made it the loveliest place in the world.

They walked holding hands, John pulling her case, towards the short term parking. They had four whole days to be together. Could anything be more wonderful? She smiled at him hoping he was as excited as she. He looked so handsome in a polo shirt and beige slacks. She hoped her summer dress and high-heels were not too formal. She searched his face. He seemed to approve. Was the bobtail a mistake?

'Every time I see you your hair is different,' he said.

'All the better to sweep you off your feet.'

She watched his smile broaden. He liked it! Then his face turned serious. He said, 'It's my turn to say we have to talk.'

Soraya had to wait until they were in his Honda before John would say more. She turned towards him and immediately felt his hands touching hers and holding them. She looked into his eyes, wondering. Could this be a proposal? Or was he about to break off their relationship? No, silly girl. It had to be something else entirely, bigger than both of them. At last he began to speak.

'Soraya, I don't just work for Roddy McKie. I'm employed by the Foreign Office in the Secret Service. So far, only Roddy and you know this, but I intend to tell your parents as well next time I see them, or you can since you will see them first.'

So matter of fact; understated; typical of him ... But how exciting! How great to be trusted. She leaned across and kissed him. 'But John, this could put you in terrible danger. You have no idea what the penalties are if you are caught ... Does your Department know that you planned to tell me?'

'Well, not the whole Department, but the key people know. Let me finish, Soraya. Our position is that we recognize Iran's right to develop nuclear energy for peaceful purposes but we want to be sure that there is no intention, State-led or otherwise, to develop nuclear weapons. So I am focused on the threat of nuclear weapons. I do not want to know Iran's commercial or strategic secrets to do with development of nuclear power as an energy source.'

Wow. This is perfect. Our positions dovetail. We can work together. Finally I can talk about it, about Anheim Mossada. She smiled back at him as he started the car.

'Listen, John,' she said, 'I suspect that there is a State-led plot but I have no proof. I haven't discussed this with anyone, not even with my parents.'

She stopped talking as John concentrated on leaving the car park and negotiating a busy roundabout. Then she told him about the execution of Anheim Mossada and what little she had learnt about him.

As they reached the Edinburgh City Bypass she said, 'I found what you said perfectly understandable but there is no guarantee that the authorities will accept your position if they catch you.'

'Well we'll just have to make sure that they don't ... Look, Soraya, you and your parents will also be in danger. So please think hard about this. I'll understand if you decide to sever connections with me and then without delay contact your Minister, Saban Kandar, to tell him what you have just learnt about me. That would be the prudent thing to do.'

'Of course we would not do that, John.'

'I knew you would say that, my Sweetheart, but I feel guilty about getting you into this.'

Soraya fell silent again. It was the first time he had used an endearment and she was revelling in the glow. Her desire for him and her sense of adventure were simultaneously aroused. Eventually she broke her silence.

'What can I do to help?' she asked.

They were now on the M9 passing Stirling. From the west they saw the Wallace Monument perched high over the city.

'Just a second, Soraya. I brought you this way to show you something. See that monument? It's for William Wallace. Remember, I was going to tell you about him. In my opinion he was the greatest Scotsman who ever lived,' said John. 'He held out for freedom, won a great battle against Edward the 1st of England at Stirling Bridge at the end of the thirteenth century, was betrayed and suffered a fearful execution. He was hanged, drawn and quartered in London.'

Soraya shuddered. 'I'll tell you later what happens at executions in present day Iran. Just as bad, I think ... But how can I help?'

She watched him take a deep breath. 'I'll tell you, Soraya. Look at it this way. We have to consider all the possibilities. One is that the West has nothing to fear: Iran is indeed committed to peaceful uses of nuclear energy and there are no maverick groups trying to make nuclear weapons.'

'Neither of us really believes that, do we John?'

He shook his head. 'The second possibility is that secretly the senior members of Iran's Governing Council, including the President, are planning to develop nuclear weapons.'

'That's what I think, John. It's why Anheim Mossada was executed.'

'You may well be right, Soraya, but that's not my immediate concern. The third and most worrying possibility is that unknown to Iran's President and his Governing Council one or more maverick groups are beginning to develop nuclear weapons. Such a maverick group, if it exists, must be headed by someone with access to the know-how, materials, personnel, facilities involved in nuclear development. My Department wants me to monitor Saban Kandar, if only to exonerate him. You and your father are as close to him professionally as anyone. Please let me know if he begins to act strangely. He is our number one suspect ... But don't tell me anything until you are sure. Remember I have no right to know about Iran's private commercial or strategic matters.'

'All right, John.'

Interesting, she thought, that John was putting greatest emphasis on the maverick option. He was surely barking up the wrong tree.

A little later John handed his mobile to Soraya and asked her to telephone Roddy to say that they had passed Dunblane and would be at the hotel in ten minutes. So Roddy was waiting in front of the green pagoda-like entrance as they walked in from the car park.

'Delighted to see you again, Soraya. You look wonderful.'

While Soraya was unpacking, Roddy and John walked towards the tennis courts. They had the path to themselves. It was strewn with faded rhododendron blooms following the high winds of the previous week.

'Have you told her yet?'

'Yes, Roddy. She understands the situation and will co-operate.'

'All right. No going back. We all must be extremely careful.'

'Quite.'

On their last day, after the conference, John drove Soraya north, car windows wide open, towards the delightful Sma' Glen. At first they talked about the conference. Roddy's paper had been the best, they decided, recommending storage of nuclear waste on the surface until the potential hazards of deep burial had been thoroughly analysed. He had scared the delegates when he showed how permeable some rock formations were, how prone to fissures, and how little was known about underground water deposits and how they might become connected. Then they discussed again the even scarier subject of the Iranian nuclear threat but made no further headway. There was so little to go on.

'Let's just enjoy today,' John said, as they entered the glen.

He was in the driver's seat, literally and metaphorically. He wanted to broach a different subject with Soraya which seemed to him equally difficult to solve. He stole glances at her, could hardly keep his eyes off her. Her lips were slightly open, her hair blowing. She looked to him like a goddess come down to inspect her handiwork and she was clearly taking pleasure in it. She was noticing everything, gesticulating and smiling across to make sure he saw it all too. What a super, loving girl. What enthusiasm. She would not let him miss any of the summer colours. He grinned back as she pointed to the reds of campion interspersed with poppies and fresh green clumps of willow herb among the white heads of cow parsley in the grasses by the river. This shall be her happiest day yet, he vowed, as they ascended to a view of open moorland. He heard her gasp. The whin had given its all but the broom had taken up the baton, keeping the hills aflame with resplendent splairges of yellow. Nearer to Dunkeld, hawthorn bushes lined the fields with thick borders of enduring may blossom, white becoming tinged with pink. He heard her take in a deep breath of admiration. The fields themselves provided a multitonal background of luxuriant green as the breeze ruffled the grass, the wheat and the barley. Every so often the road touched the edges of woods of pine, larch and silver birch where blackbirds, thrushes, diving swallows and flitting sparrows sang deliriously of the joy of being alive on this beautiful day. At one such moment he felt her fingers touch his face as he drove. Neither of them spoke.

They stopped in Dunkeld for coffee. The bustling village seemed to encourage a change of mood.

'Sma' is not dialect for small. It's short for smart, meaning beautiful,' he said. 'And while I'm on a roll Gleneagles has nothing to do with eagles. It's named after all the churches or églises in the area. But don't tell the tourists.'

'I thought I was a tourist.'

'No, Soraya. You're much more than that.'

After coffee John avoided the congestion of Pitlochry and drove round to the shore of Loch Faskally where he hired a rowing boat. He had not exercised for four days and was glad to flex his muscles. They had the loch almost to themselves.

'This loch is man-made,' he said. 'My father and grandfather used to fish exactly below where we are now. It was a river then, called the Clunie. My grandfather was in India when he heard of the hydro-electric power scheme and the flooding of his beloved river.'

He watched the beginnings of a smile develop.

'So he wrote an angry letter to the Scotsman newspaper quoting Sir Walter Scott about "the land that gave us birth". Then he came home on leave, saw the wonderful job they had made of Loch Faskally and wrote another letter apologizing for the first.'

It was great to see her laugh.

He started rowing again, upstream this time. Eventually he shipped oars.

'Soraya, I want to spend the rest of my life with you.'

Now there was a tear. 'Oh John,' she said, 'that's what I want too.'

'Thank heavens for that ... Great ...' He almost clambered across to embrace her but managed to restrain himself. 'Listen, Soraya, we'll make this work. That's a given ... But we mustn't be naïve. There are difficulties to be overcome.'

'Our religions, you mean.'

'Yes ... Look, I don't want this to sound like an inquisition. It should be a conversation ...'

'I understand, John. Ask away.'

A gentle breeze lapped small waves against the boat and they began to drift downstream again.

'Aiming for perfection is a key thing in Islam, isn't it?'

'Yes.'

'Well, I'm all for that. Who could possibly disapprove? But no one is perfect. How do you deal with human frailty?'

'We try to make up for it, John. It's a constant battle, a jihad in the best sense of that word.'

'Right. Much the same in Christianity. Bounce back. But we have a different perspective. It's about forgiveness. We're encouraged to forgive even when there has been no apology.'

Soraya paused. He could see that this was difficult ground for her. She was struggling to keep her voice calm. 'We're more committed to justice, both legal and social,' she said. 'When things go seriously wrong we make immediate corrections to preserve honour. Sometimes these are brutal. We hate losing face. We don't rate apology highly. It's because we have been underdogs for so long, I suppose.'

He gave her a gentle smile. 'I share your impatience with glib apologies. But don't you think an apology is a fine thing if it has four elements? First, you say you're sorry. That's the easy bit. Our politicians never get further than that. Second, you accept at least some of the blame, usually all of it. Third, you do what you can to make amends, and finally you demonstrate a corrective action that makes it most unlikely that the error will recur ... I suppose you have lost face but you have shown consideration, you have minimized the wrong. In an ideal world this becomes a kind of currency. You have to be ready to accept such a genuine apology if it happens the other way round.'

'That's not in the bible, is it, John? It's not in the Qur'an either. I like it though.'

'Well, that's the kind of adjustment we have to make. But, Soraya, there are lots of other differences. Take the Taleban.'

'I'm not a Taleban, John.'

'All right. They're an extreme case. But I don't like the Muslim attitude to women. I know that the prophet Muhammad improved the role of women but he still froze their second class status.'

'I'm in a privileged position, John. I have been taught to be tactful to men but I have never been made to feel inferior. But you're right. Our culture is different. I don't agree with the lesser weight given in our law to testimony by women. There are many things I don't agree with, like our refusing help to non-Muslims in times of crisis, but I understand how these practices have come about. For centuries Muslims have felt deprived. They want to turn the tide. They have a huge desire for power and territory. They want shari'a law to be the norm all over the world.'

'Quite ... You have switched to "they", Soraya.'

'Where I have reservations ... Here's something I have no reservations about. We believe that no matter how hard we try to be perfect there is no guarantee, unless we die as martyrs, that Allah, God, will accept us. He knows the future but that should not stop us from trying.'

John nodded and stuck his hands in the water, enjoying the coolness. He said, 'We also believe that we cannot be sure of getting to heaven through performing good works. For us, the only certain way is to believe that Jesus Christ took the punishment for all our shortcomings ... But to believe that is to be lost in gratitude and to try for perfection in response. Otherwise it's not really a belief. So, in practice, from different beginnings, we are both striving for perfection.'

'Yes, John. That's the essence of it.'

He gave a contented sigh and stretched his arms. But his face turned rueful as he relaxed again. He flicked a thin spray of water at her. 'It's easy to have this high-falutin' discussion while drifting merrily on a peaceful loch with a beautiful girl on a lovely summer's day,' he said. 'But some people really strive for perfection, caring for disadvantaged people, living nearly blameless lives. I mean they take it seriously, making every minute count. I'm not in their league. I want to pursue happiness as well.'

'Oh, so do I, John. There's surely nothing wrong with that unless selfishness takes over. We Muslims don't believe happiness is a gift, though. It has to be earned.'

'Right ... Soraya, for all this common ground and slight adjustment we cannot get away from the fact that our religions are mutually exclusive. If we had children would we take them to a mosque, a church, to both or neither?'

Soraya hesitated. 'I honestly don't know ... Is that a proposal, Sir?'

'Not yet, my Lovely.' John grinned at her. 'There's the small matter of saving the world first. Maybe we'll know what to do after that.'

'If you say so ... I mean "Aye aye, Sir",' said Soraya, saluting with one hand and splashing him in return with the other.

John rowed ashore and they disembarked. The wild brier roses were out, their seductive pink and white flurries blooming all over the banks. John picked a bouquet, took a sniff of their lovely perfume and presented the flowers to Soraya. She treasured them on her lap as they drove over the Muillin moors past the inviting crest of Ben y Vrackie to their left and on through Kirkmichael to the Spittal of Glenshee for a late bar lunch.

'What does Shee mean?' Soraya asked.

'Nobody knows exactly. Some say it means "peace". Others say "good luck". Still others say the place is controlled by benevolent fairies called "the good people". I think it's the nearest we can provide in Scotland to be the opposite of your number 13.'

Soraya loved the intimacy of the Spittal Hotel, the easy welcome from the staff dressed in kilts. John ordered a salmon salad for her and she had a taste of his haggis. Vaguely like ground lamb and couscous but rather different, she thought, hiding a grimace; a taste she would make an effort to acquire, some other time.

After lunch, having driven over the mountain past the Ski Centre they descended towards Braemar and parked by the rowans at the entrance to Jock's Road. Then they walked, arms around each other's waists, towards Loch Callater. It was late in the day for walkers to set out for Glen Doll at the Kirriemuir end. Those coming the other way would just have reached the far end of Loch Callater. So after rounding the first bend in the path they were alone. The heather was not yet out and there were no deer to be seen on the hills so close to the main road in summertime but still the beauty of the walk beside the rocky, chattering burn imposed its magic on them. After a couple of hundred yards they could resist each other no longer. John pulled her to him and kissed her passionately on the back of the neck. She wrapped her arms around his chest and squeezed herself against him, feeling the strength of his upper body. Then they kissed full on the lips, long and hard. Finally it was John who gently broke away saying it was time to turn back.

They skirted Perth and reached Edinburgh in the evening where Soraya would spend the night in the Airport Hilton ready for her return flights via London. John waited in the area between reception and the bar among tourists returning to the United States and Germany in the main. Some were dressed in T-shirts, shorts and sandals while the ladies in other groups appeared with coiffured hair and pearls. On the whole, John decided, the sandal wearers blended better with the decor of modern art around the walls. He did not have long to wait. Soraya had changed into her evening outfit, let her hair down and tied it into yet another shape, all down one side. All the men in the foyer gave her admiring glances as she walked across from the lift. John met her and kissed her. 'My sma' girl,' he said.

After dinner, over coffee in the lounge, Soraya forced herself to break the romantic mood by telling him the details about executions in Iran.

'I couldn't bear it if you were caught,' she said.

'Worrywart. I'll see you back there very soon.'

A quick kiss and he was gone.

As he drove back to London through the night John thought about the execution ritual. By the time he reached the M25 he had the beginnings of an idea.

Chapter 8

July 2005

The betaspodumene mine had been closed for twenty years. Saban Kandar remembered the demonstrations, quickly suppressed, to keep it going. He had been young then. Hopelessly idealistic, he supposed. He had sympathized with the workers but was powerless to help: the market had moved on. In any case he was far too junior in those days, still learning the manipulative arts. The technical details were harder to remember. Advances in some sort of transducer to keep the mirror separation constant had meant that inexpensive aluminium housings could be used for special lasers, mainly military ones. They didn't need this ultra-low-expansion material any more. Sad, but that's technology for you: comes and goes.

I'm older now, he acknowledged with a grimace as he drove southwards; but no less idealistic (he thumped the dashboard) ... and a whole lot smarter; we'll have no false modesty here. Kandar jutted his chin at a flock of sheep, daring them to contradict him. It had been a masterstroke to make use of the old mine. It provided excellent cover for the secret nuclear facility. Any aerial reconnaissance would see lorries and construction vehicles emblazoned with the logo of a mining company travelling to and from the mine and working around it. The work would be seen to continue, albeit with less activity, through the night. This was perfectly normal in commercial mining enterprises. And why shouldn't the mine be reopened? Presumably a new market had been found. Kandar chuckled. That should keep them guessing.

It was late afternoon when he arrived and the day shift construction workers and electricians were beginning to pack their tools. The cave was remarkably clean. Kandar had been expecting it to be covered in dust like a coal mine, but he observed that beta-spodumene was not a dirty mineral. This was most encouraging. He chatted to the foreman who confirmed that the reaction chamber would be completed within two weeks. Then it was just a matter of installing the centrifuges and water tanks.

As the day shift departed Kandar waved them off from the car park. He waited in his car with the doors wide open to take advantage of the breeze that tumbled down the grassy slopes high to the west. He was munching a sandwich and drinking coffee from a thermos when the late shift arrived. They had made a special effort to come early to meet him. Ali, the late shift foreman, greeted him respectfully and immediately sent two of his men into the cave to continue the electrical wiring. It was essential that the day shift should see that progress had been made overnight. Then Ali led the Minister and his three remaining men to the back of the mine where they descended into a much larger cave. This cave was in a rough condition. Great boulders of clay streaked with beta-spodumene lay across the vast floor area. Gaping holes, their edges propped by wooden struts, showed where walls had been blasted to make the cave even larger.

Kandar was appalled. There was so much more to do. 'How thick is the wall between the two caves?' he asked.

'Only two metres now, Minister. We'll finish preparing this cave and then blast a doorway.'

Kandar nodded. 'How long?'

'It's not so bad as it looks, Minister. With four of us operating the lifting gear we should have the cave clear by the end of the year. Then we can start on the radiation chambers and the wiring.'

'That's too long. I'll try to get you more help.'

Terias Shammon and his guard playacted throughout the flight. Not one word passed between them. Shammon with a permanent sneer stared straight in front. His guard decided that two could play at that game. He pulled out a paperback with a leggy girl on the cover, made sure that Shammon could see it, and laughed uproariously every ten minutes as he flipped through the pages. Both men were secretly relieved when the plane finally landed. They stayed in their seats until all the passengers and crew had left. Then a smartly dressed young Iranian carrying a briefcase came on board followed by two armed guards in military uniform. The transfer papers were signed, the two secret service men shook hands, and, still sneering, Terias Shammon was escorted into a car on the tarmac. Disallowed from leaving the plane, the MI5 guard removed his shoes and stretched out across three seats where he remained to the amusement of the cleaners who arrived soon afterwards to prepare the aircraft for the return flight.

The car took Shammon directly to the Ministry of Energy and Foreign Affairs for debriefing. His Jordanian passport was confiscated. His small case was opened and its contents were laid out on a table. He was ordered to empty his pockets and all these items joined the rest of his belongings on the table. He was allowed to keep his wrist watch, a copy of the Qur'an, and all his clothes and basic toilet utensils. His wallet and all other books and papers were put with his passport in a locker. A label was typed with his name and stuck on the door of the locker.

'These items will be returned to you in due course,' he was told. Then he was put in interview room number one. It was a basic room, not much larger than a cubicle, with a metallic table and two chairs facing each other across the table. There were bars on the window.

After a few minutes the door was opened and a different official entered. His shirt and trousers were neatly pressed. He sported a thin moustache.

'Welcome to Iran,' he said with a sardonic smile. 'How should I address you?'

'I am Mullah Shammon.'

'Well, please be seated, Mullah.'

They sat down opposite each other.

The official began to rub his hands. He had been taught that this body language would intimidate interviewees. It did not work. Shammon simply stared at him until he dropped his eyes.

Disconcerted, the official tried disarming honesty. 'Your writings will be examined by several of our mullahs. If any mullah feels he can find a use for you, you will be given the opportunity to work as his assistant.'

'And if not?'

The official recovered, using the power of silence. Then he said with as much sarcasm as he could muster, 'In that case, Mullah Shammon, you will have to work as a labourer until you have earned the respect of at least one of our mullahs.'

In line with Roddy's prediction, some half dozen lights on the clocks had failed after three months. You had to look closely to find the failures among the hundred thousand light emitting diodes; in fact, you'd never notice them. John identified them electronically using the probe Roddy had devised for this purpose. The lights were in strings of fifty. John replaced all six of the strings that had a failed light and packed the removed strings for repair back at the factory. The entire maintenance task was accomplished in less than an hour. He had the whole afternoon to wait until he could see Soraya.

He started to walk towards the city centre. The embassy district was impressive. Large buildings behind wrought-iron gates were set back from the road with well- tended lawns in between. Trees of all kinds, deciduous, fir and palm, shielded windows from inquisitive eyes. But for the palm trees he might have been in Edinburgh or even Vienna. As he descended and came closer to the centre, however, the picture changed. All the trappings of a busy metropolis began to assault his senses: billboards advertising soft drinks, the roar of traffic, the fumes of vehicles burning oil; and wherever he looked he saw columns of helmeted cyclists on their Vespa motor scooters. The streets near the hub were alive with pedestrians, many laden with baskets of over-ripe fruit, trying for last chance sales. One street was an endless bazaar. John avoided that one and took another leading diagonally to the northwest. He came upon a crowd leaving a mosque. Interested, he looked through the railings at the complex of rounded buildings. There was a car park at the rear. He could just make out the top of a large lorry. It bore the logo of a mining company.

John became aware of two large men watching him with clear distaste. He decided to take the bull by the horns. He walked over to them and gave the usual Arabic greeting, 'As-salamu 'alaikum.' This did not surprise them. Many foreigners had picked up those few words. But when he continued in faultless Farsi to ask what the mining truck was doing at a mosque he enjoyed seeing their discomfiture. Eventually one of them said, 'Karegharan napadid shodehand.' Workers of all types worship here.

Not a bad answer, John thought. He bade them farewell and returned to the hotel.

Soraya arrived by taxi punctually at 6 p.m., straight from work. She was wearing a grey midiskirt with a matching shayla. Her shoes were flat, her handbag plain but she still managed to look feminine and desirable. It was her hips in the midiskirt and the wispy blouse that did it, John decided; and her smile. He kissed her hand only for they were in the foyer in full view of the reception staff.

'Yet another hairstyle. The hidden-from-view look. But the rest of you looks smashing.'

'Thank you, I think. You're looking pretty fantastic yourself. And is that a parting I can see in your hair? Whatever next.'

John led her to a sofa and summoned a waiter. 'Which do you prefer,' he asked her, 'this place or Gleneagles?'

'They're both pretty intimidating. You weren't much more amorous in the foyer at Gleneagles.'

'Didn't want to be hanged, drawn or even quartered.'

John ordered tea and crumpets Arabian style drenched in lime juice. 'I could get used to this,' he said. 'Those crumpets go down the gullet soft and swote. That's the only Chaucer I can remember. Take my advice. Stick to the Arabian Nights, much more credible.'

They relaxed in luxury but were careful not to talk about anything important. Eventually, like several other hotel guests, they got up unhurriedly to walk in the gardens.

Early spring, when the clocks were being installed, was when the gardens had been at their authentic best with low desert flowers painting the ground. In summer the gardens were festooned with imported plants. These were no more colourful but much higher. One had to be careful at this season not to be overheard by invisible strollers. John steered Soraya to a corner bench from which they could see any approaching groups.

'Have you told your parents, Soraya?'

'Yes. They are worried for you.'

'And for you too, I'm sure.'

'My father said if we stick to the rule that we don't discuss commercial secrets but sincerely try to root out any attempt to develop nuclear weapons we should not fall foul of the authorities.'

'Well, that's the official line, I guess; and not a bad one for us to follow in foiling maverick attempts. Clearly your father hasn't thought the unthinkable. I mean ...'

'I know what you mean, John.'

'Right ... Sorry ... Anything you can tell me about Saban Kandar?'

'We haven't seen him for two days. That's not unusual.'

John paused to digest this and reached no conclusion.

'This afternoon I went for a walk, Soraya. Came upon a mosque in the northwest area. There was a lorry parked at the back. It had the logo of a mining company on it. Seemed odd.'

John waited while Soraya mulled this over. At length she said, 'John, I'm not absolutely sure but I think this is one of those commercial areas we should not talk about.'

'Right ... I'm tired of this imported grandeur. Let's go somewhere authentic for dinner. I'm in your hands.'

She took him to the Seven Esses Restaurant. The exterior was far from grand, not much more than a hole in the wall, but it opened into a large, low-ceilinged cavern of a dining area, brightly lit.

'Like the Italians we like to see what we are eating,' said Soraya.

The Head Waiter recognized Soraya at once, bowed politely to John, and led them to a corner table. A recording of a girl singing a ballad provided a soft background to the hum of Farsi conversation around them. The longer tables had rows of slim vases each holding a single tulip.

John said, 'This is exactly what I was hoping for.'

'I hope you'll like the food, John. Remember there are seven courses. You don't have to finish everything.'

But John would not be deterred. He attacked the sumac and dried fenugreek leaves with gusto, smiling at Soraya's ladylike approach to the food. He forced himself to slow down. He spoke to her in Farsi and she responded, delighted. Over the sprouted wheat kernels they chatted about their university friends, wondering when they would all meet again. Then John brought the subject round to Anheim Mossada. He sensed Soraya felt he had not shown enough interest in that lead.

'Have you come across anything he wrote, Soraya? Any technical papers?'

'Nothing yet ... but I'll keep looking.'

'I expect they are classified. Don't get caught, for heaven's sake.'

There was that beautiful smile again. He grinned back.

Five more courses to go. By the time they had polished off the meal with pomegranate sauce and yogurt curd they both felt they could take on the world.

'That was outstanding, Soraya.'

'I loved it too, John. We haven't had many proper dates, completely away from work.'

'That's true. But we'll have many more, God willing ... Shall we go?'

When Soraya woke up the next morning she knew it would be weeks before she would see John again. No good moping. She had one day to write a report prior to starting her new job. That would not take long; so she had time on her hands. She decided she had to find out more about Anheim Mossada. It was John's question, kindly meant, that stung her into action: "Have you found any of his writings?"

Let's be logical about this, she said to herself. They might have destroyed his personnel file or rewritten it to substantiate the official reason for the execution, but more likely it was now securely held in the Secret Police Building. In any event it was out of reach. His technical papers were another matter. John was right: these papers would be classified. Where would they be held? Not where someone like her father, senior but outside the inner circle, would have access. Her father, she knew, had access to classified commercial information on domestic nuclear power. Even she had been given limited access to such material. But technical papers on nuclear weapons would be stored, at least initially, in the office of a member of the inner circle. Who might that be? Saban Kandar? Not if he were masterminding a plot on his own, as John suspected. He would not go solo like that if he knew about the State-led plot. Who then?

She puzzled over this as she ate breakfast, on the bus to work, and even while writing her report. Who was in the inner circle? The Ayatollah and the President certainly. But she could hardly go barging into their offices. Who else? There was no way of knowing. Who had been in the inner circle? Maybe that was easier to guess. What about the late Energy Minister, Abdul Hanser? That seemed likely; but secret material would have been removed from his office before Saban Kandar took over. Where would it be now?

This was frustrating. Every question led to another, none of them providing an answer. She tried another tack. By now, there must be a parallel team to the one she was in. The members of that weapons team would need to have access to the technical papers in a place out of the gaze of the public. Previously, at the theoretical stage, that had probably been the office of the Energy Minister. Now, at the practical stage, it would have to be in the secret facility where they were working. Where was that? Who could lead her to it? No one she knew.

That left only one possibility. Had Anheim Mossada kept a diary, something in layman's terms to divulge to the press? If so, he would surely have made a copy in case, as probably happened, he was caught with the original. The copy would be hand-written and would probably be shorter than the original, containing the salient points only. He would have hidden it, hoping the police would not find it but trusting that someone else would. This was the only hypothesis to follow.

Soraya handed in her report and was given the afternoon off. The best place to look was back at the house where the Mossadas had lived. She had to change buses to get there. On the first bus she realized that if she could anticipate the existence of an abbreviated copy of his diary then so could the police. So any clue to its whereabouts had to be disguised in some way so that the police would leave the clue in the house and future owners of the house would leave it too. It had to look like some sort of fixture, to be taken for granted.

If it had been up to me, Soraya thought as she took a seat on the 52, her second bus, I would have tried to make the clue something that a technically trained person might recognize. Otherwise it might remain unnoticed for ever. For the rest of the journey she tried to come up with a plan for getting into the house.

As she crossed the road from the bus stop she saw Mrs Hakeem weeding the border of flowers by the front gate. Soraya called her name and waved as if they were old friends. As Mrs Hakeem straightened up, Soraya could see she was puzzled but not unreceptive.

'I came to thank you, Mrs Hakeem, for being so helpful that day when I came from the Census Bureau. A lot of people would not have been so forthcoming.'

Mrs Hakeem clearly enjoyed the compliment. 'Oh, it was nothing,' she said, 'I hope they found the information useful.'

'I expect so. I never get to hear what they make of things. I'm far too junior ... Are those African violets? Great colours.'

'No, dear, they're petunias. I expect you young people don't have much time for gardening.' She smiled.

'I'm afraid not. But I admire a beautifully tended one like yours. Do you have to read lots of books to find out about all these lovely flowers?' Soraya bent down and, avoiding the spikes, sniffed a gladiolus.

'Well, it helps. I just have two gardening books. Would you like to come in and have a look?'

'Oh yes, please, Mrs Hakeem. I'd be most interested.'

The inside of the house matched the garden for tidy brightness. Everything looked new: the rugs, the painted walls, the furniture. Mrs Hakeem led her through a kitchen gleaming with copper pots and pans to a small room at the back.

'We'll sit there, dear, on the window seat and look at the books together.'

Soraya scrutinized the window seat. It was covered with a long cushion. Evidently the seat could be lifted up, for hinges were just visible at the edge of the cushion. So the window seat doubled as storage space. It was the sort of place where you might keep toys or tennis rackets; anything really.

As Mrs Hakeem reached for her gardening books among box files and recipe books on a shelf Soraya said, 'This is awfully clever. I see the window seat lifts up to give very useful storage space.'

'That's right. I'll show you.' Mrs Hakeem raised the lid with her free hand to expose a set of neatly folded and piled bed sheets and bath towels. 'In case my brother and his family come to stay,' she said.

Soraya smiled politely but her attention was riveted to the inside of the wooden lid. Someone had carved AM 4-13.

Mrs Hakeem must have caught her gaze for she said, 'We noticed the carving when we moved in. It's on the inside; so it's not an eyesore. I suppose a little boy couldn't resist carving his initials and the date, April 13th, a long time ago, probably when he got his first penknife. Boys will be boys.' She gently lowered the seat. 'Now, I think you'll like these books. This is my favourite picture.'

After a suitable time looking through the gardening books Soraya declined the offer of tea, thanked Mrs Hakeem for her kindness and left. She knew she had seen the clue, that 4-13 was not a date, but its significance did not immediately register with her.

She stood at the bus stop. The sign on the pole had the numbers 17 and 52. Dear Allah, that was it. Those were the numbers given to Mr S and Mr P. She remembered working that out. It was too much to be a coincidence. Anheim Mossada must have solved the puzzle too. The copy of his diary had to be hidden inside the sign. Problem solved. All except for getting her hands on it. Not an operation she could attempt in broad daylight. Retrieving the copy would have to wait.

This time the 52 came first and she boarded it, feeling elated.

Chapter 9

John returned to a fraught Foreign Office that was recovering from its part in organizing the mass evacuation of British citizens from Beirut. The continuing crisis in the Lebanon was taking precedence over longer term concerns about Iran's nuclear programme. Anti-Israeli speeches from the previous Foreign Secretary blatantly challenging governmental policy could not easily be dismissed as sour grapes and required careful responses. On top of all that, parliament was officially on holiday for seventy days and key people were absent. Nevertheless, he had to concentrate on his assignment and keep busy colleagues motivated to help him. He was learning that the spying game was not all black and white. Awkward decisions had to be made. Feeling slightly guilty about possibly straying into a commercially confidential matter, John gave Peter Lipscombe a description of the logo on the lorry. This tied in with aerial reconnaissance photographs. So a mosque in Tehran had something to do with new activity at a mine in the south. Soraya had clearly known something about this, felt it was probably a classified commercial activity but was not certain. This was information to be stored. He would have to resolve it later.

In the meantime he had work to do with the technical crew at MI6. They had made him a coffin, no larger than standard size. It was a tight squeeze lying inside. He feared cramp most of all. They placed the lid on top (not nailing it down, thank goodness) and started a timer. Breathing was no problem at first. The smell of the wood was not unpleasant. He could move a little, arching his back and bending his knees, but he could not stretch to his full length. After a minute his toes registered pins and needles from the pressure on the balls of his feet against the far wall of the coffin, and his neck began to ache from the pressure at the other end. He began to sweat after two minutes. He was conscious of taking deeper breaths. After four minutes breathing was becoming uncomfortable. He flexed his body as far as he was able to stave off cramp. The smell of wood was now an annoyance. After six minutes he heard himself rasping. He imagined climbing "the ladder" at Lochnagar. Not long now to the summit.

They lifted the lid as agreed after seven minutes. John breathed in the lovely air and allowed them to help him out. He was damp and stiff.

'What do you want to do next?'

'We'll try again in an hour. Eight minutes next time.'

'Come in, Elizabeth. I'm not sure whether to offer you coffee or not.'

'I'll try to persuade you I've earned it, Tom.'

'All right. Shoot.'

They sat down at the coffee table. The Foreign Secretary looked at her hands, then up at her Prime Minister, and started to speak. 'I know you wanted to close down the current intelligence operation in Iran and why. But the situation has moved forwards, partly because of the unexpectedly early achievement of enriching uranium.'

'Surely that is all the more reason for moving quickly to stop this counterproductive intelligence.'

'But, Tom, the situation on intelligence also has changed. There is now a strong possibility that we may uncover a secret attempt to develop a nuclear bomb.'

The PM's face widened into a smile. 'I'll ring for coffee and you can tell me all about it.'

The invitation to Elspeth's wedding took them all by surprise. Betty especially was flabbergasted.

'I thought she was in Borneo,' said Nicol. 'Whom is she marrying, anyway?'

'She was. She emerged from the jungle engaged to the leader of the expedition.' Betty could not contain her excitement.

'Good for her.'

'You don't know the half of it. Said leader is the explorer, Lord Linnhe.'

'Son of a gun.'

'No, Nicol. The eldest son of a Marquis.'

Little by little, John had extended his endurance in the coffin to a full ten minutes and he had practised jumping out unaided. They had made careful comparisons of the sound of a burst blown-up paper bag, recorded outside the coffin, with that of a revolver going off, and had reached the disappointing conclusion that the sound of a fired revolver could not be satisfactorily faked.

'Maybe it's just as well,' John said. 'I might not be able to smuggle props into the coffin. Back to the drawing board.'

It would have been perfect to save the bullet for the first person to open the coffin. Now he would have to fire the revolver while nailed inside, and fake his own death without benefit of props like paint or red ink or that staple of gory films, tomato ketchup. The whole idea was becoming farcical.

Back to basics. He needed blood. Well, he had plenty of that. And if he could not shoot the first person to open the coffin, at least he could pistol whip him. That should give a second or two of shock and awe to give a surprise advantage. He'd just have to hope that the coffin would be on the ground so that a bullet fired through the bottom would not be noticed. There was still a lot of practising required.

Chapter 10

August 2005

Nicol was not enamoured of weddings. He'd had to observe too many in his final year. The marriage ceremony was much as he expected. He felt like an existentialist, detached, as he watched predictable human behaviour. They gathered outside Elspeth's church which was solid and unpretentious, suburban, a world away from the grand historic churches in the Old Town or the West End. There were about a hundred wedding guests looking like guests at any other wedding in Scotland, a smattering of kilts, a deluge of hats. They were outnumbered by an army of spectators on the opposite pavement keen to see this likeable girl from their congregation in her bridal gown; no doubt even keener to see the bridegroom, for word had to be out that she was marrying into the aristocracy. He walked into the church, trying not to glower, with Betty on his arm.

As usual the friends of the bride were in the majority. About 60/40 he estimated, craning his neck to see past the hats in the pews. Neither side seemed to know anyone from the other: there was no waving across the aisle. This was normal in his experience. They were like two rugby teams waiting to get at each other. The music was standard stuff: Handel, Mozart and (God spare us) Bach.

Betty dug him in the ribs. 'Cheer up, Misery. Just think: it's not happening to you.'

She was wearing a wide-brimmed yellow hat. She turned to John on her other side just as he leaned across to grin sympathetically at Nicol. Her hat brushed his chin and became tilted.

'Now look what you've made me do.' She glared at each of them in turn as she readjusted it. 'No Dashing White Sergeant for you two.'

Soraya had not been able to come so soon after her last visit. Her latest email had said that work was being piled on and she could not get away. So it was just the three of them; and Elspeth, of course.

John turned, as everyone did, when the music announced her arrival. She came on her father's arm, all in white. The gown was tight fitting with a long trail. She must have been wearing very high heels for she looked much taller. She was certainly slimmer than she had been at university. And she looked tanned too, although you never could tell these days. John smiled at Betty. 'Doesn't she look wonderful.'

'Of course she does,' said Nicol. 'They always do. Let me know when it's over.'

The reception was at the Braid Hills Hotel. Buses had been laid on for the guests. It was an area of Edinburgh unfamiliar to John, Nicol and Betty. This was the heartland of Napier University, of Craiglockhart College, Merchiston Castle School and the army barracks of Redford and Dreghorn.

'Very posh. Great views,' was Betty's verdict as she descended from the bus.

'Buffy, these are the friends I was telling you about from university,' said Elspeth as she introduced Betty, Nicol and John to her newly acquired husband.

Betty had never seen such a handsome man close up. He was of no more than medium height but looked very fit. This was due to the deep suntan, the clear eyes and the wiry frame. He had a mane of wavy black hair. He was probably about ten years older than all of them.

'Delighted to meet you all,' he said, shaking hands warmly and giving Betty a quick kiss. 'We must have a proper conversation later after we've said a brief hello to everyone.'

There was dancing after the speeches. Elspeth and Buffy started it off and then split up to dance with others at the high table. That duty done, they wandered round the room in opposite directions, spending time with friends at each table. Elspeth was growing effortlessly into the role of Lady Linnhe. Buffy sat down beside John, Nicol and Betty.

'I don't think you know this,' he began, 'but Elspeth saved my life ... in more ways than one. I got a snake bite, rather carelessly, when we were in Borneo. There were plenty of people on hand who thought they knew what to do - with tourniquets and pills of every size and colour known to man - but it was Elspeth who jumped in and sucked the poison out ... In case you're thinking gratitude was my motive in asking her to marry me I assure you it wasn't. Look at her. Isn't she beautiful?'

They all looked across the room. Elspeth had crouched down, knees bent, back erect, so that no one need stand up. They were all laughing at some joke. She looked so happy. Sensing their eyes on her she waved and blew a kiss.

'Clearly a rhetorical question,' said John. 'Listen, Buffy, you can trust us to keep a secret. Where are you going on honeymoon?'

'It's a busman's holiday. I've always been interested in the differences between hill folk and plains people. There has been a lot of nonsense written about this by people who haven't done proper research. For instance ... Look, this is my hobbyhorse. Elspeth keeps telling me not to bore people ...'

'Not a chance, Buffy,' said Betty. 'We're all interested.'

'All right. You asked for it. There's a glib comparison right here in Scotland between highlanders and lowlanders. Highlanders are said to be short, dark, poetic and unreliable. Lowlanders are tall, fair, balding, reliable and boring. They are said to make good surgeons and engineers ... Now I think that's hopelessly simplistic and insulting to both.'

'Especially to lowlanders,' said Nicol. 'Mind you, they deserve it. I'm a highlander, like you I think. Yes? So you plan to do the research thoroughly?'

'That's the idea. Elspeth and I want to write a book eventually, covering not just Scotland but the whole world. We're going to make a start in the Middle East.'

'Where exactly?' asked John. 'I work in that part of the world too.'

Chapter 11

September 2005

'What do you make of this Terias Shammon?'

They were in Saban Kandar's office. It was after 6 p.m. and they had the building to themselves apart from a solitary security guard.

Mullah Ahmed leaned forward eagerly. 'He's a good man. I could use him.'

Kandar nodded slowly. 'We should use him in two ways. First, let him prove himself as a labourer under your man, Ali. We need to speed up the work at the mine. Then, when the bombs are ready, we can let him loose to help you stir up the populace.'

Soraya packed her books and files in one case and changes of clothes for five days in another. The required departure from Tehran was probably the safest thing for her, she reflected. If she stayed she would be tempted to unscrew that sign one dark night and would probably be caught. She kissed her parents goodbye, saying simply that she would be back at the weekend from this new job at an unknown destination, and waited at the end of her street for the bus to pick her up. It was an impressive modern vehicle, painted blue and yellow, with under-floor storage for cases. There was even a toilet. She recognized only one of the scientists and engineers on board, not the head of her section but a clever young man whose speciality was control rods. The others must have been selected from other sites. Although she was the last to be picked up there were many vacant seats, for the passengers numbered only twelve. Being the only woman she sat by herself. After a seven-hour journey including just one break for a picnic lunch, which the driver handed out, the bus came to a stop outside a hotel whose refurbishment was long overdue, the only one apparently in the small town of Jilabad. The hotel was just big enough to accommodate them. Saban Kandar was there to greet them. He did his best over an uninspiring dinner to encourage them to bond as a team. He himself would stay with them for the first week. In the morning, he told them, the bus would take them all to the secret location where they would start work. Dramatically, with a hushed voice, he explained that the secret location was, in fact, a disused beta-spodumene mine which had been refurbished for them.

In the tiny bedroom which had been allocated to her for the week, Soraya had much on her mind. That mosque in the northwest sector of Tehran where John had seen the lorry had to be Mullah Ahmed's mosque. Therefore the mullah must be involved in the venture at the beta-spodumene mine. That could hardly happen without Saban Kandar's knowledge. So Kandar and the mullah were co-operating.

All right, slow down, she told herself. This does not necessarily mean that anything sinister is happening at the mine. On the other hand, it may be the first sign of the maverick group that John is worried about.

Could John be right after all?

It did not take long for Terias Shammon to bond with Ali and the others. They were his kind of people, tough and dedicated. Nor did he take long to figure out what the work was all about. At last he was doing something useful, something that would make a difference, a highly dramatic difference. Every time he helped to set off a blasting explosion in the large cave he imagined with relish the nuclear explosion that would transform the Middle East physically, culturally and above all religiously.

The first week passed uneventfully for Soraya. The installation team had cleaned the cave beautifully and had laid it out as a replica of the work area which Soraya had designed in Number Two Facility. There was just one difference. It was as if everything had been mounted on a turntable that had been rotated half-way round. She would have had the entire installation rotated through 180° but it was too late to change that now. Anyway, there were arguments on both sides. In her way, the enriched uranium would have ended at the entrance for easy addition to the arriving control rods rather than against the wall at the far end. On the other hand, this way made it more convenient for loading basic materials from the lift. That must have been the thinking.

The twelve of them quickly got to work testing the installation. One of the centrifuges made protesting noises when the power was increased. This was easily diagnosed: a shaft had become slightly bent – probably damaged in transit – and this in turn had damaged a bearing. Replacement parts would have to be procured from the massive storage site called Number One Facility. This was just beyond the suburban district of Tehran, about a mile from Soraya's home. If she had been able to contact either of her parents she could have asked one of them to go there, withdraw the spares from stores, and have them driven down; but that was not possible in the climate of secrecy. Instead, the rigorous protocol implying queuing times would have to be followed. This meant some days of delay in procuring the replacement parts. In all other respects the installation was passed fit by the end of Wednesday. There was nothing more to be achieved by working the next day. The best plan, willingly agreed to by Saban Kandar, was to take advantage of a short first week, go home and return refreshed ready to start in earnest processing uranium on the Sunday morning.

When the bus dropped her off home on Thursday evening Soraya was tired. The work had not been demanding, the meals at the hotel had improved slightly, the bus was comfortable, but the mental strain of looking for definitive clues to reveal the real purpose of the mine - and not finding any – had left her exhausted. Her mother, Aisha, was immediately concerned.

'Is it terribly hard work, Soraya? I don't like seeing you so tired.'

'It's not too bad, Mother. Must be the long journey. I'm glad to be home. Two nights in my own bed. Plenty time to get my washing done.'

'Oh Soraya.' Aisha was disappointed. 'You mean you have to go back on Saturday this time. They're working you too hard. We'll just have to make the most of our time with you.'

Her parents did not ask where she had been and Soraya did not volunteer the information. They all knew the rules.

Blasting holes in the walls was great fun but lifting the debris was much less enjoyable. With five of them at it things were happening more quickly but it would be months before the job was done. Ali had been told that the technocrats had already started in the smaller cave and that the first week had gone without any significant hitch. He passed this information to his team, hoping to encourage them. But it had the opposite effect. Terias Shammon expressed the reason for disquiet.

'We are all working like Trojans but the project is out of kilter. There will soon be nothing more for them to do next door.'

Ali tried to exert his authority. 'We have to leave the management to Mullah Ahmed and the Minister,' he said. 'Saban Kandar is adamant about preserving secrecy for as long as possible.'

Shammon was quick to pick an opening. 'You mean Mullah Ahmed is not so strong on the need for secrecy?'

'I didn't say that.'

'Listen, Ali, you're a great foreman and I'd trust you with my life. But we all have responsibility here to move the project along. We are strong enough to control these technocrats, especially if Mullah Ahmed joins us, and we could set them to work labouring with us. Do them a power of good, I'd say.'

There were supportive noises from the others who had downed tools to listen to the debate.

Shammon continued. 'Let's force the issue. Let's blow the doorway now. You can blame it on me. Then we'll bring them through to this side as soon as they arrive next week ... Can you get us rifles in time, not that we could not manage without them, eh?'

Soraya had had no chance to return to the bus stop. When she arrived at the mine with the others on Sunday morning she was the first to enter the cave from the lift. The installation was exactly as they had left it but there was now a large jagged hole in the wall at the back. She could not see what lay beyond the hole for it was in darkness. But she knew at once what it meant. The rotation of the layout now made awful sense. Their installation was just the first stage. The uranium would be successively enriched on the other side of that wall. They had all been co-opted into the manufacture of a nuclear bomb.

She looked back to the lift and heard the grinding sound it made when ascending. The others caught her anxious mood. They all stared, mesmerized, at the lift station. The change of sound told them the lift was descending again. The doors opened to reveal eight large men with rifles and a terrified bus driver. Two of the men, smiling broadly, carried a coffin. They placed it on the floor about ten metres from the lift and removed the lid, placing it on the floor also. The coffin was empty except for a hammer and some nails. One of the men, grinning fiendishly, laid a revolver inside. Then all but one of them stood behind the coffin across the entrance while the Mullah Ahmed strode into the cave and, using sharp gestures only, lined up the scientists and engineers and the bus driver in front of the centrifuges.

'It is time for you to know the truth,' he said. 'You, we, are here to make nuclear bombs.'

Most of the scientists and engineers had already realized this since entering the cave, but to three of them the news came as a shock.

The mullah continued, 'I see that some of you have received this information better than others. Each of you will be interviewed so that we can determine whether to treat you as a willing worker or as a hostile one. It really makes little difference since all of you will work hard, or end up inside that box.'

He paused to let this sink in. There was no reaction from the technocrats. Good, they were learning.

'I shall start with the strongest looking of you, for the first task is manual labour.'

Soraya was the last to be interviewed. By this time everyone else was at work in the larger cave.

'You may sit, Miss al-Jerad.'

'Thank you, Mullah Ahmed, but I shall stand like you.'

'Very well. There are good things and bad things about you. You are undoubtedly clever and useful but I have been concerned about your pro-Western leanings. You must remember that you are first and foremost an Iranian.'

Soraya said nothing, just looked straight ahead as if she were a junior soldier being given a dressing-down by her commanding officer.

The mullah noted her silence but gave no sign as to whether he approved or disapproved. 'I am particularly displeased with your relationship with John Russell.'

This produced an intake of breath but no further reaction.

'I require that you sever connections with that young man.'

Now she had to speak. 'Mullah Ahmed, I understand your concern and I am in no position to argue. You pointed out a moment ago that my loyalty to Iran should be paramount. I have never been disloyal to Iran. If I must break contact with John Russell, my friend from university, allow me to do so in a manner that will prove to you that I am a proud Iranian and that I pour disdain on the falsity of Western ideals.'

'And exactly how do you propose to do these things?'

'Let me send him my favourite book, a version in English of the Arabian Nights, and let me inscribe it with the words, Take the fifth, my friend.' She spat these last words.

The mullah laughed. 'Yes, I see what you mean. You give him the brush off, tell him to keep his mouth shut, and remind him that our ancestors were just as cultured as his ... Do you have the book with you here?'

'Yes. It goes wherever I go, or has done till now.'

'Bring it to me then. I'll have to check that there are no other messages inscribed.'

Saban Kandar rang for his secretary.

'See if you can get me an appointment with the Mullah Ahmed.'

After a few minutes the secretary returned to his office. She told him that there had been no reply at the mosque.

This was strange. Ahmed would surely want to know how things had gone in the first week.

'Keep trying,' he said.

Satisfied that his men had everything under control, the Mullah Ahmed drove back north on Sunday night. He had the packet for John Russell ready to post when the main Post Office in Tehran opened at 9 a.m. He certainly was not going to post it locally. He would make it in plenty of time. He snatched a couple of hours' sleep in his car.

Having mailed the book he returned to his quarters at the mosque. He took time to freshen up with a shower and clean clothes. Now to break the news to Saban Kandar. Better invite him to the privacy of the mosque.

It was an explosive meeting at first but Kandar was nothing if not a pragmatist and he soon calmed down to think through the next steps. On the positive side, the large cave would now be ready in six weeks. Long before that time had expired there was bound to be concern from relatives of the scientists, engineers and bus driver about their whereabouts. He would have to be proactive in heading that off. So a plausible story had to be concocted. He himself would have to remain squeaky clean, working to keep a single facility secret in the national interest but unaware that it had been hijacked to make nuclear bombs. He would take the relatives into his confidence and swear them to secrecy without disclosing the location of the mine. That had better be done over the next couple of days before they became anxious about non-returning loved ones. Then the technocrats at the mine would expect him to put in an appearance by the end of the week. He'd arrive, be shocked, and they'd have to take him prisoner too. That was the best course. It might just work.

Chapter 12

The packet was addressed to John at his flat in Heston. There was no cover letter, just the book. He knew how much Soraya treasured that book. So, given the inscription Take the fifth, my friend, it had the hallmark of a despondent farewell gesture: she had decided after all that their relationship was impossibly dangerous and she was urging him to clam up. No, that couldn't be right. The Soraya he knew would not do that. He turned the page and saw the full title displayed: The Arabian Nights or tales told by Sheherezade during a thousand nights and one night. Then he understood. Clever girl. He reached for his mobile and dialled Peter Lipscombe's home number.

Later that morning he was called to attend a meeting with Lipscombe in the Minister's office. She looked very alert and businesslike.

'Explain to me in words of one syllable what this communication from Soraya al-Jerad means. I understand she sent you a book with a cryptic inscription. Is that right?'

'Yes.'

'Well?'

'The inscription was Take the fifth, my friend.'

'Advising silence, presumably.'

'No, Minister. I mean, that is what her captors thought she meant, that she was advising me to pull up stakes, but her message is quite different. You see, the alternative title to the Arabian Nights is Tales told by Sheherezade during one thousand nights and one night.'

'We all know that. So what?'

'When Soraya wrote Take the fifth she was referring to the fifth power series of integers, something she and I had studied at university.'

The minister made a face.

'Look, I'll write it on this flip chart, if I may ... The first term is 1. Then comes 2 to the power five. That's 32. Then 3 to the power five. That's 243. And so on.'

'All right, but what's your point?'

Lipscombe coughed politely. 'This is where it becomes interesting, Minister.'

'Well,' John said, 'if you add the terms together you have to go as far as the thirteenth term before the sum is a square, and that square is 1001 squared. Soraya, under pressure, had to think of a way of transmitting to me the number thirteen.'

'Which, we all know, means mortal danger. I see.'

Lipscombe took up the running. 'What it means, Minister, is not just that Soraya is in mortal danger but that she is a captive. Why else would she have had to resort to this complicated communication? Put that with what we know about the mine in the south and it is a fair bet that she and others are being held there against their wills. Why? To develop nuclear bombs of course.'

The minister gave her hand signal for a period of reflection.

At length she said, 'That is very plausible. It must be verified. Off you go, you two, and work out how to do it.'

'Come in, Elizabeth, and tell me all about it.'

The PM was in an expansive mood. It had been a terribly long, hot summer with scandals galore not to mention the crisis in Lebanon and plots to oust him but now his popularity was rising again. He had wowed them at the Party Conference. The Party had come to the realization that they needed him more than ever to ensure the continuity of electoral wins. Once again, his word was law.

She sank into an armchair opposite him and immediately adjusted her skirt, feeling at a disadvantage. 'I thought you should know this right away, Tom. Around midnight tonight, one of our agents will land by parachute close to a mine in the south of Iran to confirm our suspicions that it is being used in the development of a nuclear bomb.'

'Excellent. When will he get word to us?'

'We'll have to give him a few days to escape.'

'Escape?'

'Oh yes. He plans to be captured first.'

The PM shook his head and exhaled in admiration. 'Well, if he can pull this off we'll have all the ammunition we need. Who is it, by the way?'

'John Russell.'

'Ah yes, the clock man.'

'Well, the real clock man, the inventor, is someone else. It was my predecessor's idea to latch on to him.' The Foreign Minister again straightened her skirt. She had been careful not to mention Robert by name. She was dressed in yellow today. She had taken to wearing bright colours since her promotion and she did not want to revert to navy blue and dark grey.

'Does this inventor know anything about nuclear physics?'

'Yes. He gave a paper at the Gleneagles conference in June.'

'I'd like to meet him. I think he could be useful.'

John's plane, a Hercules C130J, took off from Brize Norton that evening. The first leg was to Cyprus for rapid refuelling and collection of the parachute and gear he had requested from the specialist hangar. Then they were off again. He tried to snatch some sleep but he was too excited. This was the real thing: a high level flight over Iraq and then a leap in the dark, literally. Peter Lipscombe and he had planned as well as they could but in the end it was all going to be up to him: his reactions, his rapid decisions. These would have to be perfect, every one, for Soraya's sake as well as his own.

The plane droned on. He dosed off, leaning against the corner formed by his seat and the fuselage. There was just one row of seats on each side to leave room for paras to sprint down the middle for a mass jump. Tonight, however, he'd be the only jumper.

They roused him with a cup of black coffee.

'Feeling OK? You have ten minutes.'

'Right.'

He made the coffee last. It was black and tasted bitter. Maybe they had found that milk made first-timers sick. They opened the trap door and hooked him up.

'Three, Two, One ...'

He jumped into the night sky.

Chapter 13

John landed on a downhill slope. He managed to lift his legs and slide on his bottom for about twenty yards. The slope was grassy with a sprinkling of small stones and did not hurt much. He pulled in his black parachute and weighted it down with his rucksack and some stones. Then he dug a hole with the small spade he had brought and buried the parachute. It would be dawn in one hour.

He put on night vision goggles and surveyed the scene. He made out the shapes of hills around him. There was a hut about a quarter of a mile to his left but no other sign of habitation near him. Down in the valley lay the mine. A bus, a car and six assorted lorries and construction vehicles were parked beside it. By the light of a small torch he checked his bearings with map and compass. Then he put everything save the torch and a penknife back into the rucksack: map, compass, goggles; and buried the rucksack and spade with the parachute. By hand he covered up most of the bare earth with a scattering of stones. He felt like young Lochinvar, all unarmed and alone, as he began the descent.

It was still dark when he reached the mine. He crept around the vehicles in the parking lot. There was no one there. He set to work puncturing the tyres of all the vehicles except the bus and the car. Then he waited.

Soon after dawn a man emerged from the mine entrance. He was carrying a rifle. John recognized him as one of the two he had conversed with outside the mosque. The man had a cursory look around. He must have been satisfied that the place was deserted as expected for he propped his rifle against the wall near the entrance, walked a few yards farther up, and started to urinate against the wall.

John knocked him unconscious with a stone against the back of the head. He dragged him to the second lorry and dumped him in the back. Then he tied him securely, wrists and ankles together, using rope from the back of the lorry, and gagged him with material cut from the man's trousers. Then he raced back to the rifle. He removed the magazine, hid it behind one of the flat tyres and left the rifle standing against the wall. Well, that was one less to worry about. He took a deep breath, entered the mine, walked into the lift and pressed the button to descend.

There was no reception committee as he walked into the cave for they had been expecting the return of their lookout man. John had about five seconds to take in the scene. It was in uproar. One of the engineers, a fragile young man, was being frogmarched towards the coffin. The others were screaming at the guards to let him go. A man with a large beard, clearly the authority figure, was looking on impassively. John surmised that the fragile young man had been sentenced to death at dawn for failing to comply. He had just enough time to see Soraya in the background, yelling with the best of them, and was that Saban Kandar with a gash across his forehead looking disconsolate among the captives?

Suddenly the yelling stopped as everyone realized that a Caucasian intruder had entered. The guards who had been manhandling the engineer ran over to John and grabbed him instead.

'Good morning,' said John in Farsi, addressing the authority figure. 'I think it's going to be another lovely day.'

The Mullah Ahmed laughed. 'I rather think not ... So, this is John Russell.' He looked at Soraya and back at John. 'You would have done better to heed the warning. Now we shall see just how brave you really are.'

'A last request?'

'Very well. You may speak to Miss al-Jerad for a final time ... Release him. He cannot escape.'

John walked over to Soraya through the captive engineers. 'Pretend to be more frightened than you really are,' he whispered to them. 'Get close to the guards. When they open the coffin, that's our moment. Do your best to grab the rifles then. I'll need just a few seconds. Pass it on.'

He took Soraya's hand and kissed it. 'We can win this, my Sweetheart.' Then he walked over to the coffin and allowed himself to be bundled inside. They tossed in the revolver, put the lid on, and he heard the nails being banged down.

Keep calm, he told himself. You've done this many times. Start counting the seconds. The only real surprise is Saban Kandar on the wrong side of the fence. Can't fathom that yet. He flexed his back. All's well. Early days ...

Coming up to five hundred seconds. Aches and pains arriving on schedule. We'll go for seven hundred this time. Put on a show, right? Funny thing, all that mathematics: comes down to counting in a coffin. Missed a trick when old Fischer asked me what four and thirteen meant. Should have told him a double dose of mortal danger. That's right. Four is what golfers shout. Beware. Fore ... The Fauré Requiem ... Requiem for a Wren ... Neville Shute. Wake up! You've got to shoot.

John bit into the middle finger of his right hand and tore off some skin. He didn't need to squeeze out the blood. It came gushing. He coated his right temple liberally. The blood streaked down his cheek and on to the collar of his shirt. He raised himself on his left elbow and fired the revolver through the bottom of the coffin. The sound was deafening in the enclosed space. He shook his head and yawned to clear his ears. Then he took up the dead position, on his back, head turned to show the wound, the revolver in his right hand, his left arm lying limply across his body.

They were beginning to prize off the lid. It would take them another twenty seconds. Count out fifteen. Then a very deep breath.

Everyone in the cave crowded around the coffin. It had been a long wait: almost twelve minutes. It was a relief when they heard the shot.

The Mullah Ahmed was the first to peer inside the coffin. The body looked peaceful except for the blood running down from the head. The cleric leaned in, reached for John's left wrist and started to check the pulse. John grabbed the beard with his left hand, pulled the cleric in on top of him and whacked him across the temple with the flat of the pistol. Then, with a tremendous effort, he pushed the mullah upwards and started his own spring out of the coffin. At that precise moment a shot rang out fired by Terias Shammon who had managed to wrest his rifle back from the engineer who had grappled for it. The bullet caught the mullah in the back and entered his heart. In mid-leap, John managed to grab the mullah's rifle. He landed with a somersault and came out of it firing at Shammon who was about to fire at him again. Shammon dropped to the ground, shot through the forehead.

John yelled to the other guards who were still struggling to keep control of their rifles. 'Let go or I'll kill you too.'

With both their official and their unofficial leader dead so suddenly Ali and his remaining men gave up. John ordered them to lie face down on the floor with their hands behind their backs. He showed the engineers how to tie them with ropes. Then he smiled at Soraya. 'Any chance of a cup of tea?'

In answer she ran to him, flung her arms around his neck and kissed him unashamedly. Then she recovered her poise.

'I'll make us all tea,' she said. 'Just this once.'

While she was in a corner setting water to boil, the scientists and engineers, having examined the motionless bodies of Ahmed and Shammon, gathered around John to shake his hand. The fragile young man was in tears.

'Thank you, thank you,' was all he could say.

John told him that he must have been very brave to defy the captors.

'Which brings up an important point,' he said, getting instant attention. 'Was this the only one of you who refused to co-operate?'

'No,' came back the chorus. Then the oldest one said, 'They picked on him because he was the smallest. We all pretended to co-operate at first, working very slowly, trying to be non-productive. When they realized what we were doing they decided to make an example of him. There was a semblance of a trial. The rest you know.'

'Right,' said John. 'Now comes a delicate question. Whose side is the Minister, Saban Kandar, on?'

The spokesman for the engineers looked at Saban Kandar for a moment. Then he said, 'As far as we know, the Minister is on our side. He was deceived by the Mullah Ahmed as we all were.'

'Not true,' came a voice from one of the men tied up on the floor. 'I am Ali, the foreman. Saban Kandar and the mullah were in it together. They planned the whole thing.'

'Utter nonsense,' said Saban Kandar.

John smiled at him. 'You do see my difficulty, Minister. All I can say for sure is that one of you is lying. No doubt the truth will emerge.'

Soraya called out that the tea was ready.

'We'll serve the prisoners first,' said John. 'That reminds me. There's another one in the back of a lorry. I must check on him ... Minister, would you please accompany me? We must discuss what happens next. And Soraya, would you come too?'

They left the others to revive themselves with tea and entered the lift.

John addressed Saban Kandar. 'You do understand that we must blow up the mine and everything in it.'

For a fraction of a second John caught a flicker of venom in Kandar's eyes. But Kandar answered equably, 'Of course.'

At the top, John and Soraya, holding hands, went out first followed by the minister. Kandar spotted the rifle against the wall, lunged for it and had it in his hands before either John or Soraya turned round. He pointed it at John and then with a cunning smile at Soraya.

'I don't think, brave John Russell, you'll let me shoot Soraya ... Careless of you. Too arrogant by half. Now I'll tell you what we'll all do. The bombs shall be made.'

John shook his head and walked towards him. Kandar, puzzled, pointed the rifle back at him and pulled the trigger. There was a click but nothing more.

'Told you the truth would come out.' John took the rifle from him and flung it across the parking lot. 'Now perhaps we can have a serious discussion, or do you want me to tie you up too? ... First, Soraya, would you see if the man in the lorry is all right? You could take his gag off. I probably needn't have put it on.

'Now, Mr Kandar, you are in an unenviable position but there may be a way out for you. The scientists and engineers, apart from Soraya - and let's not forget the bus driver - may suspect you but they cannot be sure that you were not duped as they were by the late Mullah Ahmed and his ruffians. I'm going to let these ruffians loose. They will lie low if they have any sense and should not cause you a problem. The only people who might are the scientists and engineers – and Soraya and I, of course. So you have to win them over. If we hear that any harm has come to them we will expose you.'

Kandar looked into John's eyes and saw that he meant it.

John continued, 'You could use your authority to order proper burials followed by the destruction of the rifles and the blowing up of the mine. That should tilt the balance in your favour in the eyes of the scientists and engineers. Then go back with them on the bus to Tehran, leaving your car for Soraya and me. We'll wave you goodbye, like the best of friends. When you report to the President you run the risk that he will have you executed if only because you did not take him into your confidence. On the other hand he may see an advantage in keeping you on. You know him. I don't.'

Kandar sighed. 'All right. Quite generous in the circumstances ... What will you do?'

'Think of us as an insurance policy to keep you honest. We shall simply disappear, temporarily. But we'll be watching you.'

'John, you're driving East. Britain's back that way. So is the airport at Shiraz.'

'Trust me, Soraya. The airport's too obvious. The earth is round. We can get to Britain this way too.'

Although it was already autumn the heat was unrelenting across the salt flats. There was no road. As they bumped their dusty way ever eastwards Soraya told him about finding the clue which Anheim Mossada had left and of her conclusion that the copy of his diary was hidden in the sign at the bus stop. She was delighted to see the look of admiration on John's face.

'I always knew you were brilliant, Soraya, but that's amazing ... Promise me, though, that you won't try to retrieve it. Leave that to me. I have an idea already.'

'All right, John,' she briefly touched his hand on the steering wheel, 'but suppose the diary proves the existence of a State-led plot to develop nuclear weapons. What should we do about it? Presumably the development is now underway.'

'I'm sure you're right but I think they will still have a long way to go. We have some time. Let's not go off half-cocked. We need absolute proof. Best not to tell anyone yet.'

Soraya nodded. 'I agree with you, John. But we mustn't wait too long.'

'My feelings exactly, on quite another matter,' he said with a grin.

Lord and Lady Linnhe had put up a tent beside their Land Rover to escape the midday sun. Looking across the desert through the open flaps they saw a tiny dust cloud. As they watched, it grew bigger, sometimes waxing fatter in the distorting atmosphere close to ground.

'I'll get the old gun out, Elspeth, just to be on the safe side. The natives are supposed to be friendly but you never know.'

Elspeth crawled out of the tent with him and stood up to get a better view.

'I think it's a car, Buffy, a solitary car ... They've seen us. They're waving out the windows ... Good heavens. It's Soraya and John. You'll love Soraya, Buffy.'

The car came to a shuddering stop. John and Soraya got out and ran across to Elspeth.

'Not too late for luncheon I hope?'

There were vigorous embraces all round, in spite of the heat.

John and Soraya were extremely hungry and thirsty. Elspeth and Buffy kept the food and water coming, opening tin after tin, bottle after bottle.

'Sorry you couldn't make it to the wedding, Soraya. This is not up to wedding breakfast standards.'

'Believe me, Elspeth, it's delicious. I feel human again. Thank you so much.'

'Yes, thank you both very much,' said John. 'Buffy, can I prevail further on your hospitality, talk you into a spot of people smuggling?'

'Ra-ther. Where to?'

'The British Embassy back across the water in Oman.'

'You're on, old man ... Elspeth, you don't mind going back a day early, do you? I think we've seen everything this place has to offer.'

On the evening of the next day a Land Rover that had taken the return ferry crossing from Ormuz to Muscat was driven up to the gates of the British Embassy. The driver, Lord Linnhe, was recognized by the sentry from his "check-in" visit the previous week and the vehicle was admitted into the compound. Two passengers who had been hidden in the back under a ground sheet among the clobber of tripods, boots, rucksacks and camping equipment got out, a man and a woman. As they stretched their aching limbs they joked with the driver and his passenger about their disreputable appearance and likely reception. Then they all kissed goodbye. The Land Rover departed, waved off by the couple with grimy faces and dirty clothes. They were smiling as they walked, holding hands, towards the front door of the embassy.

Chapter 14

John and Soraya had some difficulty in convincing the Consular Attaché of their credentials. The Consul had already left for an evening of bridge and did not want to be contacted except in emergency. John had deliberately brought no identification. Soraya had her Iranian Civil Service badge which was simply a photograph with her employment number and her rank, Junior Scientific Officer. This, at first, seemed to do more harm than good. The Attaché was plainly disturbed and out of his depth. John persuaded him to telephone the Foreign Office and insist on speaking to Peter Lipscombe. It was early afternoon in London. Lipscombe answered his phone and evidently told the Attaché to give them every assistance. The Attaché said that Lipscombe wanted John to send his report in code forthwith.

Lipscombe had taught John to be brief when using code. The longer the message, the easier to decode. But this message had to be detailed. So John wrote Suspicions confirmed. Two ringleaders dead: Mullah Ahmed and Terias Shammon. Facility destroyed. The Minister, Saban Kandar, pretends he was deceived. Under threat of exposure by Soraya and me he has returned to Tehran with innocent scientists who give him benefit of doubt. Soraya with me at Oman embassy. Awaiting instructions.

As he had been ordered, Lipscombe immediately took the decoded message to the Foreign Secretary. He caught her just before she left for a Departmental meeting.

'All right,' she said. 'This is sufficiently important for an early meeting with the Prime Minister. Make an appointment for me as soon as possible. Pull me out of the conference hall if you have to.'

The PM was not amused.

'He has exceeded his brief. He was not supposed to blow the place up, just to report that it was a bomb factory ... Now we're back where we were. No ammunition.'

The Foreign Secretary's defence mechanism kicked in. She wanted to diffuse the situation with humour, something like I take it coffee is out of the question then, but a further glance at his furious face dissuaded her. Instead she said, 'Look at it this way, Tom. We've nullified the immediate threat and can now concentrate full time on their non-clandestine facilities. We know where all fifteen of their operating facilities are. Unusual activity at any one of them will be noticed.'

'And then I suppose you'll send in your John Russell to blow it up. I don't think so. Next time we'll sort all fifteen out, the way we planned from the start in a combined operation with our Allies ... But you're right, Elizabeth, about one thing. Concentrate full time. Let's pull in another expert. Get me this McKie fellow. Tomorrow morning will do.'

That evening Roddy was in his study organizing his trip to Tehran, in John's absence, for the six-monthly maintenance when the telephone rang. He had to quieten Dougal to hear what was being said. He made out the words, 'I shall put the Foreign Secretary on the line, if you would hold for just a moment.'

He grabbed Dougal's collar, pushed him out on to the landing, fondled his ear and shut the door. Dougal gave one protesting high-pitched moan and lay down noisily, taking his time about it. At last he was silent.

'Good evening, Mr McKie, this is Elizabeth Andrews. The Prime Minister asked me to see if you could come to a meeting with us in Downing Street tomorrow morning at ten. He apologizes for the short notice,' (she thought she had better throw that in) 'but feels confident you will understand that your expertness in certain fields is urgently required. Can I tell him that you are able to come?'

'Certainly, Minister. Should I bring any papers or materials with me?'

'No. Just your good self. I look forward to meeting you. Goodbye.'

Roddy raced downstairs with Dougal in hot pursuit.

'The plot thickens,' he said to Margaret who was ironing his shirts in the kitchen. 'You'll never guess ...'

'Let's see,' said Margaret. 'It's not Mr Lipscombe. Must be someone more senior ... Her Majesty the Queen?'

'Almost,' Roddy laughed. 'It was the Foreign Secretary ...'

Margaret's face registered her astonishment and pride.

'Arranging a meeting with the Prime Minister.'

'You'll be needing your good shirt then.'

Roddy was admitted immediately to Number 10 and was escorted upstairs to a conference room. There were no security checks, at least none of which he was aware. He did not have to show his passport and was not required to wear a badge. Perhaps they tailed me from the airport, he thought. Sent on a digital photograph.

His escort retreated downstairs as Roddy entered the room. It was spacious, set up with a projector and screen, like Ove Arup's boardroom. When you've seen one ... The Foreign Secretary advanced to meet him.

'How good of you to come, Mr McKie. Come and meet the Prime Minister.'

'How do you do, Mr McKie. And this is Brian Skelton, my Private Secretary, who will take notes.

'Now, first things first. Coffee after your journey.'

They all sat down around the tray of coffee and biscuits. Brian Skelton did the pouring, serving Roddy first, the Foreign Secretary next and the PM last. Finally he poured one for himself.

'Elizabeth has kept me informed of your progress with these clever clocks which have proved to be so helpful in Iran.' The PM got right into it. He disdained small talk. 'But this meeting is not about your clocks, or only peripherally. We want your advice and impressions on Iran's nuclear capability. Now, before you say anything, Brian is going to show us slides of aerial reconnaissance photographs of their facilities.'

There was a pause while Brian Skelton walked round to the projector and dimmed the lights.

'Iran has fifteen nuclear facilities,' he said, 'sixteen if you count their storage facility. They are scattered across the country as you might expect and all have easy access. In two cases, roads had to be built to link up with major arterial routes.'

Skelton then put up sixteen slides in succession, pausing without comment for about ten seconds on each, for they were clearly labelled.

'As you see, there has been no attempt at disguise or camouflage. This is consistent with Iran's openness about their nuclear programme.'

The PM interrupted irritably. 'Yes, well I think we'll let our expert reach his own conclusion about that.'

'Of course, Prime Minister. Can I provide anything further for you, Mr McKie?'

'I'd like to take a closer and longer look at these photographs. Could I see the originals, please, and would you mark the location of each facility on a map? Let me examine them for half an hour on my own. Then I'll tell you what I think.'

'Meeting adjourned,' said the PM. 'I am tied up for the rest of the day. Please work with Brian to give a written report of your conclusions. Then I'd be grateful if you would spend the afternoon with Elizabeth at the Foreign Office to go over the consequences; in other words, to make recommendations. She and I will meet again this evening. We may need you down here again soon.'

Roddy and Brian had a working lunch as they prepared a one-page report.

'It's the short ones that take longest,' said Brian. 'But this should give them something to think about.'

Then Roddy took a taxi to the Foreign Office and delivered a copy of the report. He was admitted to the Foreign Secretary's office within five minutes. It was small, designed for no more than three people. Her only concession to femininity was a dark blue vase of spider-mums beside the telephone on her desk.

'I have read your expertise, Mr McKie. Fascinating. Admirably brief. But I'd like you to amplify a little.'

'Three of the sixteen facilities deserve special attention because they are or seem to be disproportionately large. This may amount to nothing, you understand, Minister. There may be innocent explanations. But I'll go over them in order. Facility Number One, close to Tehran, is the storage facility. It presents a contradiction. It is unnecessarily large, as if they haven't heard of Just-in-Time stock control. Yet from the number and size of vans and lorries buzzing about I estimate it is being run on a Just-in-Time basis ...'

'Meaning frequent deliveries of small quantities?'

'Yes. Little and often. So we have old-fashioned, Just-in-Case storage operated in the modern way. An innocent explanation may be related to long delivery times of sensitive components.'

'And what about the next case?'

'This is Facility Number Nine in the industrial belt. It is huge, an obvious target. I would have had three or four smaller facilities distributed across the industrial region.'

'Yes. Too many eggs in one basket, you think?'

'Precisely ... The third one is Facility Number Fourteen. It is in the back of beyond, close to the border with Afghanistan, one of the two that needed to have access roads built. The only reason I can think of having such a large facility in such a remote location is to serve planned conurbations.'

'New towns in the desert? Doesn't seem likely.'

'I agree. That one should be monitored thoroughly. I think all three should.'

The minister took a deep breath. 'Let's have a short break.'

'What do you mean "monitored"?' she asked when they reconvened. 'We can keep up the aerial reconnaissance but our resources on the ground are limited.'

'I think we've got to see inside these facilities. Don't ask me how.'

'All right ... Let's broaden the subject.'

The minister opened a drawer in her desk, pulled out a sheet of paper and handed it to Roddy. 'That's John Russell's report. As you see, he has escaped to Oman and is safe with Soraya in the embassy. The interesting thing is that he has let Saban Kandar go.'

Roddy took a moment to digest what John had achieved.

'That's most impressive,' was his first reaction. 'So-o,' he paused, concentrating hard. 'We know that Kandar organized this attempt to make a nuclear bomb, but everyone in Iran thinks he was simply trying to get another facility up and running for peaceful purposes in case the rest were destroyed.'

'Yes. It puts us in a strong position. We can afford to wait a little. Let's see how Tehran reacts.'

Chapter 15

On the bus, Saban Kandar worked hard to keep the scientists and engineers on side, believing in his innocence. He stood near the front hanging on to the frames of seats on both sides and spoke solicitously to them about the frightening experiences at the mine. As they approached Jilabad, Kandar said they would have to stop at the hotel briefly so that he could pay the bill and he took orders for food for the journey to be included.

Once at the reception desk, Kandar called Security at Shiraz Airport to intercept Soraya and John whom he described. He would have liked to spread the net wider but he had had to co-operate in the preparation of the bill and by the time the bill had been paid the sandwiches for the journey were ready. He could not then afford to raise suspicions in the minds of the passengers by dallying on the telephone.

Satisfied that he had done all he could, he tried to relax in his seat for the rest of the journey north. His mind was working furiously, however. He must appear to the parents of the technocrats as a guardian angel. So he must deliver them to their houses personally. Then, before going to his own house to shower and change, he should telephone the President's office and ask for an audience. Coming direct from the field would surely add to his credibility and gain him a sympathy vote.

He was asked to report not to the President's office but to the building of the Secret Police. They ushered him into an interview room where the President was waiting. So this was not going to be a cosy tête à tête but an observed interview that would be pulled apart later. Utmost caution was required.

The President started affably enough. He was dressed in a sports jacket and flannel trousers. The shirt was open-necked and did not quite go with the jacket. Someone should teach the man how to dress.

'Sit down, Saban. You look as if you have been through the mill. Why don't you tell me about it?'

Kandar cleared his throat. Best to be formal, he decided.

'Mr President, as your Minister for Energy and Foreign Affairs,' he began, 'I took very seriously the threats from Western Powers to eliminate our nuclear facilities. Indeed, in the interests of absolute secrecy, I took it upon myself to arrange the clandestine construction of one more facility. Then not all would be lost if the others were destroyed.'

Kandar was delighted to see a nod of understanding from his President. He picked up speed as he recited the details. 'In this endeavour I had the assistance of the Mullah Ahmed and some of his followers. They did much of the manual work to prepare the site, a disused beta-spodumene mine which served as a disguise, and I picked a team of scientists and engineers who were exceptionally competent and enthused by the policy of protecting our development of nuclear energy for peaceful purposes. Unfortunately the mullah had a different agenda. He deceived me by hijacking the facility to make nuclear bombs.'

The President made as if to interrupt but changed his mind. 'Go on,' he said.

'When we were taken prisoner by the Mullah Ahmed and his men one of my team of scientists, Miss Soraya al-Jerad, managed to get a message to a British Secret Agent with whom she had made friends, perfectly innocently, at university in Edinburgh. This man, to his eternal credit, single-handedly performed a daring trick of surprise at the mine. The Mullah Ahmed and one of his underlings were killed. The rest surrendered and have gone into hiding. Without their leader they will cause no further problems.

'Mr President, the rest is merely an account of tidying up. I organized burials, destruction of weapons and, which was most important, the blowing up of the facility. I saw to it that all the scientists and engineers were safely returned to their homes, all, that is, except Miss al-Jerad who, understandably I feel, chose to help the British Secret Agent leave the country.'

'And who, do we know, is this British Secret Agent?'

'His name is John Russell. I had met him at the Arabian Nights Hotel. He posed as a member of the installation team for the clocks.'

'And do we know where he and Miss al-Jerad are now?'

'No, Mr President.'

'I see. Well thank you for that very clear account of your activities. Please wait here.'

The President left the room and ominously locked and bolted the door behind him.

Upstairs, in the Briefing Room, the President was joined by the Chief of Secret Police.

'Well, what do you make of that?' he asked.

'He's very polished, isn't he, Mr President ... I think we can turn all this to our advantage.'

'Go on.'

'We scare him first, of course, for going it alone, but keep him on to publicize his story. The West must believe they have foiled a plot that we knew nothing about. This will reinforce the perception that our motive is entirely peaceful.'

'That's good, but what about Soraya and this John Russell?'

'Mr President, we need to get them back, talk to them, find out what they really know. I suggest we offer to present them with a national honour – perhaps the Purple Crescent, if you agree. This can only help our relations with the West.'

Soraya and John were each given a bedroom at the embassy. They found a suit in the Consul's wardrobe, somewhat on the small side for John. Soraya had to make do with a blouse and frock from the receptionist. These were kindly provided and gratefully received. After languishing in baths and changing into fresh clothes they were treated to an excellent dinner. The Consular Attaché did his best to redeem himself by bringing in candles to their table and dimming the lights. He asked what music they would like and put on the closest approximation he could find. Peter Lipscombe had made it abundantly clear that he, the Attaché, was extremely privileged to be serving a truly heroic couple and that nothing was too good for them.

After serving dessert the Attaché brought in a large pot of coffee and bid them goodnight. They were finally alone in the large dining room, enjoying the soft music.

'Soraya, we're no more incompatible than a Christian and an Atheist and these get married all the time.'

Soraya smiled, one eyebrow raised. 'Is that a proposal, Sir, or don't you think we've saved the world yet?'

'You know we haven't, my Darling. But I want to marry you anyway. I can't wait much longer ... Soraya, please will you marry me?'

'What about all these children we're going to have?'

'How many did you have in mind?'

'That's not the point, John. Have you worked out what to do, how to bring them up?'

'Still working on it, Soraya.'

'So am I, John ... I want it to be perfect, my Darling. No loose ends. We've waited so long. Just a little longer ... I promise.'

'All right, Soraya ... Let me hold you at least. Let's dance.'

Lipscombe sent John a coded holding message. Stay put. Enjoy. Waiting game.

Two days of being waited on hand and foot was all that Soraya and John could stand. So they asked to see the Consul, commended the Consular Attaché for his diligence, and asked to be left to their own devices.

'Of course. Just as long as you don't leave the compound. They'll have my guts if anything happens to you two. Try to be patient. Do you play bridge, by the way?

'Regretfully no.'

Chapter 16

The letter from the President of Iran caused quite a stir in Downing Street and the Foreign Office.

Dear Prime Minister,

Greetings from Iran. You will understand that we do not normally welcome secret agents. This, however, is an exceptional situation. I am sure you are aware of the excellent work performed by your Secret Service Agent, Mr John Russell, in discovering and eliminating a clandestine attempt to make nuclear bombs at a mine in Southern Iran. As you know, I have repeatedly maintained that Iran's nuclear ambitions are entirely peaceful. It was an embarrassment to learn of this secret activity but it is comforting to know that the ringleaders were killed in the skirmish at the mine.

In order to show our appreciation, we, the Governing Council of Iran, would like to honour your Mr John Russell and one of our own, Miss Soraya al-Jerad, for their brave contributions to our security by awarding each of them the Purple Crescent which is Iran's highest non-military award.

If you will allow this, we ask you to send a guest list of some ten or twenty people whom you would like to attend the ceremony. We shall then issue invitations. We propose the date of 16th December.

Prior to that event, I should be grateful if you would assure the two "fugitives from Iran" that they have nothing to fear and are welcome to return.

With all good wishes,

Yours etc.

The Foreign Secretary called Lipscombe to her office.

'What do you make of the letter?' she asked.

'A number of things. There is no mention of Saban Kandar. Therefore he is not regarded as a ringleader, for otherwise they would have exposed him for greater impact. I expect he will continue in his post. Second, they want to close out this issue as a one-off and use it to reinforce the message that their nuclear programme is purely for domestic energy. Third, they're in a hurry. They want Soraya back pronto.'

'So should we go along?'

'Oh yes. Sweetness and light, but carry a big stick.'

Back in his office, Lipscombe sent a final coded message to John at the embassy in Oman. Take her home. All is forgiven. Keep up your guard.

A courier brought a case of John's clothes with his passport and a change of clothes for Soraya from Marks and Spencer. The embassy negotiated visas and provided money, airline tickets from Muscat to Tehran and an open ticket for John's return to London. After profuse thanks they took their leave of the embassy staff and were driven to the airport. During the flight they decided not to expose Saban Kandar provided he had kept his part of the bargain not to harm the scientists and engineers.

It was mid-afternoon when a taxi dropped them off at Soraya's house. It was locked. They waited in the front garden until Aisha appeared carrying a basket of groceries. She put down the basket, ran to Soraya and embraced her. Then she kissed John too.

'I can't thank you enough, John, for bringing her home safely,' she said. 'Let's go inside.'

John retrieved the basket. Some of the fruit on top was already overripe. Shopping late in the day made the produce cheaper but you couldn't be too choosy.

'I'll put the kettle on and you must tell me all about it. Did you know you're famous? It's in the newspaper. Saban Kandar put out a press release, but I want to know the full story. I'm so proud of you both.'

'First of all, Mrs al-Jerad ...'

'John, you must now call me Aisha, please.'

'Thank you, Aisha ... Can you tell us if the scientists and engineers got back safely.'

'Oh yes, I think so. I'm sure they are back at work in the facilities they came from. All back to normal. It wasn't their fault. I suppose you will have to return to work tomorrow, Soraya?'

'I expect so, Mother ... That's all right. I'm well rested.'

'Where have you been? ... Ah, there's the kettle.'

'I'll do the tea, Mother. You talk to John.'

John asked to see the press release. Kandar had been generous in his praise and accurate if you ignored his protestation that he had been duped by the Mullah Ahmed. He did admit to organizing the site as a secret facility but only for peaceful purposes. John told Aisha how Soraya had cleverly sent her crie de coeur, how with the help of aerial reconnaissance photographs he had discovered the mine. He glossed over the coffin episode, saying simply that the tables had been turned and confirmed that the ringleaders had met their deaths. In the uncertainty immediately following the blowing up of the mine, until Saban Kandar's report was accepted, Soraya and he felt they should seek a haven. He told them of their escape to Oman and made her laugh when he described the clothes they had had to wear at the embassy. 'All's well that ends well,' he concluded.

Nasher arrived from work a few hours later after they had prepared dinner. John had to recount the tale. They insisted he stay in their spare room overnight. Nasher drove him to the airport the next morning saying mysteriously that he looked forward to seeing John again as a celebrity very soon.

John waved goodbye as he walked into the terminal building. He counted up to fifty. Then he came out again and joined the queue for taxis. Aisha would not buy overripe fruit.

The taxi dropped him off at the Arabian Nights Hotel. He walked round the back to the staff car park. The managers and their assistants had been assigned spaces near the rear entrance. The rest of the car park was about three-quarters full. There were at least twenty Vespas in a long rack under a corrugated roof. He returned to the front entrance and walked over to reception.

'I'm back to check on the clock,' he said. 'Can I book a room for tonight?'

'Certainly, Sir. You'll find your colleague in the ballroom. He arrived yesterday.'

So Roddy was here doing the maintenance himself. That made things easier.

John checked in and found Roddy in overalls at the top of a step ladder.

'How's it going, Roddy?'

'John, what a great surprise. The disease is following its expected course. Eight failures this time.'

'Let me give you a hand. Is the locker open?'

'No. Here are the keys.'

John caught the keys and trotted over to the service corridor. He found a set of overalls in the locker and put them on. Then he went to the kitchen where white-clad workers were cutting food in readiness for the evening meal. He spoke to them in Farsi, hoping that the overalls would engender a spirit of solidarity.

'Hi there. I wonder if any of you could help me. I want to nip across town to visit a friend tomorrow morning before my boss appears. Could I borrow a Vespa just for a couple of hours. I'll pay of course.'

'Okay, mate. I'll be here at 7 a.m. That give you enough time?'

'Yes. Perfect. And may I use your helmet and goggles?'

'Sure ... Is she very pretty?'

John winked and ran back to the ballroom just in time to hand Roddy up the last of the eight replacement strings of LEDs. That afternoon they brought each other up to date with their exploits and suspicions. Roddy agreed to take a long time over breakfast.

Next morning a helmeted and goggled John sat astride the Vespa a few doors down from Soraya's house. The first to leave was Soraya herself. She was dressed for work as she had been when she met him at the hotel. She walked to the end of the street and waited for a bus. He wanted to drive up and surprise her. Whisk her away, anywhere. Instead he watched as she boarded the bus. Heigh-ho. Five minutes later Nasher entered his BMW which was parked on the street and drove down past John. Heigh-ho again. Now for the interesting one.

After a further fifteen minutes Aisha came out of the house and locked the door behind her. She looked every inch the respectable, sophisticated wife and mother out to do the day's shopping. She carried the basket, now empty.

John followed her about a hundred metres behind on the Vespa. She walked towards the suburban shopping area until her house was no longer in view. Then she turned into a side street where a gleaming Mercedes was parked. A chauffeur opened the back door for her and she quickly got inside. John tailed them towards the city centre. They seemed to be arguing. Aisha was doing most of the talking. They drove up to the front entrance of a tall office building. John watched from the other side of the street. The chauffeur opened the door for her and she got out without her basket. As she came to the front entrance a uniformed guard opened the door for her. She disappeared inside.

John stopped a pedestrian. 'That's a fine building. What's it for?'

'You want to steer clear of that, mate. It's the home of the Secret Police.'

Crikey, John thought, what a revelation. Bash on. No time like the present. You'll never have a better opportunity. He rode the Vespa through the last of the rush-hour traffic out of the city centre to the south-west sector. He located the avenue and the bus stop across from number 29 with the pristine front garden just as Soraya had described it all. Still wearing the helmet and goggles he parked the Vespa against the post on which the sign showing the bus numbers was mounted. He removed his jacket so that people would see the belt of tools around his waist. He stood on the saddle and examined the screws holding the plate with the two bus numbers to the frame. They were large Phillips screws. He had them loose in no time.

'What's going on? They're not changing the bus routes are they?' It was a woman wearing just a scarf over her head. She must have come running out of her house.

'No, madam, nothing like that. Just routine maintenance: inspecting for rust. Sometimes we have to replace the screws ... These are all right. See.' He held the four screws towards her in the palm of his hand while holding the freed number plate tightly in place with his other hand.

'Right you are,' she said happily enough.

When she had gone John tilted the number plate about its base and felt inside. He removed a black plastic envelope and pushed it inside his overalls. Then he quickly screwed the sign together, jumped down, donned his jacket and rode calmly to the hotel.

They went to Roddy's room to open the envelope. There were seven pages of foolscap filled with neat writing and diagrams. Roddy examined the diagrams and asked John to translate some of the words. It was definitely a commentary about plans for a nuclear weapons factory.

'Does he say where?' Roddy asked.

'No. He would have said if he knew.'

Roddy made a grimace. 'So this is blowing the whistle on a feasibility study only.'

'You sound disappointed.'

'Well I am, in a way. Without knowing where I don't see how we can stop it ... But we now know for sure that there is a State-led plot. Well done, you and Soraya.'

'Let's not forget Anheim Mossada.'

Roddy nodded in respectful silence. At length he said, 'I take it we are the only ones on the side of the angels who know this.'

John nodded.

'How are you going to let Soraya know?'

'I can't until we meet face to face. It's too risky to send a message. Then I'll have to tell her about her mother. I'm not looking forward to that.'

Chapter 17

As Saban ascended the half dozen marble steps leading from the elevator to the President's mezzanine floor he did not know what to expect. It could go either way: promotion or execution. Whether from worry or exertion he was perspiring by the time he reached the landing. He was asked to wait in the anteroom. Too tense to sit he walked to the window looking north. He thought he saw snow on the mountains in the far distance but it may have been white clouds; there was usually more than one interpretation for any observation. The trick was to steer the audience in the preferred direction, and that was his forte, worked for him nearly every time. But no one could spin the Inner Circle.

They remained seated when he was ushered in. Saban walked forward to the centre of the room, resigned to his fate. He bowed to the Ayatollah. There were only four of them: the Ayatollah, the President, the Minister for Internal Affairs with whom Saban had shared many light-hearted moments and, disturbingly, Soraya's mother, Aisha al-Jerad. Aisha, looking severe, was presumably here as his accuser on behalf of her daughter. He wished he had not pointed the rifle at Soraya.

The Ayatollah spoke first. 'Saban Kandar, you have exhibited little faith. Never again shall you plot in isolation. The penalty will be death.'

'Will be, your Eminence?' A ray of hope. Was this torture or a reprieve?

'Will certainly be.' The Ayatollah smiled. Then he turned to the President who took up the running.

'Saban, we are unanimous in deciding that your heart is true. You have proved that. Now you must learn to work in a team. You will be our fifth member. Have faith,' he smiled back at the Ayatollah, 'we are working more effectively than you were able to on the issue closest to your heart.'

So it was going to be all right. Better than that, the mission was alive and he would be part of it. Saban exhaled in relief and satisfaction. Then he quickly recovered, wouldn't do to seem overly emotional. 'Thank you all for this honour,' he said.

They came forward then to shake his hand.

'You will naturally be wondering what role Mrs al-Jerad has,' the President said. 'She is the head of the Fedayin-e Islam.'

What an amazing morning. Saban bowed as he shook Aisha's hand and returned her quizzical smile.

As the Minister for Internal Affairs shook hands he said, 'We heard from Aisha that your car had gone missing, Saban. So we have provided you with another. It's parked outside. And your salary has been increased. Treat yourself to a celebration. Welcome aboard.'

The car was a Ferrari, scarlet and gleaming. Saban opened the door and sat in the driver's seat. They had already adjusted the seat position for him. He waved to the office window on the mezzanine floor. They would be watching. He caressed the steering wheel. After putting the gear lever through all twelve forward positions he fine-tuned the angles of the side mirrors. What a car, the ultimate in fashion. As he adjusted the main mirror he briefly saw his face reflected. On an impulse he drove straight to the private hospital nearest his apartment. 'I want a nose job,' he said.

Chapter18

Peter Lipscombe shook John warmly by the hand.

'Well done at the mine. The MI6 guys are cock-a-hoop. I'll tell Her Ladyship you're back.'

'Wait a moment, please, Peter. There's something else.' John handed over Anheim Mossada's hand-written pages and gave a quick summary.

Lipscombe locked the papers in his desk for future study. 'Dynamite,' was all he said, but he put his finger to his lips.

The Foreign Secretary came over to Lipscombe's office. 'Congratulations, John. We were so worried. Thank God you made it.' She almost kissed him but recovered just in time. 'We should have a proper debriefing. My office at 11?'

'Peter, this is getting complicated. Would you please take notes. Now, John, you're saying that Soraya's mother is a member of their Secret Police?'

'A senior member, Minister. Possibly the head.'

'Amazing. That does put a new complexion on things ... Any ideas, Peter?'

'I'm as gobsmacked as you are, Minister. I'm trying to think how many people she has deceived, if it's possible her husband and daughter don't know.'

'That's an interesting thought.' The Minister began to rock in her chair. 'What do you think, John?'

John took his time. He and Roddy had been struggling with this very question on the flight back to London.

'I think they are a very interesting family, all of them brilliant, all loyal to Iran but in different ways. Each is so focused, so used to keeping minor secrets, not asking too many questions, that it is possible one of them could keep a major secret from the other two. One thing is clear, Peter. You and I have to abandon our working hypothesis. If there is a State-led plot to develop nuclear weapons then Aisha – that's Soraya's mother, Minister – is part of it.'

The Foreign Minister leaned forward in her chair. 'Mr McKie, I assume, has told you his analysis of the aerial photographs?'

'Yes.'

'He says we have to see inside the three large facilities.'

'I wouldn't know what to look for.'

'Then, John, you'd better get that information from Mr McKie. Maybe you'll have to take him with you ... Oh, I almost forgot. The Governing Council of Iran is going to present medals to you and Soraya a week before Christmas. You may take some friends. Perhaps you can do covert work then. Anyway, off you go, you two, and out-scheme the schemers.'

It took a while for news of the death of Terias Shammon to reach the Home Office. Iran did not volunteer the information, nor did the Foreign Office. Governmental departments jealously guard their hard-won information. What triggered the admission was the routine follow-up by the Home Office three months after Shammon's deportation. A brief statement of regret from Iran's Department of Energy and Foreign Affairs was received within a week. It stated that the writings of Shammon had found favour with one of their mullahs, Mullah Ahmed, who had co-opted Shammon into his subversive organization. Both men died from gunshot wounds during the overthrow of the organization at a mine in the south of the country.

Betty was appalled. She felt she had sent Shammon to his death.

'You have nothing to reproach yourself for,' she was assured by her Section Head. 'This kind of thing happens all the time. He would have got into bad company anywhere, if not Iran then somewhere else. He was a disaster waiting ...'

Betty put her hands over her ears and ran from the room.

Nicol found the right words later at their flat.

'Come to bed,' he said.

John and Peter were pouring over a map in Lipscombe's office.

'How fit is Roddy McKie?' Lipscombe asked. 'Fit enough to ride a camel?'

'Sure.'

'Well I think the pair of you should make a dash for it, crossing the border somewhere near Islam Qala. We can get you into Afghanistan easily enough and escort you to the border but after that you'll be on your own.'

'Fine. That's Facility Number 14 taken care of. What about the other two?'

'Rein in your camel, John. One at a time.'

John rang the doorbell at Betty-and-Nicol's flat in Wandsworth.

'John!'

Betty flung her arms around his neck.

'Nicol. Look who's here.'

'Hey, John. C'mon in.'

They sat down around a table in the kitchen. Nicol opened a bottle of wine and Betty produced some nuts and crisps.

'Betty, I know about Terias Shammon.'

'How? They said he died at a mine in Southern Iran.'

'Betty, I was there. I killed him. It was self-defence.'

Betty turned pale. She put down her glass. She needed both hands to do it.

'My God. I nearly had you killed too.'

John got up and put his hands on her shoulders, leaning over her chair. He kissed her hair. 'No, Betty. Let me tell you how it happened. Then you'll understand and can put it behind you.'

John told the story of the mine once more, leaving out the duplicity of Saban Kandar.

'Can both of you get away for a long weekend in Tehran in December, all expenses paid? It's a chance to see Soraya. They're giving us medals, would you believe, on the 16th and we can bring our friends. Best kind of closure there is, Betty.'

Chapter 19

October 2005

The pale blue sky was peppered with stratocumulus clouds. It was noticeably colder on the hands and in the lungs. Geese giving directional squawks were on their training flights south over the Fife peninsula and back. Pairs of laverock were playing chases low and high over the stubble field. Roddy returned with Dougal into the driveway from their morning walk. They delighted in the crunching sound as they trod on the spate of chestnuts, kernels and leaves lying on the gravel. The driveway was streaked with shafts of sunlight through the trees. They walked round to the back door, taking in the view of the lawns, the turning trees, the hedgerow, the fields, and the sea beyond. Low sunshine painted the autumnal scene around them, bringing out the lushness of the grass under a scattering of colourful leaves, here lit, there in shadow.

Roddy took a last look before entering the house. It was unbearably beautiful, far too much to risk losing. But John was offering him the chance to put some real excitement into his life before it was too late. Only a coward would turn down such an opportunity. He squared his shoulders and strode inside.

A quick breakfast, Dougal first, and then action stations. Never wear brown shoes south of Perth. Roddy polished his black pair, showered and shaved, put on his Sunday suit, received an approving glance and a kiss from Margaret and set off for Edinburgh Airport to pick up John. They drove to Dreghorn Barracks. Two extremely young-looking soldiers on guard duty, wearing black hackles, asked them to park just inside the barrier and to go to the guard room. A corporal had them sign in, gave them a car pass for inside the windscreen, welcomed them on behalf of the First Battalion of the Royal Regiment of Scotland and asked them to drive over to the Officers' Mess where Major Phillips would be waiting.

As they drove past an expanse of grassy slopes they noticed the square largely filled with military vehicles being loaded by soldiers in battle dress.

'We're off to Gareloch tomorrow for fieldcraft training,' said Major Phillips after briefly shaking hands. He had impossibly broad shoulders and a grip of iron. He led them inside. The hallway was full of bergers. 'Sorry about the mess in here. State of flux. Let's go into my office.'

The office, like the officer, was very tidy but seemed too small for him. He quickly and effortlessly lifted over a second chair to join the one already there in front of his desk. Must be used to one on one meetings, Roddy thought. Wouldn't like to be on the receiving end.

They got down to business immediately. The major explained that One-SCOT Battalion, the recently amalgamated Royal Scots Borderers, was going through standard training procedures. They had spent a week at Barry Buddon on target practice and had a planned programme of exercises in the Pentlands, Gareloch and Wales.

'Wish I had more time,' he said. 'I'd like to get my new Company thoroughly gelled before we are deployed. But I understand you have a pressing requirement in Afghanistan.'

'Have you personally served in Afghanistan?' John asked.

'No. But I have been there on a rece with Sixteen Brigade, with the Third Paras in particular. As you know, they're about to leave Helmand Province. They showed me around not just in Helmand but all the way across to the Iranian border. It's bandit country. Worse than South Armagh in its heyday.'

John and Roddy nodded sombrely.

'From what I've heard and already seen,' the major continued, 'the Taleban are highly aggressive fighters, preferring pursuit to retreat. We may use that against them. What plan has been proposed by the Foreign Office?'

'Not much of one,' said John. 'Just to make a dash for it across the border near Islam Qala.'

Major Phillips laughed. 'Typical ... We'll have to flesh that out ... You do realize that it is impossible to cross the border unobserved. Even if there is no moon you will be seen. They have the best of night vision equipment.'

'So what do you suggest?' Roddy asked.

'For getting you in or bringing you back? Both, I take it.' He gave them a wink. 'Let me think for a minute.'

John and Roddy waited patiently while the major turned away from them the better to concentrate. He took a full minute staring at a map.

'We'll need to dress you up as Taleban and set you off on camels. Eight of us will chase you, firing to miss. The Taleban will cheer you on and come gunning for us. So we'll pull most of them away from the area. I'll set up the rest of my volunteers to ambush them just as they are about to catch us. Somewhere near Kenar-e Kapeh, I fancy.'

'So we get in,' John said, 'and do our stuff. What about the return journey?'

'I was just coming to that ... Not all of the Taleban will have chased us. There will be a few left wearing their night vision goggles. So more deception is called for. ...'

Chapter 20

Roddy asked for a day to get used to his camel. He needed all of that. So did John, for that matter.

'You're both unco' gentle,' said Sergeant Thomas of the Third Parachute Battalion who had stayed behind to teach them. 'Camels are belligerent beasts. Y'have to boss them around.'

They were at Camp Bastion in the north of Helmand province. The field where they were receiving instruction was more like a beach, half sandy, half stony. Flies buzzed around their heads: the camels seemed to attract them. Beyond the field they could see ruined buildings the colour of sand crumbling back to the dusty land. A shepherd wearing a brown turban was leading a resigned flock of sheep through this scene of desolation. Roddy and John took careful note of the shepherd's attire. They would soon have to look just like him.

The sergeant took it slowly. All he had them do for the first hour was mount and dismount again and again. Then they practised riding at walking pace followed by a little trotting. One good thing was that wherever Roddy's camel went John's would follow. So at least they stayed together. At the end of the morning's practice it was obvious that John was the better rider. Roddy was finding it difficult to grip tightly enough. His dodgy knee was playing up.

They took a break for lunch in a marquee. It was not especially hot outside. The benefit of the marquee was to escape from the dust and the flies. The food was not bad, standard barracks fare with no concession to the dramatic change in location from the cold skies of Edinburgh. There was a choice of curry or lasagne with tinned peaches to follow, all cooked and dished out cheerfully enough by soldiers who had drawn the short straw, for the Mess staff from a private firm did not go with the battalion on active duty.

'You know the story of the Bedouin tribesmen?' Sergeant Thomas asked this as they were finishing their meal. 'No? Well these two tribesmen each had a camel and each man was convinced that his camel was the slowest in the world. It was their only claim to fame and they went around boasting about it. One fine day they met and challenged each other to a race. The course was agreed: from a store at the edge of Cairo out into the desert, round an oasis, and back to Cairo.'

'So both of them were hoping to lose the race?' John gave Roddy's foot a tap under the table. He was sure Roddy would have heard it too. But it was better to stay on the right side of their instructor. He'd be putting them through it all afternoon.

'You've got it. But the riders cheated, holding their camels back, and so they soon ran out of food and water and were nearly deid by the time they reached the oasis. Fortunately a famous philosopher was there watering his camel. Each rider told the philosopher the truth, saying he was willing to die to prove his point, but would prefer not to. The philosopher gave them just two words of advice. The men leapt on the camels right away and went haring back to Cairo ... What were the two words?'

'We give up.'

'Change camels,' said the sergeant. 'And that's what you gentlemen should do. Then all you'll have to do, Mr McKie, is hing on ... So then, if you've had enough to eat, we'll try going a wee bit faster with Ali Baba and Sesame.'

"Hinging on" at high speed over a contrived slalom course was not easy. Both of them fell off many times. They got no sympathy from the sergeant.

'Get back on, quick as you like.'

By the end of a long, painful afternoon, however, they felt much more competent and thanked the sergeant.

'You're not finished yet. There's a wee trick y'have to learn.'

Major Phillips joined them in the field. He was carrying two rucksacks.

'You'll be wearing these on the outward journey,' he said. 'Shouldn't affect your balance too much. Better give them a dry run though.'

John and Roddy donned the rucksacks and mounted their camels. They performed a couple of high speed runs through the slalom course. All went well.

'Now open them up.'

'Hey, that's clever,' said Roddy who was first to pull the assemblage of dummy and straps from his rucksack. 'Where did you get these made?'

'It's Sergeant Thomas and some of his platoon you have to thank for these. He's not just a teller of riddles ... He'll show you how to attach them.'

It was easy to strap the dummies on: one loop towards the front and the other about three feet farther back behind the hump. The dummy was then unfolded and raised to the vertical sitting position on the saddle by sliding a crossbar into position and tightening a clamp. From a distance through night vision goggles they would look convincing.

Sergeant Thomas walked eighty paces away from them. He signalled that he was ready. John and Roddy pointed their camels at him and gave them a whack on the rump. They ran over to the sergeant who rewarded them each with a few dates. Then he walked the camels back and asked John and Roddy to remove the dummies, wait two minutes and strap them on again. The performance was repeated. In fact at the sergeant's insistence they repeated it five times, gradually increasing the distance.

Late in the following afternoon ten men and two camels boarded a Chinook. Flying high in a northerly direction they were soon out of Helmand province. As they headed towards Herat and later westwards to Ghurian they had several glimpses of Taleban soldiers in single file on mountain trails. They also saw peasants working. It was impossible to tell the difference since both dressed identically.

'That's one of the things that makes it difficult,' said Major Phillips. 'We surround a village where some atrocity has been committed and find no enemy soldiers, only decent, hard-working peasants ... That's why I'm particularly looking forward to this. There's a kind of symmetry about it.'

Roddy tried in vain to identify the symmetry. Maybe the major had meant poetic justice; but there was no poetry either, only bathos perhaps. Roddy looked across the bay at John and suppressed a laugh. He looked like an actor about to go on stage, a stranger in paradise. They had even given him a false beard to hide his fair complexion. But this was no fancy-dress party. It was deadly serious. Some of these relaxed soldiers might be killed before the night was out, all to help a couple of wayward mathematicians on a pet project. Most serious mathematicians, Roddy reflected, had found the benefits of symmetry to be overplayed. Was it Sylvester who had said, 'Symmetry is like an eastern garment: although pleasing to the eye it impedes progress'? Well, this robe had better not impede progress. The consequences did not bear thinking about.

They landed just beyond Ghurian where the rest of the Company had set up a temporary field position about fifty miles from the Iranian border. Everything was in place: armoured lorries and jeeps and a horse box for the camels. After a meal of field rations they set out at sunset in three convoys, the largest convoy heading southwest and the smaller ones west and slightly north of west.

The small convoy consisting of those who had come by Chinook stopped five miles from the border.

'This is as close as we dare go with the vehicles. Take it slowly for the first three or four miles until we are out in the open. Then go for it. No more talking.'

It was almost pitch dark. John took the lead on Ali Baba. They came upon a dried-up river bed and used it for a time for cover. Then they emerged into scrubland dotted with large bushes of juniper. In other circumstances and in daylight it would have been a delightful outing, the sort of holiday safari you might pay for. The dominant scent was the smell of the camels but occasionally John's head was stroked with a wisp of leaves at the end of a branch and that scent could be bottled. It made him think of Soraya. Sooner or later she would find out about her mother. What a test of loyalties ... but back to the present. Open ground or not, the moment he sensed they were observed he had to start the mad gallop.

They made it through the juniper bushes without incident. Sergeant Thomas came up and fed the camels a final titbit.

'That should bring them back,' he whispered. 'You'll be fine.'

John turned and nodded to Roddy. They kicked their camels into a gallop. Shots rang out behind them as they raced across the open ground. It was about a mile and a half to the border. They should be across in four minutes.

Now they were a quarter of a mile ahead of the pursuing soldiers. They would soon be out of range. The camels raced on. John and Roddy heard shots from another direction, over to their right. John had to pull hard on the right rein to keep Ali Baba on course. The shots were not directed at them, however. So the plan was working. The Taleban were protecting them with covering fire.

The sound of gunfire behind them became more frenzied as they approached the border. God help Major Phillips and his men. He had told them the border was indicated by a series of unconnected posts about two hundred metres apart, each supporting a sign bearing the single word, Iran. As they hurtled across they saw just one of these posts: not very welcoming, Roddy thought. If this had been Scotland the sign would have said, 'Welcome to the best small country in the world.' Still, there was no border patrol. That was the main thing.

They raced on for another half mile until the ground took a sharp descent. Only then did they ease the exhausted camels into a walk. It was eerily quiet. The only sound was of distant gunfire behind them and farther to the south. Looking ahead they saw lights from a village far in the distance.

'That'll be Tayyebad,' said John. 'So Facility Number 14 is up this way.'

He steered his camel to the right. Sinbad obediently followed. Roddy relaxed and massaged his left knee: so far so good.

After the tension of the gallop the even walking pace of the camels through the darkness over the sandy soil lulled their senses. It was the sudden clattering sound of Ali Baba's hoofs on tarmac that told them they had hit the road. John immediately steered him off it, back to the sand. They strained their eyes to follow the line of the road from as far away as possible, which was only twenty metres. The sand was not deep and with any luck their tracks would not be noticed. After a mile they came upon a chain-link fence. John guided them fifty metres along the fence farther from the road and dismounted. Holding a stirrup by its leather strap he pushed the metal against the fence. There was no flash. He gestured to Roddy to dismount. They tied their camels to the fence, took off their rucksacks which they left with the camels, and unpacked torches. Then, having remounted the camels and now standing on the saddles, they heaved themselves to the top of the fence and listened. Following John's example Roddy landed evenly on both feet. His left knee jarred but did not buckle.

Hearing no sound they crept down the side of the fence towards the main gate. There were no sentries. The gate was closed but unlocked. They walked into a car park. They counted six cars. So perhaps there was a skeleton crew on night shift. They tiptoed to the front entrance and opened the door. The place was in darkness. John flashed his torch. The floor was unpaved. He flashed it again, straight ahead this time. Nothing came into view. He switched it on full and began to scan the area.

'Roddy, the place seems empty and deserted. Let's walk. You go that way, I'll go this way.'

The area was huge. It must have covered a hundred acres. They spent the next two hours inspecting it thoroughly. It consisted of sixteen buildings connected by passageways. There was nothing inside. The buildings were empty shells.

'But why the cars?' Roddy asked when they had returned to the front entrance.

'All part of the illusion. They probably drive them in with a bus from Tayyebad every morning and come back in the evening to drive most of them back. Nice work if you can get it.'

They returned to the camels and rode them around the north side of the facility. John set a course east by northeast. After an hour they came to the steep rise that indicated the border was half a mile away. Just below the top of the rise they strapped on the dummies and buried the rucksacks and one of the torches. John checked his watch.

'Two fifteen. Perfect. We said between two and three. Ready for this?'

'Never better.'

They pointed Ali Baba and Sinbad in a south-easterly direction at an angle of forty-five degrees across the open ground to the border and gave them a whack. The camels took off, half in fear, and presumably half in expectation of a treat at the other end. If the camels kept galloping on that line and were not noticed until they crossed the border then they would not be intercepted by any Taleban observers running out from the bushes for almost six minutes. That was already a lot of ifs, though.

John gave the camels a half-minute start. To have gone sooner would have increased the risk that he and Roddy would be noticed before the Taleban's attention was focused on the camels. Then, carrying his torch like a baton and holding his pocket compass in his other hand, he set off at a steady seven-minute-mile pace towards the northeast, at a right angle to the direction the camels had taken. By the time the dummies were discovered Roddy and he would be almost at the border. Then they would have to maintain that pace for the next couple of miles in order to keep at least two miles between them and the Taleban giving chase on foot from where they intercepted the camels. What if the Taleban signalled to another group nearer to them? The two-mile safety margin might then be drastically reduced. John wanted to set a faster pace but knew he was already asking for as much as Roddy could give.

Roddy strove to keep up. His knee was protesting but he knew it would feel better once he had warmed up. That would be when the pain in his lungs and the heaviness in his arms and legs took precedence over any discomfort in his knee. He concentrated on giving full strides.

The ground was not perfectly flat: there were numerous minor undulations. Their eyes were sufficiently accustomed to the darkness to see the changes in level before their feet hit the ground. That was not the problem. But John had the demanding habit of accelerating every time they had a few uphill strides. He was beginning to leave Roddy behind.

They were across the border. The ground was flatter now. Roddy picked up the skirt of his robe and lifted his knees more. He managed to catch up with John and heard a cheerful 'Well done, old man.' He wanted to say, 'Patronizing git,' but was too tired to reply. He tried to think of other things than running. He wondered what would happen to the camels, how the Taleban would treat them. They'd probably kill them hallal-style for meat.

'We have almost certainly been seen by now,' John said. 'But with any luck they're well to the south of us ... How are you feeling?'

'Fine ... Sorry for the camels.'

'Quite ... Let me know if you see anything ... Our soldiers will be watching us too ... They'll flash a light when we get closer.'

John did a quick check with his compass. They were still on course.

'Less than a mile to the scrubland ... What's that noise?'

They stopped briefly to listen. It was the sound of galloping hoofs coming towards them. There was nowhere to hide.

'Stand still,' John said. 'Remember they may think we're Taleban. I'll do the talking.'

Two men on camels arrived in a cloud of dust. They were holding rifles. They pulled the camels to a stop. Just then there was a shout in English.

'Hit the deck.'

John and Roddy immediately fell on their faces. Two shots were fired. The riders slumped and fell to the ground. John bounded up and grabbed the reins of Ali Baba and then of Sinbad. Six soldiers came bursting on the scene.

'The rest of them are running this way but we've plenty time.' The young captain grinned at them. 'Hop on the camels, Gentlemen, and we'll run along beside you.'

As they got underway Roddy spoke to the captain who was running beside Sinbad. 'We thought they'd kill the camels, but of course it was cleverer of them to use them to catch us.'

'I know. We saw the whole thing. Realized we'd have to break cover to reach you in time.'

'Thank God you did.'

They were now among the juniper bushes and immediately felt safer but the captain signed no more talking. He led them half a mile to a camouflaged army lorry.

'We pushed it here the last mile. Hop in, camels and all. Quickly now.'

The sudden sound of the engine betrayed their position but they were out of the scrubland after a few minutes and barrelling along towards Ghurian where the Chinook was waiting.

It was dawn when they touched down at Camp Bastion. John sent Peter a coded message by satellite. Facility empty, a decoy. All well. They were given a full delicious breakfast and retired to sleep.

In the late afternoon they were awakened by the sound of a convoy of vehicles entering the camp. John and Roddy got up and dressed quickly.

'How did it go?' Major Phillips asked. 'You found what you were looking for?'

'Yes, thanks. The facility is a decoy.'

'Really ... Well I suppose it was worth it.'

'Are all your men okay?'

The major smiled. 'We made it without casualties. The ambush worked ... I must write it up. See you later.'

Over in the field Sergeant Thomas was nuzzling Ali Baba and Sesame. He had two large carrots in each hand.

Chapter 21

November 2005

John needed to think. After the successful investigation of Facility Number 14 Peter Lipscombe had given him a free hand to plan the operation on the storage facility.

'It's better that I don't know the details, John. I'd have to report upwards. If the PM hears about it he'll want to go in with all guns blazing. Try to resolve it quietly.'

John went for a walk along the Embankment. It was a blustery day causing strings of white waves to crop up randomly across the Thames. For a time his thoughts were like that, in snatches, disordered, becoming panicky. He turned his face away from the river and looked resolutely towards Westminster. He must put his thoughts in order. Soraya, she was the starting point, the beginning of the piece of string as old Fischer would say. How to tell her, when to tell her, what to tell her: it all had to be done lovingly and carefully or he would lose her.

He could fly over to see her using the pretext of the nine-month maintenance of the clock. But everyone in authority would know that he was a British Secret Service agent and that the clock was just a ruse. His cover was well and truly blown. He could be open and say he needed to see Soraya, couldn't bear to be away from her. God knows that was the truth. And they might well allow him to visit. After all, they were going to honour him as a hero in a few weeks. He could take Soraya somewhere quiet and break the terrible news to her: tell her that her mother led a double life, that there was a State-led plot and that she would be involved in it. If Soraya managed to recover from that bombshell he could go on to talk about the need to smuggle Roddy into the storage facility and ask for her help. This would mean deceiving her father also, for they must assume that he knew nothing of his wife's covert activities and would have to be kept oblivious of them. Soraya would have to keep these secrets from her parents for weeks until the matter was resolved. It was too much to expect of her. She was only human. She would not be able to conceal her shock and unhappiness from the parents in whom she had such trust.

No. Soraya must not learn these things until the last moment, for her own safety. So he would have to plan with the help of their friends how to smuggle Roddy into the facility, and bring Soraya up to speed later. This meant their friends would know of her predicament before she did. Would she ever forgive him?

Nicol closed the front door noisily behind him.

'What was your day like, Betty?'

'Unremarkable. Yours?'

'Bloody awful. Those accountants can't speak English. Christopher Robin could do better ... The Greeks and the Romans were there for a reason ... Humour me, Gorgeous Crumpet.'

'Let's see ... But basics they left are defiled every season ... Will that do?'

'Too right ... There's "centred around", well we'll list just a few ...'

'Gosh ... hang on ... "Affinity with" and "oblivious to" ...'

'Good girl ... I've got it ... High treason.'

The next day Nicol came home in a better mood to be greeted by an excited Betty waving two invitations. The first was very grand from the Governing Council of Iran requesting the pleasure of their company at the medals ceremony at the Presidential Palace on 16th December at 5 p.m. and afterwards at a Ball at the Arabian Nights Hotel. Two airline tickets and hotel vouchers were enclosed. Limousines would be provided for all transport.

'You did arrange the Friday off, Nicol?'

'Eh, what Fri ... Of course.'

'That wasn't funny ... And you'll help me choose a dress?'

'If you insist.'

The second invitation was hand written on a simple white card: drinks and nibbles on Friday evening at seven-thirty with Elspeth and Buffy at their house on Bywater Street.

'I know the street,' said Nicol. 'Chelsea. Off the King's Road. Very nice.'

Buffy led them down a stylish wrought-iron staircase to the basement dining room where Elspeth, John and an older couple were standing and chatting as they sipped wine. Betty and Nicol kissed Elspeth, and then John introduced Roddy and Margaret, saying simply that Roddy and he worked together in Iran. Betty and Margaret quickly made friends, remarking on the splendid layout of food. The table was groaning under the weight of delicacies from all over the world: macadamia nuts, quails' eggs, caviar, anchovies, serrano ham, bratwurst, haggis, cuscus, oatcakes, salads, col slaw, tomatoes on the vine, a huge variety of cheeses and breads, authentic turkish delight and chocolates.

'Margaret and Betty, you must lead the way. We'll be right behind you. Red or white, Betty? They're from M and S round the corner. We've always found their wines to be good.'

'Red please, Buffy. This is a super spread, Elspeth.'

When they reached the coffee stage John got to his feet.

'I'd like to thank Elspeth and Buffy for inviting us to their lovely London home and for the wonderful food and wine.'

'Here, here,' Nicol and Roddy joined in.

'But, Nicol and Betty, I have to confess to having an ulterior motive. Roddy and Margaret know about it, and so far Elspeth and Buffy know only that I wanted a secure place to discuss with you all something very delicate. I couldn't risk my own flat. I'm going to ask a tremendous favour from all of you.'

'Is this something to do with Soraya?' Elspeth asked.

'Oh, I hope so,' said Betty. 'Are you two going to tie the knot?'

'I sincerely hope so,' said John, 'but that's not what this is about. Soraya doesn't yet know what I'm about to tell you.'

Betty inched back in her chair. She had never seen John so serious.

Chapter 22

It was not until after nine on the evening of Friday 15th December that they had signed in at the Arabian Nights Hotel. The manager, Mr Abdollah, came through to Reception to greet them. John introduced his friends and went up with them to their rooms leaving Nicol with Roddy who then drew the manager aside.

'Mr Abdollah, it's good to see you again. How's the clock? Still ticking away?'

'Mr McKie, you know your clock does not tick. Yes, it is continuing well I think.'

'I have left the maintenance a little late since I knew we were coming for the medals ceremony. We're all tired this evening and tomorrow is a big day, sight-seeing and then the medals ceremony and Ball. I plan to do the maintenance on Sunday after all the festivities. But it is important that the clock should be working well at the Ball tomorrow evening. So please don't hesitate to telephone for me if it should break down before then, no matter where I am. I'll come myself if I can or I'll send my new assistant, Mr Anderson here. It must be perfect.'

'Of course, Mr McKie.'

'We'll give it a quick check now before we have dinner.'

Soraya came over by taxi to join them for coffee after dinner. Under a hooded cape which she left in the ladies' cloakroom she came in Western dress to put her friends at their ease. She wore a beige light quilted jacket over a black sweater with a rollneck collar. Her trousers were black and elastic with a low waistband through which was threaded an elegant gold chain belt with medallions and pendants. Her hair had grown longer and reached her shoulders. She looked like a top model.

John was surprised and delighted to see her in Western dress. He walked quickly and met her in front of Reception, kissing her hand.

'You look gorgeous,' he said.

'Thank you, kind Sir ... You look troubled, John. Is everything all right? Where are the others?'

'They're all here. We'll meet them later. First we have to talk.'

He led her into the floodlit garden which was deserted. It was cold. Snow was forecast.

'Soraya, my love, I have to tell you disturbing things. They are intelligence matters. So they are partly guesswork, not like mathematics where we have absolute proof.'

Soraya nodded. She looked into his eyes with a sense of foreboding.

'All along, you and I have been on the same wavelength about Iran's nuclear aspirations. Our only concern has been against those who would develop nuclear weapons.'

'And you think there is another plot?'

'Yes. Anheim Mossada's papers – that abbreviated diary – prove at the very least that there was a secret feasibility study done.' He saw her look of admiration and wanted to hug her. If only that were all he had to tell her.

'You managed to retrieve it, John. At the bus stop?'

'Exactly where you said it would be ... But listen, Soraya, there's more.' He took her hand and looked at her tenderly before continuing.

'I think your father is exactly what he appears to be: a clever, dedicated, senior man who is trying to establish Iran's nuclear facilities for peaceful purposes. Soraya ... your mother, on the other hand, is a truly amazing woman. She has kept a secret from you and, I think, from your father. She is a senior member, possibly the chief, of the Fedayin-e Islam.'

Soraya let go of John's hand. He had been half expecting her to say that that was ridiculous, that it could not be. But, as he watched, something inside her, some quick logic about past unexplained experiences, made her accept the news. She gave a low moan.

'Tell me how you know,' she said, tears rolling down her face.

'Oh Soraya, there is no easy way to tell you. I suspected something the last time we were together, the day I brought you home from Oman. The fruit in your mother's basket was overripe. That did not fit with the Aisha I knew. I followed her the next day after you and your father had left the house. She walked for a little way and then was driven to the Secret Police building. I think she has been in that routine for many years.'

'So she is your enemy?'

John hesitated.

'Well, is she?'

'Yes, Soraya.'

Soraya turned away and wept uncontrollably. John stood frozen.

After a full minute Soraya's breathing began to return to normal. She turned back to John and hugged him.

'Help me to understand. Please help me to understand.'

John squeezed her gently and then held her away from him, looking into her eyes. 'Your mother is a fine lady, dedicated in a different way. If there is a plot to develop nuclear weapons, and we think there probably is, then she is part of it and so is the President and a few senior members of the Governing Council.'

'Where do you think they are doing this development?'

'We're not sure yet. We have aerial photographs. Three of the facilities are large enough to be nuclear bomb factories. Roddy and I checked one out, close to the Afghan border. It was a decoy. We think the storage facility, the least likely one you might think, so close to Tehran, is very possibly where bomb development is going on. We need to get Roddy inside to have a look.'

'I take it you have a plan?'

'Yes, Soraya. I'll be watched the whole time. So I need the help of our friends ... I had to tell them about it, not everything, not about your mother, Soraya.'

Soraya bit her lip, fighting away the tears.

'Then I'll tell them, John. They must know in case they make a mistake.' She hugged him again. 'Thank you for holding that back until we talked. I'm on your side, my love. I trust you ... Be kind to my mother, as kind as you can be in the circumstances.'

They walked slowly back into the hotel and found the others in a corner of the lounge. The embraces were heart-felt. Everyone knew that Soraya had just heard about the new suspected nuclear plot. They could see that she had been crying.

'Let's all go up to the roof,' John said. 'Bring your wraps, ladies, it's cold and bug-free in both senses but you'll love the hurl up and the view, and I'm sure we'll have the place to ourselves. We have a lot to talk about.'

Chapter 23

December 2005

It was like a wedding reception at first. Soraya arrived with her parents. Nasher parked his BMW in the car park at the Presidential Palace and escorted his wife and daughter up the steps to the marble hallway. He took off his hat and coat. Soraya offered to check them in with her mother's coat and her own in the cloakroom and received three tickets which she kept in her purse. They walked on up the staircase. Nasher pointed out the stained glass windows and the carvings on the ceiling. He was beginning to take it all for granted, having mounted these steps once a week for many years, but he wanted his wife and daughter to enjoy the magnificence as they saw it so rarely.

The President stood at the top of the stairs to greet everyone. For once he was sartorially elegant in evening dress with medals all over his chest. He shook hands with all the men and bowed to the women. With Aisha and Soraya he made more of a fuss, kissing their hands. This drew everybody's attention. A ripple of applause broke out as they walked into the antechamber to receive their glasses of champagne.

John and the other friends were already there. Soraya led her parents over to them for handshakes, kisses and introductions. The sound level was high and it was difficult to communicate without speaking unnaturally loudly.

'Just wait till the music starts,' said Nasher. 'Then it will be impossible.'

Saban Kandar joined their group. He looked different. He was no less full in the face but his nose was no longer hooked but aquiline. He shook Roddy's hand and gave a startled Margaret a peck on her cheek. 'I hope this evening to have another dance with you, Mrs McKie.' Then John introduced the others. Kandar was delighted to meet Lord and Lady Linnhe and clearly wanted to quiz them about smuggling Soraya and John out of the country. He also seemed to be particularly taken with Betty in her slinky black number. Their conversation was interrupted by a fanfare of buglers. Then they were invited to enter the chamber and take their seats for the ceremony.

Margaret whispered to Soraya that she needed to visit the ladies' room before the ceremony started. Soraya took her hand with an "excuse us" smile and led her down the stairs. They went to the cloakroom.

'My friend needs a breath of fresh air,' Soraya said. 'Could she have her coat?'

Margaret handed over her ticket.

'And my father thinks he has left his spectacle case in his coat pocket. Could I have a look?'

Soraya showed all three tickets. She was handed her father's coat. Turning her back she felt inside. Good. The keys were there. She exchanged them for her own bunch of keys in case the difference in weight might be noticed. She put her father's keys in her handbag with the tickets and handed back the coat.

'It's not there. It must have fallen out of his pocket, probably in the car. We'll find it later. Thank you.'

While Margaret walked out into the parking lot Soraya returned upstairs to rejoin the crowd as they milled into the chamber. Their group was seated in the front row, along from the President in the midst of the senior members of the Governing Council whose seats extended to the second and third rows. Soraya dropped her handbag. Roddy retrieved it for her and pocketed the keys.

The ceremony started promptly at 5 o' clock. The President went to the lectern which had been installed for the occasion below the dais where he usually sat.

'Distinguished guests, ladies and gentlemen,' he began, reading from a prepared speech...

Nicol glanced at his watch and received a reproving look from Roddy.

'Relax,' he whispered out of the corner of his mouth.

The President droned on.

At 5.05 there was an interruption. A uniformed servitor walked up the aisle bearing a note. When he reached the front he bowed to the President and asked it to be passed along the row to Mr McKie. The President stopped in mid-sentence. Roddy opened the envelope, read the note and immediately stood up.

'My apologies, Mr President. The clock beckons. Please excuse us.'

Nicol and he followed the servitor out of the chamber. Behind them they could hear Saban Kandar trying to diffuse the situation with a joke, something about "the exigencies of time". By the time they reached the top of the stairs the President had resumed his speech.

At the cloakroom the servitor told them that the hotel had sent a limousine. So they quickly retrieved their coats and Roddy's hat (which looked remarkably like Nasher's) and entered the limousine. Just before they reached the main gate Roddy tapped the driver on the shoulder.

'On second thoughts I should go back to the ceremony,' he told the driver. 'My assistant will surely manage on his own. I'll come away early as soon as the formal proceedings are over.'

'Would you like me to come back for you, Sir?'

'No, thank you. I don't know how long the ceremony will last. Quite a long time, I think, judging by the first speech.' He grinned at the driver who smiled back. 'I'll take a taxi. Don't worry.'

The limousine departed with a wave from Nicol.

Roddy walked briskly through the car park to Margaret who was standing beside Nasher's BMW. She had hidden her hair under a scarf. Roddy pressed the key button and they got in. Margaret removed the eyebrows, moustache and back-and-sides hairpiece from her handbag and stuck them on her husband.

'A whole new man,' she said. 'I think I'm in love.'

'All right, Mrs al-Jerad ... Remember to look authoritative. The guards at the gate may know you're really in charge. Wave them away if they become too curious.'

Roddy looked across at his wife and smiled. She was trying not to look frightened.

'It'll be much less intimidating than you might think. There won't be soldiers or any show of force. They've got to make it look like nothing more than a storage facility.'

He drove the long way round the car park to avoid being seen from the front entrance of the palace.

It took less than five minutes to reach Number One Facility. There were street lights at the barrier and the kiosk inside was well lit with two uniformed guards inside. They recognized the car with Mr and Mrs al-Jerad inside and opened the boom immediately. One of them came out and courteously indicated a suitable place to park by the front entrance.

Roddy smiled his thanks and Margaret gave a stern nod. Roddy got out of the car. The guard was twenty metres away. He started walking towards the front door, reaching for his keys, but Roddy held up his own keys and the guard retreated with something between a wave and a salute. Margaret sat ramrod straight watching the guard in a wing mirror as he re-entered the kiosk.

Roddy looked at the lock. It needed a Yale key. There were two on Nasher's key chain; presumably one was the master key for all the facilities and the other was a house key. He picked the newer one. Bingo. He was in. He had to hurry. Must put on the downstairs lights. The guards would expect that. Done. Need a bird's eye view: find the stairs, he told himself. Using his torch sparingly he ran up metal stairs, not much more than a ladder, to the top floor. It was a typical storage area: dexion frames and shelves, metal cupboards, everything labelled and neatly laid out. He walked towards the centre. It was a long way in. There were railings after thirty metres. He shone his torch over the top. It *was* a factory. He ran along the edge, grabbing the railings for support. The beam from his torch revealed three columns of six sets of centrifuges leading to a large reaction chamber. That was all he needed to know. He raced back downstairs and switched off his torch. Now what could he find to take out?

He entered the open office area. A printer was chugging away, making a trail of stock records. He tore off the first six sheets, took a pen from his pocket and marked two items on sheets four and six with large red circles. The boss was doing a spot check of their record keeping and had found them wanting. He switched off the lights and left the building, pulling the door firmly behind him. As he walked towards the car he held the long print-out for the guards to see. Then he wrapped the bundle under his left arm and made the sign of slitting his throat with his right forefinger. The guards nodded and laughed. They had the barrier open well before he drove through.

It was now 5.31. As they drove towards the hotel Margaret tore the bundle of papers into small sections taking care not to drop any of the pieces. They found a litter basket by a bus stop and deposited the fragments. They drove on. Roddy stopped the car about fifty metres short of the hotel. Margaret tore off his disguise, checked that there were no tell-tale residues, said she preferred the original after all and gave him a quick kiss. She moved over to the driver's seat as Roddy got out.

'Don't forget to dump the bits of disguise, Mrs al-Jerad. See you soon.'

Margaret reached the Presidential Palace without incident having found a different litter bin for the disguise. She drove round the parking lot as Roddy had done, reparked Nasher's car and locked it. It was 5.55 as she removed her headscarf into a pocket of her coat and entered the building. A band upstairs was playing God Save the Queen. Margaret nearly burst out laughing. The relief. She was back in time. She left her coat with the cloakroom attendants. As she mounted the stairs she heard the Iranian National Anthem. So Soraya was receiving her medal. Margaret stood at the back of the chamber and watched. She would transfer the keys into Soraya's bag when she congratulated her. It had all been too easy. She could get used to this.

'What a pity that both you and your husband had to miss the ceremony, Mrs McKie.'

It was Saban Kandar. He had come up behind her at the back of the chamber.

'I, too, felt the need of fresh air. My new nose is still a little sensitive. It's sometimes a bit stuffy in here. I had to miss the actual presentations after listening to the three interminable speeches. Did you see John receiving his medal?'

'No. I came in again just as the national anthems were being played.'

'And, you can tell me, Mrs McKie, which of the speeches did you find the most boring? I assume you were listening to them from the back of the chamber between your breaths of fresh air.'

'Now, Minister, I couldn't possibly say. I am a guest in your country.'

'Well said, Mrs McKie.'

Everyone stood up as the President led the Governing Council down the aisle of the chamber and out to their limousines. Then Soraya, John and the al-Jerad's followed by Elspeth, Betty and Buffy were next to leave past the smiling rows of diplomats and Iranian civil servants. When they reached the far end of the chamber Saban Kandar shook hands with all of them and demanded at least one dance with each lady in the forthcoming Ball. Margaret delayed her hug of Soraya until Kandar was greeting Aisha. Under John's instruction they had practised this move. With one arm around each other's back they had their inner arms hidden. Soraya opened her handbag and Margaret dropped in the keys.

As Soraya collected the coats and her father's hat Aisha headed for the ladies' room. She telephoned the hotel and asked to speak to the manager.

'Did the clock really break down?'

'Oh yes, Mrs al-Jerad. It had gone haywire. The lights were out in one of the carpets and the rest were pulsing randomly.'

'And did they manage to fix it?'

'Yes. It took the young man some time but it's working perfectly again.'

'Mr McKie and the young man are both there, are they?'

'Yes, Mrs al-Jerad. Both of them are here.'

Before changing for the Ball the friends who were staying at the hotel had another council of war on the roof. Snow had begun to fall and it was slippery. The expanse of whitening roofs and trees below them bordering the lit streets added to the fairytale atmosphere. They formed a huddle in the middle, the way some rugby teams do. Roddy wasted no time.

'The facility is laid out for making bombs. No doubt about it.'

'Right,' said John. 'How could Soraya's father not have known?'

'The perimeter really is a storage facility. Unless you go to the top and walk in thirty yards you would never know. Nasher would have no reason to do that. And remember, the Secret Police would have people there to distract him back from the brink if he ever went upstairs.'

'Good. So there's still no reason to suspect Nasher. It's just Aisha we have to worry about. And the President and Saban Kandar. Not to mention selected members of the Governing Council.'

Buffy broke the silence which was threatening to become ominous. 'Can we say it has all gone well, then? No problems?'

'Saban Kandar gave me a fright at the end,' said Margaret. 'By the way, how many speeches were there?'

'Two,' said Betty.

'The bastard tried to trick me.'

Roddy gave her a kiss. 'He's no match for you,' he said. 'But listen, everybody. The point is they are suspicious of us. Too many unusual things happened: the clock breaking down; three of us absent from the ceremony ... We may have got away with it so far. But as soon as they check with the guards at the storage facility they will know we've been there.'

'But they are in an awkward position,' said John. 'Remember they are trying to present themselves to the world as developers of nuclear power for peaceful purposes. They won't want to make a scene at the Ball ... I think they probably already know about the impersonations to get Roddy into the facility. It would only take one phone call.'

Roddy interrupted. 'If they haven't checked yet, they are bound to find out tomorrow when they see that some of the print-out is missing ... It seemed a good idea at the time to justify my visit in the eyes of the guards.'

'Quite,' said John. 'So, either way, we're probably safe until the Ball is over but early tomorrow morning, maybe immediately after the Ball, they'll converge on us... Therefore at least one of us must escape before the Ball is over.'

Elspeth looked puzzled. 'One of us?' she asked.

'Yes, Elspeth. At least one. It only takes one to pass the news to our Foreign Office. Then all hell would break loose. We've got to be able to threaten them with that. That will put the rest of us in a strong negotiating position.'

'Why not telephone the Foreign Office right now?'

'Because we want to resolve this peaceably. We're the only ones who know. In case you don't know it, you've all been temporarily co-opted into the British Secret Service: just a bit of it, in the lower echelons.' John smiled at them. 'My immediate boss, Mr Perspicacity, does not want to know, because he doesn't want the politicians to know and risk another war. The real powers here are we, the bottom end of the British Secret Service, and they, the top end of the Iranian Secret Police and a few of their top politicians. We hold all the cards, provided one of us can escape.'

'It's better than that,' said Roddy. 'They just have to think that at least one of us has escaped.'

'Who?' Nicol asked.

'Nicol, I think you and Betty should make a break for it to the British Embassy. It's an unaccompanied posting these days – no wives or families – so you'll have to pretend to be servants of some kind.'

'How?'

'All right. Here's an idea off the top of my head. Feel free to adjust it. Take your passports and some local money but leave your good clothes behind. You can retrieve them later. I'll obtain a Vespa for you. I've done it before. They'll not recognize you under a helmet and goggles, Nicol, or Betty under a niqab; trust me. Leave with the Staff after the Ball. Ride to Soraya's house. She'll give you a key. I'll come for you before the al-Jerads arrive if the negotiations break up early. Otherwise, at first light, go to the bazaars and buy some fruit and bread. Just point to what you want. Then ride to the British Embassy and go in with the early deliveries. Have them contact Peter Lipscombe at the Foreign Office. He'll tell you what to do next.'

'Right,' said Nicol.

Betty looked at him in surprise and admiration. No questions, no discourse. He was turning into a man of few words.

'Have you ever ridden a Vespa?' she challenged.

'Cut out the negative waves, Gorgeous Crumpet. You'll love it.'

John grinned at them. They all looked cold. He decided to cut the meeting short.

'Buffy and Elspeth, you're the experts on people smuggling, but this time escape is impossible. So I suggest you stay here openly and act the injured innocents. Come to think of it, you really are innocent. Your key roles will come later when we negotiate. Roddy, you're a genius, and Margaret is even smarter than you are. Make them think you've escaped but hide in the hotel for as long as possible. That will take some of the heat off Nicol and Betty. I'll leave the details to you. I'm too cold to think any more. Let's go down and enjoy the Ball.'

On the drive back to their house Aisha silently went over her conversation with the hotel manager. There was a loose end. She should have interrogated him more thoroughly. That Mr McKie may not have been there all the time. To be on the safe side she decided to telephone the guards at the facility as soon as she was back home.

She called from her dressing room. This time she made no mistake. Barely containing her anger she learnt from the puzzled guards that Mr al-Jerad and she had been the only visitors that evening: that they had come by car, yes their own car, that while she sat in the car her husband had entered the building using his master key to do a stock check, that he had found a couple of mistakes in the print-out and had made a joke about it. He had been in the building only ten or fifteen minutes.

'Did you have any conversation with him?'

'No, Mrs al-Jerad, but you saw that, surely.'

'Of course. Thank you. One can't be too careful.'

She hung up. Her hands were trembling as she worked through the consequences. So they know about the bomb factory. By this time all seven of them must know. And Soraya. Oh Blessed Allah, my own daughter is one of them. She must have connived in procuring the keys, and replacing them. I must protect her. But I must stop word going back to London. They do not have secure communications equipment with them and there has been no report of contact via open channels. Too risky for them anyway... There's still time to stop them, discreetly, after the Ball, when the diplomats have left. What if they try to get word out through the diplomats? I must make that impossible. Call in full strength surveillance. Never let the opportunity arise ... As soon as the diplomats have left interrogate them in the hotel. Scare the living daylights out of them. Lay down the law but get Soraya off the hook.

She made several phone calls to her juniors but decided not to tell the President yet. It was good to be back in control.

Chapter 24

As Master of Ceremonies, Saban Kandar promised there would be no more speeches. He invited John and Soraya to lead off the dancing with a snowball waltz. 'In deference to the weather,' he couldn't help adding.

John led Soraya to the middle of the floor between the carpets of lights. There were cheers and applause.

'Just as if we were married,' he said.

'A small matter to attend to first. What was Roddy's verdict?'

'Suspicion confirmed.'

'Ah ... So what next?'

'You and I and Buffy and Elspeth stay put. Act normal. The others will escape, or pretend to. Give Nicol your house key.' John spoke quickly. They'd soon have to part and pick new partners. 'The Iranian Secret Service is here in force. See all the strong silent types.' He executed a left-hand turn to give her a sweeping view. 'They probably think we'll try to send a message through the diplomats who are here. So don't dance with any diplomats; I've already told the others. That will puzzle them and help to build our case for later.'

They split and chose new partners. John walked towards the wife of the British Consul but chose the President's daughter instead. Just as in Hamilton House, he reflected cheekily: selling a dummy. Soraya picked out one of the silent brigade. He danced awkwardly and was glad when she selected one of his cronies next. Soon the floor was swarming with dancing couples. A Spanish diplomat tried to get a dance with Betty but she started coughing and with a smiled apology headed for the ladies' room.

Aisha observed all of this while chatting with a group of civil servants off the dance floor. Surely they would try to speak to the diplomats. The snowball waltz was a golden opportunity. What were they playing at?

As the evening progressed the friends danced exclusively with Iranian civil servants. Whenever a diplomat approached to ask Margaret, Elspeth, Betty or Soraya for a dance he was beaten to the draw by a tough-looking Iranian. The ladies gave no sign of disappointment but welcomed their dancing partners with vivacious smiles. The diplomats shrugged their shoulders and danced yet again among themselves. Aisha made a point of mingling with them and had a few dances. She could detect no undue urgency on their part to dance with the new faces, nothing beyond natural curiosity and a desire to add variety to the routine.

Around 10.30 when the food trolleys were being wheeled back to the kitchen Betty started to yawn. The President was dancing. So Nicol immediately led her to where Aisha, Nasher and Saban Kandar were chatting and they took their leave with thanks and apologies.

'Betty never really adjusted to the time change,' Nicol explained.

They were accompanied in the lift by two stalwart Iranians who followed them along the corridor towards their room. The Secret Service men were still in sight, making no attempt at subterfuge, as Betty and Nicol turned the last corner to their room. Once inside, they immediately changed into jeans, sweaters and jackets. Nicol picked up the keys, helmet and goggles which John had laid on the bed and handed up to Betty a headscarf and full veil courtesy of Soraya. They opened the French doors, closed them behind them and went on to the fire escape, feeling the sudden change in temperature.

'What will we be charged with if they catch us?' Betty asked. Her teeth were chattering but whether from cold or excitement she could not immediately tell; fear, almost certainly: it was a long way down.

'Well it can't be high treason,' said Nicol. 'Your English is too good.'

This won him a brave smile.

They followed the fire escape round the corner to Roddy-and-Margaret's room. Betty pushed against the French doors. They had been left off the latch and opened easily. They gingerly opened the door to the corridor: no Secret Service agents in sight; they would still be camped round the corner outside their room. They tiptoed along the corridor to the service lift. As the lift descended Nicol put on the helmet and goggles. Betty had already donned Soraya's niqab. They mingled with the departing kitchen Staff leaving a path of overlapping footprints in the snow as they walked to the shelter for the Vespas.

Nicol watched as others started their machines and drove off spraying muddy snow behind them. He copied them confidently. Soon Betty and he were in a convoy heading downtown.

When the first of the diplomatic contingent showed signs of leaving, Roddy and Margaret also made to leave. This spurred the Secret Police into action. In the queues to shake hands with the President and Saban Kandar they skilfully interposed their bodies between the couple and any stray diplomats.

John, Soraya, Elspeth and Buffy all remained at the Ball, dancing every dance, ignoring the departing diplomats, giving every appearance of enjoying themselves hugely. This kept most of the Secret Police downstairs in the ballroom, but some half dozen followed Roddy and Margaret up to their room.

As soon as they were inside Margaret kicked off her high heels leaving them untidily on the carpet and put on another pair of dress shoes. While she was doing this Roddy opened the French doors wide leading to the fire escape. The wind made the net curtains billow into the room and drove in flurries of snowflakes which melted on the carpet. Then they hid behind a full length velvet curtain over the box window that took up one wall by the bed.

There was a knock on the door. They ignored it. Another knock sounded, louder this time. A voice bellowed, 'Open up. Police.' They remained motionless behind the curtain.

There was some discussion outside the door. Roddy recognized the word for "the manager". Then impatience prevailed. The door began to shudder. Someone was giving it shoulder charges. On the fifth attempt it burst open. Six men came charging in, saw the high-heeled shoes lying haphazardly on the carpet, the wide-open French doors, the flying curtains. Three of them went down the fire escape and the other three used it to climb up to the roof. A helicopter obligingly was flying towards the airport.

Roddy and Margaret left their room and took the lift down to the first floor. Below them, in the ballroom, the orchestra stopped playing.

Chapter 25

Aisha waited until a few minutes after the last of the diplomatic contingent had left the ballroom. Some of them were such dithers, sure to have forgotten gloves or a handbag. At last she was satisfied that they had left for good. She walked over to the orchestral conductor who quickly and elegantly brought the dance number to a close. Family members of officials had already left with the diplomats. She waved off the remaining civil servants and all but ten of the Secret Police. These ten formed a circle around John, Soraya, Buffy and Elspeth. She sent one of the ten upstairs to pass the message that it was time to bring down the other two couples. Then, for the first time, speaking quietly to the President with her husband by her side, she told him what had happened and how she had the situation under control.

Soraya watched her father's face. It registered bewilderment. She wanted so much to go to him, to explain, to comfort him.

The messenger returned, walking quickly into the ballroom and stopping in an empty space. He bowed to Aisha and gave a nervous gesture beckoning her to come to him.

Aisha walked over. The unfortunate messenger whispered the news that both couples had disappeared. Aisha was clearly furious but she delivered rapid instructions. 'Alert airport security. Search the hotel ... discreetly. Do not disturb other guests at this stage. Keep me informed.'

Her composure regained, she walked back to the middle of the ballroom and addressed John.

'It is only a matter of time till we find your missing friends. In the meantime we have much to talk about. I have booked a conference room.'

With that she led the way out of the ballroom to the stairs. Her entourage followed consisting of the President, Saban Kandar, her husband Nasher, and John, Soraya, Buffy and Elspeth ushered by the nine members of the Secret Police. They mounted the stairs to the first floor and walked round the stairwell to a beautifully carved door. Aisha went in first and put on the lights.

'Ah, there you are,' said Roddy looking the genial host with Margaret by his side at the head of the conference table. 'We have been expecting you. I took the liberty of ordering coffee and sandwiches. Thought we all could do with a little refreshment. Shall we sit down?'

Chapter 26

It was a cold ride on the Vespa. They had not brought gloves. Betty hugged Nicol and buried her fingers in the cuffs of her jacket. Nicol tried to steer with one hand at a time, sitting on the other to warm it. But after an alarming skid he abandoned that practice and kept both hands on the handlebars. He followed the Vespa in front of him at a distance of ten metres. Any closer and the spray would be in his face. Tonight the convoy rode in single file following muddy tracks. Virgin snow near the middle of the road was too treacherous to ride on.

As they approached the centre, riders began to peel off. Nicol stayed with the main group. They rode through the deserted downtown area and out towards the suburbs. The last of the riders ahead of them turned at a junction waving goodbye. Now there was no avoiding the virgin snow. Nicol had to stop to warm his hands.

'How much further?' asked Betty.

'Farther, Crumpet ... Only a couple of miles I think. We'll soon be warm and it's the last place they'll look.'

They took their seats around the conference table. The President, half-way down one side, took command. He dismissed the secret agents who had been hovering by the door.

'Mr McKie, all of you in fact, you have some style, I'll give you that, but you clearly do not appreciate the ... ah ... delicacy of your situation. You all have either committed espionage or have aided and abetted in it. Either way, that is a capital offence. Put it another way. You are all in mortal danger.'

'As the only bona fide spy here, on the British side that is, may I answer that, Mr President?'

'Please do.'

'I used the term bona fide deliberately. I want you to trust our good faith. My immediate superior in the Foreign Office gave me full authority to resolve this peaceably. He does not want to be kept informed until there is a satisfactory result to report. Your secret is safe with us. If we do not return safely, however, the UK authorities will know that you are planning to develop nuclear bombs, they will announce this to their allies and together they will take severe military action. We, sitting around this table, can prevent that.'

Aisha gestured to her President and received permission to speak.

'Why, then, did you find it necessary for your young friends to run away?'

'Because we wanted insurance against the possibility that you would stage an accident, shed crocodile tears and continue unabashed ... One accident you might explain away. More than one would stretch credibility.'

The President gave a hollow laugh. 'So you appear to have thought of everything ... I have just one question for you. What makes you think that it is acceptable for the United Kingdom to have nuclear weapons but unacceptable for us in Iran to have them?'

John paused to make eye contact with his interrogator.

'In principle, there is no reason why the UK should be favoured over Iran. But I ask you, with an open mind, to examine the psychology. How likely is it that having nuclear weapons Iran would not use them? With respect, Mr President, this is all about attitudes to suicide, mass suicide.'

'No, young man, you misjudge us. There is a world of difference between setting off a conventional suicide bomb and authorizing a nuclear attack in the certainty that it condemns one's own population to death. We are just as capable as you of managing détente.'

The President looked hard at John and at his friends. None of them seemed to be reassured. He tried another tack. 'I feel you are all missing the point. Look at any map of the Middle East. Israelis are hopelessly outnumbered. They are squeezed into a tiny tip of territory and have no friendly land to escape to. Eventually Iran and the Arab nations will overcome Israel in conventional warfare. Israel already experienced more than it bargained for in the Lebanon. A major conventional war will stretch them to breaking point. Israel will seek to end the war by resorting to its nuclear weapons just as the US did against the Japanese. We therefore need a nuclear deterrent.'

There was a pause while everyone around the table digested the President's words.

It was broken by a knock on the door heralding the arrival of two trolleys of coffee and sandwiches. Roddy thanked the waiters and dismissed them. Margaret poured the coffee and Roddy passed round the sandwiches. Observing reluctance to eat or drink, Roddy conspicuously drank from one of the cups and took a bite out of a sandwich. With some embarrassment the President did the same and everyone followed his lead.

Seizing the initiative, Buffy stood up. 'May I say a few words, Mr President?'

'Certainly, Lord Linnhe.'

'None of us in this room is an Israeli, but I would like to respond on behalf of the West with regard to Israel. Rather than war against Israel we think a better solution for the Middle Eastern nations is to accept the State of Israel as an established fact. Much money has been poured into Israel by the West: much less into Palestine, the Arab nations and Iran despite their vastly greater size. We want to help Palestine in particular - and the other nations also - to do well economically, for that is the right thing to do and it is good for trade. That is the peaceful way forward. The reason so little progress has been made is the stated desire of nations or of powerful groups within them to drive Israel into the sea. Abandon that and all things are possible. More to the point of why we are here, nuclear weapons are then unnecessary.'

'So what do you suggest?'

'Trust us, John Russell whom you know, and the rest of us, his friends. We sincerely want Iran to develop nuclear energy for peaceful purposes if that is what Iran wants. Iran's oil will become a lasting source of income to Iran, particularly if we outsiders have the sense to purchase it for lubrication and not as fuel. Speedily dismantle the bomb factory. Allow us to arrange routine inspection of your facilities which can be discreetly combined with technical assistance if you want it. Amongst us, we have all the necessary contacts. Encourage your Arab neighbours to accept Israel and in return to receive genuine co-operation.'

'May I add,' John said, 'that the UK Foreign Office and hence the UK government will know only that you have agreed to routine inspections and technical support in expanding peaceful uses of nuclear energy. This will be consistent with the international posture you have always presented. You will have to deal formally with the usual governmental contacts, but we are always available to you to sort out any muddles. Please regard us as your friends.'

The President chuckled. 'Touching speeches, but not practicable. Inspections are humiliating and can lead to an excuse for war. Look at Iraq ... Do you really think that we in Iran will suddenly be persuaded by your idealistic arguments to reverse our policies? Certainly not.'

The door was opened and the secret agent whom Aisha had used earlier as a messenger entered the room and handed her a note. She read it quickly and passed it to the President. He read it, crumpled it into a ball and threw it accurately into a waste paper basket five metres away.

Emboldened by that "basket" the President continued, 'It is clear we are not going to reach intellectual agreement this evening even if we have an all-night session. I have listened to you and you have listened to me. For the foreseeable future we must agree to differ. Now let us focus on the matter in hand.'

Margaret caught Elspeth's eye and they each went half-way round the table offering to fill up coffee cups. Soraya and Roddy followed, each carrying a plate of sandwiches.

The President accepted a sandwich and took a bite. 'As I said at the outset, you Britishers certainly have style.' He cleared his throat and looked across the table at Aisha and then at Saban Kandar and at Nasher who were seated on either side of him. He put his hand on Nasher's shoulder and whispered that they must talk later. Then he addressed John and his friends. 'We must concede that you have won a battle, but not the war. We do not feel that you have the moral high ground. But we are practical people. In order to avoid violent repercussions we shall dismantle the factory in question. There shall be no formal inspection: we will not allow that; but we shall allow informal inspection in the name of technical co-operation provided that you, John Russell, are in charge. Come back after your Christmas holidays and you will find no trace of the factory. All of you, including your absent friends, are welcome in Iran at any time. You will be regarded as friendly protagonists.' He smiled at each of them in turn.

'Thank you, Mr President,' said John. 'May I ask...'

'Oh, your young friends. We still don't know where they are. Retrieve the note if you like.'

'May I bring them in?'

'From the cold, as it were,' said Saban Kandar.

Everybody laughed politely.

'Of course,' said the President.

The party began to break up. The President drew Aisha aside and gave whispered instructions. 'Tighten the cordon around the British Embassy. That must be where they're headed.'

At the same time John whispered to Roddy, 'We can take no chances. There's too much at stake for them to give in so easily. We must not all be in the same place at once. In fact they must never know where all of us are. Pack up and leave for the airport with Margaret, Elspeth and Buffy as soon as you can. Take the first flight. Once you're in the air we're all safe. I'll get a later flight with Nicol and Betty. We'll do the maintenance. That's a good excuse.'

Aisha left the room briefly and returned as Roddy, Margaret, Elspeth and Buffy took their leave, shaking hands with the President and waving goodbye to the others. The President put an arm round Nasher and led him to the far end of the room. He spoke gently and reassuringly as far as John could tell. Then the President and Saban Kandar left together, leaving John, Soraya, Nasher and Aisha alone.

Nasher broke the silence with great dignity. 'John, would you please take Soraya home? Aisha and I will come later.'

John asked the night porter to summon a taxi. He led Soraya to a sofa to wait.

'That must have been very trying for you, my Sweetheart.'

'Much worse for my father.'

'Well, your parents have a chance to talk now. We'll soon know how they've managed.'

The taxi's headlights made a fleeting pattern on the wall in front of them as it swept to a halt at the hotel entrance. It had finally stopped snowing but for the past hour snow had fallen steadily and now covered most of the mud and slush which the earlier vehicles had created. Having given the address John closed the window behind the driver's head for privacy. The driver gave no reaction. It was pleasantly warm in the taxi. John put his arm around Soraya and kissed her. This allowed them to talk seriously while giving the impression of whispering sweet nothings.

'We may have only twenty minutes before your parents arrive. We'll have to hide Nicol and Betty. Any ideas?'

'For how long?'

'Until 8 a.m. at least. That's when Roddy and co. take off. I've scrubbed the idea of getting Nicol and Betty into the British Embassy. It will be too closely watched.'

'I'm thinking,' said Soraya.

John watched her. Her brow did not furrow. If anything her face became more relaxed. She seemed to be in a trance. Then she smiled at him and gave her analysis.

'The first problem is to get me inside the house without a key and without the taxi driver noticing I'm being let in. So you have to drop me off and immediately go off in the taxi to be out of sight before I reach the front door.'

'Right. I'll have him drop me downtown. That will focus their attention away from the house. I can always run back. It's not too far.'

'Good. Now the next question is will my parents come together to the house or will my father drive back alone? If they come together it probably means the Secret Police have given up chasing us. But we expect him to come alone because my mother will want to stay at the hotel hoping to have you and Nicol and Betty taken prisoner when you naïvely return with them. In either case, I'll just hide Nicol and Betty in my room until you let me know it's safe ... How will you know that Roddy and the others are actually on the plane and that it has taken off?'

'I'll have to go to the airport. Can't risk a taxi. I'll come back for the Vespa. Have Nicol put it behind the garden shed if it's not there already, with the helmet and goggles, and his jacket. I'll call your mobile from the airport. You can bring them in by taxi and we'll have a late breakfast at the hotel. We'll soon finish the clock maintenance and fly back in the afternoon. Will you come with us, Soraya? Christmas and New Year in Scotland are not to be missed. You know that.'

'I'd love to, John, but I need to see that my parents are all right first. I'll email you in a few days.'

'Right. Here we are. See you later.'

He kissed her once more, opened the door to let her out and asked the taxi driver to take him downtown as quickly as possible.

There was no one about as John paid off the taxi driver. John made a point of walking purposefully down the first side street. His footprints left a clear trail. He rounded the next corner and waited in the sheltered forecourt of a petrol station. As expected the taxi came down the side street he had just left, paused at the corner and sped off.

Disappearing in a deserted city centre covered in snow is not easy. Footprints are the problem. There is only one way. Up.

John climbed up a drainpipe to the flat roof above the petrol pumps. From there he was able to ascend to the roof over the shop. He had a good view of the downtown area. He plotted a course over the rooftops, minimizing the number of times he'd have to descend to cross a street. It was too complicated. He crouched behind a chimney.

He did not have to wait long before a fleet of cars arrived on the scene. The first car parked at the petrol station. The driver got out and waved the others on, one at a time. As each car drew level he spoke to the driver. Soon cars were parked at all the intersections surrounding the petrol station. Four people got out of each car. They began to patrol the stretches of street between the cars, looking in doorways, behind walls and hedges. John watched them from the roof, rubbing his hands. Footprints were no longer a problem. He just had to outwait them.

Eventually the search was called off. The cars were driven back in the direction of the hotel. One car was coming in the opposite direction. That had to be Nasher, with or without Aisha. For a moment John was tempted to intercept him, for he was bound to be alone; the search proved that. There would be just enough time for him to clamber down and run to the junction with the boulevard. But that would force Nasher out of his neutral position. It would not be fair.

John climbed down and walked carefully along the footprints made by the Secret Police until he reached the boulevard along which Nasher had driven. Then he ran in the tracks made by the nearside wheels of Nasher's BMW. He was at Soraya's house in forty minutes. It was 3.50 a.m.

Whatever conversation had passed between Soraya and her father was clearly over for the house was in darkness. There were footprints leading to the front door. John looked for wheel tracks from the Vespa. There were faint ruts, not at all obvious. So Nicol had wheeled the Vespa round to the back long before it had stopped snowing. John tiptoed to the back. The fruit trees looked like ghosts waiting to envelop him. The Vespa was there behind the garden shed and so were the helmet and goggles and Nicol's jacket. He put these on and picked up the Vespa. He carried it out to the front, still on tiptoe, and set it down on its stand in the BMW's track. Then he went again to the back of the house using the toeprints. Walking backwards he did his best to smooth over the toeprints. He surveyed his handiwork. It would do.

He wheeled the Vespa to the end of the street before mounting and starting it. The tank was half full. He told himself to remember to leave extra money to cover the petrol. So much to think about. It would be a bonus if they could keep secret from Soraya's parents the fact that Nicol and Betty had spent the night there. He was too tired to think how to do that. Leave it to Soraya. She'd solve it. Must stay awake. Coffee and food would help. As he entered the motorway he was pleased to see lights from long-distance lorries. There was bound to be an all-night truck stop somewhere ahead.

It was just after 5am when he saw the sign to the truck stop. He decided to risk it. There was a super-tanker accompanied by two supermarket lorries in the parking lot. He left the Vespa beside the less brightly lit side wall and walked up to the counter. The three drivers were in separate booths, reading newspapers as they tucked in to all-day breakfasts. Still wearing his helmet and goggles John ordered a mug of coffee and toast and a newspaper. He took these over to a vacant booth. He removed his helmet and goggles, opened the newspaper and hid behind it. It was quiet. He closed his eyes and fell asleep.

He was awakened at 6.30 a.m. as another lorry driver came in. John forced himself to drink the cold coffee and eat the cold toast. Just what the doctor ordered, he told himself. Putting on the helmet and goggles he went to the toilet and left with a wave to the lady behind the counter. It was still too early to risk appearing at the airport. To kill time he walked around the parking lot a few times and did some free-standing exercises. Finally, feeling refreshed, he rode to the airport and left the Vespa in short term parking.

He checked the Departures. "Final boarding" was the sign against their flight. Good. Ten minutes to go. They were probably on the plane already. He scanned the check-in area, trying to identify the Secret Police. They would become tense about now. This was the moment of truth. Surely they would be told to stand down. Nicol and Betty were safely hidden, weren't they? And anyway, no one had apprehended him.

'You'll damage your eyesight, John, wearing these goggles indoors.'

It was Saban Kandar. John gaped at him as he removed his helmet and goggles.

'We knew you'd come. Don't worry. Your friends are about to leave. Come with me. There's just enough time to see them on board.'

Kandar spoke into his mobile phone as they ascended on the escalator towards Departures. They were waved through Security and directed to Gate 17.

'No need to run. They'll wait for us,' Kandar blurted out, walking quickly. 'By the way, you can tell me now, where are your other two friends, Nicol and Betty?'

'Nice try,' said John.

Kandar laughed. 'You have a far too suspicious mind, John Russell.'

They boarded the aircraft. On seeing John escorted by Kandar the friends feared the worst but were quickly reassured.

'All is well,' John said. 'Have a good flight. Nicol, Betty and I will come on the afternoon flight ... Let's all have a holiday to celebrate. Soraya will come too if she can. I'll be in touch.'

John watched the take-off. Then he telephoned Soraya from an airport telephone while Kandar was in the toilet. Her mother had not yet returned to the house. Her father had left for work saying he had to go through the motions of normality. Neither would know where Nicol and Betty had spent the night. She would bring Nicol and Betty to the hotel, walking some way first and then taking a taxi.

Kandar emerged all smiles. John had to admit that the nose job had improved his looks. He insisted that John put the Vespa in the boot of his Ferrari even though the handlebars and front wheel stuck out under the open lid.

'You've earned a bit of luxury. I'll drop you at the hotel.'

John replaced the Vespa in its rack and left an envelope stuffed with money in the pocket under the seat. He entered the hotel by the back entrance. There was no sign of Aisha. The Secret Police had departed too. A taxi bearing Soraya, Nicol and Betty arrived. The four friends relaxed over a splendid late breakfast. Then John checked the clock. With Nicol's help he replaced three strands of LEDs while Soraya went up with Betty to help her pack. They passed the bedroom of Roddy and Margaret. The door had been propped up. Betty giggled.

'Temper, temper,' she said.

Chapter 27

Nasher returned from work on the Sunday evening to find Aisha asleep in her room. Soraya had left a note saying she would stay at the airport for a few hours, have dinner there and return around 8 p.m. Nasher started to prepare a meal. This was not his forte; he had been looked after too well. He decided to make tea and toast and to boil some eggs. He tried to work quietly, lifting pans out of the cupboard as noiselessly as possible until he found one of the right size, but there was no way to minimize the sound of running water or of the noise it made as it approached the boiling point. Aisha joined him in her dressing gown and slippers.

'I'll do that for you, Nasher,' she said.

'It's all right, my love. I can manage this much.'

They sat together on a sofa in the den adjoining the kitchen as they sipped tea and cracked open their eggs.

'What do you think, Nasher?' Aisha looked sadly into her husband's eyes.

'It's a lot to take in, Aisha, to find out for the first time that we have not been pulling together.'

'I know, I know ... Nasher, I believe in what I'm doing. I wish I could persuade you. Now that the secret's out couldn't you and Soraya ...'

'No, Aisha ... We're on opposite sides. I'm so worried about how this will end. I desperately don't want to lose you.'

They put down their cups and plates and embraced tearfully. Then they simply sat with his arm protectively around her shoulders.

Soraya found them like that, in darkness. She said nothing, embraced them in turn, and started to walk to her room.

Aisha called out, 'Soraya, please come back. I want to tell you something.'

Soraya returned.

'Put on the lights, Soraya. We're rested now.'

Nasher rubbed his eyes. He stood up but it was Aisha who continued to speak.

'Your father and I are at peace, Soraya, even though we take opposite sides on the nuclear issue. You must follow your own path. Never doubt that we both love you.'

Tears rolled down Soraya's cheeks.

'I know,' she said. 'Goodnight.'

On the following day the President summoned Aisha and Saban Kandar to the Presidential Palace. He laid into them for having been so comprehensively outwitted.

'You have one last chance to redeem yourselves,' he said. 'I have bought you time. They think they have won. They will relax.'

The President looked hard and not unkindly at Aisha.

'I know this is especially difficult for you, Aisha, but this is a defining moment not only for our nation but for the entire region. I make only one concession: Soraya may be brought back unharmed; but the rest of them, all seven, must die.

'For you, Saban, it is a final opportunity to redress the ignominy of your previous defeats at the hand of John Russell. I will hold both of you to account if you fail yet again.'

Saban felt perspiration trickle down his forehead but his voice was firm.

'A tragic accident shall befall them in their own country, Mr President.'

'Very well. Spare me the details ... In the meantime there shall be no dismantling. On the contrary, see to it that work in the factory proceeds at full speed.'

Chapter 28

John took the tube into work on the Monday morning, refreshed and thoroughly pleased with the way things had gone. His high spirits were infectious as he greeted his colleagues at the Foreign Office on the way to his desk. There was an email from Soraya: Domestic scene sad but stable. Can come. Let me know when and where. XxS. John's spirits rose even higher. That was the best possible news.

Peter Lipscombe arrived. He waved to John, beckoning him into his office.

'You seem mighty pleased with yourself. I take it all went well in Tehran.'

'Yes, as well as I could have hoped. I think the matter has been resolved, with a lot of help from my friends.'

'You think ...'

'Yes. You don't want to know yet, do you? I'll be able to give you a full report of the fait accompli following an informal inspection after the winter break.'

'Got it ... I can see they will need a little time ... Don't worry. You haven't told me anything ... But in another sense, please do worry. Keep up your guard. They will take this right to the wire.'

John refused to relinquish his happy mood. 'There's not a lot they can do now, Peter. Anyway, if it's all right with you, may I disappear with my friends over Christmas and New Year?'

'Certainly.'

'And I mean a Scottish New Year. Don't expect me back on the 2nd of January, or even the 3rd.'

'All right ... Where are you planning to go?'

'There's a fishermen's hotel on Loch Tay, near Killin. I'll see if it's available.'

'Well, have a super time. It sounds as if you've earned it.'

As John returned to his computer, no doubt to arrange the winter holiday, Lipscombe watched him go. There was a spring in his step. This did not bring a smile to Lipscombe's face. He picked up the telephone...

Chapter 29

Saban Kandar telephoned Aisha.

'Your place or mine?'

'I'll come to your office.'

They were under great pressure. They could hardly fly to Britain unrecognized to take charge. The Iranian embassy in London was poorly staffed and closely watched. The chance of delegating a successful operation to be run from there was close to zero.

'The only solution,' said Aisha, 'is to employ local talent ... but how?'

Saban Kandar shrugged his shoulders and shook his head.

'Think underworld connections,' Aisha prompted. 'C'mon, Saban, we haven't much time.'

'Don't rush me, Aisha ... Let's have some coffee. We'll probably both think better after that.'

Kandar was right. The coffee helped. He had an idea.

'The best man, apart from John Russell of course ...' Too late he saw the pained look on Aisha's face. 'I'm sorry, Aisha ... What I was trying to say was the late Terias Shammon was the best contact we ever had from the UK. I read his writings. He had a colleague, name of Kasim al-Zaman, like minded, tough.'

Aisha perked up. 'How could we contact him?'

'Good. Now we're back in unison ... I have his contact details. Shammon was thorough.'

Aisha stood up and walked to the window, graceful as ever.

'Their intelligence services will monitor all communications to him ... We might as well use the telephone. I'll do it. Give me the number.

'Hallo ... Kasim? This is your auntie from Tehran. Auntie Asla, that's right. I have terrible news ... It's about your brother ... Kasim, my dear, he died this morning ... Fell off a ladder ... I'm so sorry ... Can you come to the funeral? I'll meet you at the airport.'

Aisha hung up. 'He'll be on the next plane,' she said.

The telephone rang in Peter Lipscombe's office. It was the Foreign Secretary. 'Come to my office,' she said. She sounded annoyed.

When Lipscombe dutifully appeared she began without preamble, 'What is going on? You have left me in the lurch.'

'I am sorry, Minister. There is very little to report.'

'Oh ... Let's have it anyway.'

'You remember there were three facilities under suspicion, that the one on the Afghan border was a decoy and that we decided to concentrate our efforts on the facility closest to Tehran?'

'Yes, yes. So what happened?'

'I wanted to resolve this peaceably if at all possible. So I gave the project to John Russell with the instruction not to raise the temperature prematurely.'

'Hm ... And?'

'So far I have no definitive information from John that the building in question is anything other than a storage facility.'

'Hm. Where is John now?'

'He is taking some well-earned leave.'

'Where, I asked.'

'I believe he plans to spend a few days with his friends at a hotel on Loch Tay.'

The Foreign Secretary paused, motionless for once. 'These are the same friends who attended the medals ceremony in Tehran?'

'I expect so, Minister.'

'Then they may be in danger. You had better arrange protective surveillance.'

'I've already done so, Minister.'

'All right.' Finally she gave an approving smile.

Chapter 30

Buffy and Elspeth understandably wanted to spend their first Christmas together at their highland home near Spean Bridge. This suited Nicol and Betty whose parents were to be in London over the Christmas period and wanted to take them to performances of ballet and theatre. Roddy and Margaret said they would fit in with whatever worked best for the rest of the group. So the friends agreed to delay the start of their joint holiday until the 29th. For the few days leading up to New Year John was able to book the Fishermen's Hotel exclusively for themselves. The hotel would be officially shut from 7 p.m. on New Year's Eve until 7 p.m. on New Year's Day but the proprietor, who came from Crianlarich, knew John from previous holidays with his parents and said they could stay, with access to the bar, larder and kitchen, to bring in the New Year if they did not mind looking after themselves. Soraya said she would fly over on the 28th so that John could collect her from the Edinburgh Airport Hilton on the following morning.

Rather than cool his heels in London over Christmas, John took the opportunity to visit his parents and brother and sister in California. He left from Edinburgh so that his car would be in the right place when he returned to meet Soraya.

On the 29th, Nicol and Betty were met bright and early by Roddy at ten past six at Arbroath station off the night train.

'Hope you don't mind the doggy smell. You'll meet the culprit soon. I hope you're hungry. Margaret will have started the bacon and eggs.'

They drove in Roddy's Renault Laguna westwards out of Arbroath and through Arbirlot.

'What a lovely Christmas-cardy village,' said Betty.

'Looks even better in the snow. You didn't see any on the way up. No? There's bound to be some where we're going or else Dougal will complain.'

'As long as we're adequately supplied with fine wine and good whisky I'll not complain,' said Nicol.

Soon they were on the hill road passing farms and the village school. The view over the mouths of the Tay and the Forth was crystal clear.

'You can almost see into England,' said Roddy. 'That blue smudge as far as the eye can see is Eyemouth ... But you know that we'll have even better views where we're going.'

After a full Scottish breakfast they drove, Roddy and Margaret in front, Nicol and Betty sharing the larger portion of the back seat to leave an area for Dougal over the converted portion behind Margaret. Dougal, however, had other ideas. When tired of looking out of the window he gradually wriggled his way to lie across the knees of his new best friends and ended, supremely comfortable, with his head on Betty's lap. By common consent they took the shortest route by Crieff and Lochearnhead. They all were familiar with the scenery but simply had to stop at St Fillans to look up Loch Earn mirroring the surrounding hills which had snow above 1,000 feet. They pressed on to Killin and stopped again to take photographs from the bridge at the falls of Dochart.

'Simply magnificent, isn't it?' said Margaret.

Betty squeezed her hand. Such an expanse of white water. Roddy kept Dougal on a tight lead in case he was tempted to jump in. Margaret and Betty turned to look downstream. Close to the bridge an island caused the river to split. The two sets of tumbling waves were competing to reach the other side of the island first. On the island there was a weathered stone archway largely overgrown with ivy. In the dark interior Betty could just make out an iron gate marking the entrance to a building but it was impossible to gauge the building's extent because it was surrounded with overlapping branches. A sign in front of this sinister ancient construction stated CLAN MACNAB, BURIAL GROUND. Underneath a smaller sign said, "Access At Own Risk." Betty burst out laughing. 'Look, Nicol, Burke and Hare are alive and well in Killin.'

'Ready to MacNab you,' said Margaret, advancing like a ghost to scare her husband and to take Dougal from him.

Nicol and Roddy put on indulgent facial expressions. Then they turned their backs to examine the pub at the south end of the bridge. Nicol could not believe what he read. "Sorry, no alcohol."

'What kind of a place has John brought us to?'

Roddy explained. 'It's a standing joke in the village. Two ladies bought the pub but filled in the licence application incorrectly. They have to wait till next year to try again, just a few more days. Don't worry. There will be plenty of booze at the hotel. I could murder a pint right now.'

'Why don't you two drive on and start unloading?' Margaret called out. 'Betty and I will walk up with Dougal. He needs the exercise.'

They watched the Laguna disappear round a bend.

'Now, Betty, tell me all about you and Nicol.'

'Oh, Margaret. Where to start. Love at first sight and we've been together ever since ... He's honest and true.'

'Well, you're ten percent of the way, then.'

Betty laughed. 'The other 90% is pretty good too.'

'Thought it might be ... Don't you want to get married?'

'Nicol's not crazy about weddings.'

'What about you?'

'Sure. But he hasn't asked.'

Margaret made a face and pulled Dougal to a halt.

'Men can be so obtuse,' she said. 'We women are stuck with the convention that they have to ask. Why, for heaven's sake? But over the centuries it has become the accepted norm. So we compensate. Our mothers encourage us to enjoy being girls. We dress up and make ourselves attractive. Nothing happens, well, not on the proposal front. After a while we make do with compliments from other women. We end up dressing for other women. It makes me cross.'

'Are you saying I should propose?'

'No. Heavens no. He'd run a mile I should think ... The only time I've known that to work was in Dundee a few years ago. A librarian was head over heels in love with a distinguished writer, an older man, very handsome, with a kind, lived-in face. They had met over the years at literary events and had taken to flirting, for both had a good sense of humour. Anyway, this writer came to do a book event at the university. He had a big audience, including, of course, the librarian. The question and answer session was going well when she put up her hand.

"Yes, Sandra."

"I don't have a question, but I have an answer."

'Everyone started clapping. Two months later they were married.'

Betty laughed again. 'I'm not so clever. I'll stick to the long-suffering route.'

Margaret gave her a hug. Dougal, not to be left out, joined in and required a hug from each of them.

'Maybe something will happen,' Margaret said, 'to wake him up.'

Once they were out of the village and saw the road clear and devoid of sheep Margaret let Dougal off the leash. He raced ahead to join Roddy and Nicol in the bar and to explore the rest of the hotel.

Buffy and Elspeth came south through Glencoe to Crianlarich and thence to Killin. They saw Margaret and Betty on the road ahead.

'Hop in unless you're determined to walk,' said Buffy.

When they reached the hotel Margaret saw that the Laguna had not been unpacked.

'Your Nicol's a bad influence,' she said.

'So am I,' said Buffy. 'Our cases can wait too.'

Dougal came out to meet them and gave them each a warm, wet welcome. They joined Roddy and Nicol in the bar and relaxed, watching the sunshine on the loch, as they recounted what they had done over Christmas.

Having collected his case and walked over to the Hilton, John telephoned Soraya's room. Over breakfast he asked, very concerned, if the family situation was bearable.

'It's very loving, John, but very sad. My mother will not be persuaded to change her views ... You know she likes you very much ... But the intellectual side of her is so dominant. She would sacrifice everything, including all of us.'

'Surely not you, Soraya.'

'Of course she would do her best not to have to. But in extremis I think her conviction would take precedence.'

John fell silent for a moment, shaking his head. What a contrast with his own family visit. He said, 'On a happier note, my parents are really looking forward to meeting you, Soraya.'

'Oh that's lovely. Let's not talk about my mother. Let's just enjoy this break, John.'

They squeezed each other's hands under the table.

John and Soraya were the last to arrive. John had brought her via Aberfeldy and Kenmore. Then he drove along the north side of Loch Tay through Lawers village.

'Proper climbers start the ascent of Ben Lawers from here,' he told her. 'It's a Munro. They feel honour bound to do at least 3,000 feet. But we don't have to. We can drive half-way up ... Come to think of it, we don't have to climb it at all. We're on our holidays. Let's have another kiss.'

Blissfully unaware of the Vauxhall Astra that had been following them from the airport they drove on past the Loch Tay Marina and the Boathouse Restaurant. Soon Soraya had her first view of the village, predominantly white-walled houses with grey slate roofs, nestled beneath the hills at the head of the loch. As they drove through she saw a shop window with clocks in the foreground and knick-knacks all around. It was called "Killin time".

'They must have known Roddy was coming,' she said.

It was lunchtime when John parked his Honda beside the others' vehicles. The Astra, slowing only a fraction, continued past the hotel heading back to Kenmore along the south side of the loch. Dougal ran out to meet the new arrivals. Sensing that Soraya was unused to dogs Dougal ignored her and jumped around John instead; but later, when they were seated for lunch around a table in the bar he chose to sit at Soraya's feet. By the end of the first afternoon Dougal had forsaken Roddy in favour of Soraya.

'Happens to me all the time. Unfaithful hound.'

'A dog of taste and discrimination,' said John.

That evening over dinner they talked and talked, recounting their adventures in Tehran.

'Do you think they're really dismantling the bomb factory?' Buffy asked.

'They don't have much option,' John said. 'What do you think, Soraya?'

Soraya pursed her lips and tilted her head. She used to like it when John asked for her opinion. Now she was not so sure. It always made her appear the serious one. She needed practice in light conversation; she had so much to learn from Betty and Margaret. But this question called for a serious analysis.

'They'll be most reluctant to start dismantling: it has obviously been a major project for them. But they know John will report if the factory has not been dismantled when he visits early in the New

Year; and all of us are John's insurance policy. It's checkmate. We've won.'

'Unless they zap us all here,' said Nicol.

Betty wagged her finger at him. 'There's no such word as "zap",' she said.

In the morning they walked down from the hotel to see the site of the largest crannog, a man-made island that had been built as a fortress in the Iron Age before the time of the Picts. It was officially closed during the holiday period but Elspeth had worked at this architectural site while at university and was able to point out the main features.

'They lived off the land in the woods around the loch,' she said, 'but when danger threatened they retreated to their island fort. Same principle as Horatio on the bridge.'

Nicol looked puzzled.

Buffy said, 'I with two to help me will hold the foe in play.'

Betty finished it off. 'For I'm to be queen of the May, Mother, I'm to be queen of the May.'

Nicol looked even more puzzled.

'It's from the hodgepodge of "The boy stood on the burning deck", Ignoramus. Didn't you do that at school, or were they too busy teaching grammar?'

Nicol could not think of a response. Betty pressed her advantage. 'See, Discursive Genius, I'm better educated than you. Aren't I?'

Nicol recovered. 'Amn't I,' he said.

Elspeth cleared her throat, governess style. 'We're not here to have fun, boys and girls ... Would you believe there are twenty-eight crannogs on the loch? There's another big one at the Kenmore end.'

'Surely they couldn't withstand a sustained attack,' John said.

'They didn't have to, John,' said Elspeth. 'It was all about clan warfare. Not really warfare at all, just skirmishes. The attackers couldn't afford to leave their encampments for more than a day at a time in case their own homes were attacked. They had to keep watching their backs in those days.'

The next morning, hogmanay, they noticed three military dinghies making sizeable wakes on the loch.

'Probably the SBS out for a training session,' said John. 'That's the Special Boat Service, Soraya. Very tough guys, like the Special Air Service. I know the SAS used this area a lot during the foot and mouth epidemic. Maybe they can't stay away. Can't say I blame them. I'd rather bust my gut here than in Hereford.' He turned again to Soraya. 'Perhaps we should climb Ben Lawers after all.'

'Speaking of busting guts,' said Roddy, 'let's not do that today. A civilized coffee break is first on the menu.'

'I vote for the coffee too,' said Soraya.

This won her a smile from Elspeth, a pat on the back from Margaret and a thumbs-up from Betty.

'I don't think we are taking our situation seriously enough,' said Buffy as they lounged in the Drummond Hotel at St Fillans looking up the length of Loch Earn. 'It's hogmanay. We must have a ceilidh.'

'Too late to book a band, my dear,' said Elspeth.

'No, I mean a proper ceilidh, home-made, not one of those ghastly modern ones with imported entertainment.'

'I'm afraid I've long forgotten any party pieces I had,' said Roddy.

'Good, because set pieces are disallowed in the best ceilidhs. Everything has to be spontaneous.'

'You mean I don't get to recite The Boy Stood on the Burning Deck?' Betty looked disconsolate, bringing a smile to Soraya's face. She wanted so much to fit in, to play her part in contributing to the party mood.

'I'm afraid not,' Buffy responded, always the gentleman. 'I've been giving this a lot of thought while the rest of you have been, if I may say so, whittling away the hours. We'll take turns. Roll a die. You have to say something interesting, set a puzzle or invent a game.

If the die comes up 1, it has to be something to do with English; 2 for Mathematics; 3 for Physics; 4 for History; 5 for Geography; and if you roll a 6 then you can choose any one of the five ... It's vaguely like Trivial Pursuit.'

'Sounds horribly intellectual,' said Margaret.

'Don't forget we'll be wining and dining into the small hours. So our critical faculties will not be razor sharp. And we'll think we're becoming more and more brilliant.'

'Buffy, have you played this before?' Betty asked.

'Never.'

There was a pregnant silence.

'Sounds great,' said John.

They were served an early dinner back at the Fishermen's Hotel. Then, by agreement, the Staff departed leaving the kitchen and bar open for them on an honour's system. So the friends had the hotel absolutely to themselves until dinner-time on New Year's Day.

Buffy rolled the die. It came up 5.

'Ha, Geography,' he said. 'Well if there's one resource we have a lot of around here, it's water. So the first game is to come up with the best name for the water in this glass.'

Betty took a sip and made a face.

'Vin ordinaire,' she said.

Margaret picked up the glass and sniffed. Then she dipped in a forefinger, spread some droplets on her upturned wrist and took another sniff.

'Eau de Killin.'

'Game, set and match.' Buffy passed the die to Roddy. 'Your turn, old man.'

Roddy threw a 3 for Physics.

'About that test bomb which North Korea set off, what is the question the media failed to ask?'

'Why on earth?' said Margaret.

'No. They should have asked if the bomb was atomic or nuclear ... In the Cold War Harold Macmillan passed off an atomic test as a nuclear one to gain prestige. The North Koreans may have done the same.'

'Even so, it's still bad news,' said John.

'Yes,' said Betty, 'but not as bad.'

'Not so bad, you Awful Person,' said Nicol.

'C'mon, you two,' said Elspeth. 'A truce ... Don't you think Iran will take encouragement from North Korea's test, whatever it was?'

'They would certainly like to,' said John, 'but there's nothing they can do. They must be having a frustrating hogmanay.'

He looked quickly at Soraya and mouthed the word, 'Sorry.'

She gave him a forgiving smile.

He refilled everyone's glass. It was comfortable around the fireplace.

'Who's next?'

'I'll go,' said Betty.

She threw a one.

'All right, people,' she said. 'You've asked for it. We're going to write a poem, an alphabet poem.'

Soraya said, 'This is definitely not my strong suit. If I do one on maths later will you let me out of this English one? Just let me listen.'

'Righty-ho,' said Betty, 'provided the maths is not too difficult ... I'll kick it off, then ... A is for alternative; there's only one of these. Over to you, Buffy.'

'The next in line is B for both. Two straws, Sir, if you please.'

Soraya laughed. 'Very good,' she said.

Roddy, who was sitting beside Buffy, went next.

'C's for can and not for may. We *can* say who done it, but daren't.'

'I object,' said Nicol. 'It's always harder for the second person.'

'Overruled,' said Betty. 'Get on with it, Maestro.'

'Disint'rested D's for judges and such but rarely describes a parent.'

'How like a schoolmarm,' said Betty. 'Trump him, Margaret.'

'E's for escapee; from whom the bird has flown.'

John said, 'So, Madam Lawyer, we're the escapers and they're the escapees. The Foreign Office will never understand if I put that in my report ... Are we allowed more on E? After all, it's the most common letter.'

'All right,' said Betty. 'Since it's you, John.'

'Well it's a pet peeve of her ladyship ... Oh, sorry, Elspeth, I don't mean you ... the Foreign Minister. E also stands for expertness, not expertise alone.'

'You have to go again, John,' Betty ruled, 'because that was not entirely your own work.'

'If you insist ... F is used for fast; not to be run, but stuck;'

'Thank you, John,' said Elspeth. 'You're forgiven because you've given me an easy one ... And G's for the ghost of times past when grammar was not down to luck.'

'Oh, it's me again.'

'I again,' said Nicol.

'Then go ahead,' said Betty.

'Not at all. Ladies first.'

'H highlights misuse, fighting hopefully's reign of terror.'

Buffy finished the new couplet with a flourish, 'Our questions are induced, for begging is mostly in error.' He won applause from Margaret.

Roddy said, 'Just watch for extra words, like imports from abroad;'

Nicol ended the verse, 'And kindly note that farther north is cardinal, not odd.'

'Let's have a breather,' said Margaret. 'My head is beginning to spin.'

'Overruled. We're not even half-way.'

'Is she always like this, Nicol?'

'Invariably.'

'Well, take my advice. Settle your differences out of court. Look out for legalese chatter, for you may let rip with an oath ... We charge by the word count, you know.'

John said, 'M is for subject or matter, just one of them, not both ... C'mon, Elspeth.'

'N's for no forward plans, or warnings that come in advance.'

'That's suspiciously like something Nicol said to me many moons ago, but I'll let it pass, Elspeth, because you've kept the kettle boiling on unnecessary words ... O is on one hand: the the is flowery romance.'

'Ah, I'm glad the P falls to me,' said Buffy. 'Our esteemed Prime Minister is always talking about periods of time ... Period starts with P, ending timelessly with a full stop.'

'Time for a scientific one,' said Roddy. 'Q's a quantum leap? No giant has such a short hop.'

'This one's discursive,' said Nicol. 'Relatively is effete. Its worth is overstated ...'

'Where strangers come complete, and further exacerbated,' said Margaret.

'A toast,' said John. 'May all unwelcome strangers be exacerbated ... T's for too, meaning bad. So avoid tautological crime.'

'John, you'll have to explain that one, please,' said Soraya.

'Too many sweets are bad for you. That's a tautology. Too already implies bad.'

'I'm glad you asked,' said Elspeth. 'I had no idea either ... Thought the toast had been one too many for him ... Leave hyperbole to the sad: understatement will work every time.'

'It's I again,' said Betty turning up her nose at Nicol. 'V's for verbal gloom: use oral for speech or a yell.'

Buffy rounded it off. 'Who does not stand in for whom. Accusingly tolls the bell.'

'Sounds ominous ... We just need two lines to finish the poem but there are three letters left. If I do X and Y together, do I get a bonus point?' Roddy looked at Betty as a midfielder appealing to a referee.

'No.'

Roddy hunched his shoulders. Then he straightened up. 'Xylographers can't make amends but you can erase every howler.'

Nicol had the last word. 'Please maximize IZE ends. Don't take it from me. Look up Fowler.'

Soraya, their only human audience, applauded. Dougal, at her side, barked twice. They topped up their glasses again, feeling very pleased with themselves.

'All right, Soraya, you need a 2 or a 6.'

It came up six.

'Thank goodness,' she said. 'Mathematics.' She looked at John. 'I'm making this up. It didn't really happen this way.'

'Since you didn't throw a 4 for History we'll allow a bit of fiction,' said Buffy.

'Thank you, Buffy ... The last time I flew over here I was able to catch an earlier connecting flight out of London and reached Edinburgh Airport an hour early. There had not been time to alert John. So, of course, he was not there to meet me. Since it was a lovely sunny day I walked out of the airport trundling my case behind me. I kept walking towards the Bypass. Eventually I saw John's car coming towards me and hopped in. We embarrassed Roddy at Gleneagles by arriving twenty minutes too soon. For how long did I walk?'

There was no immediate answer.

Soraya said, 'They set a similar question to the final year psychology class at the University of Edinburgh. Only one of the twenty-five in the class got it right. So I've cheated. It's really a psychology question ... The question was propounded in terms of my movements. To find the solution you have to consider the situation from John's point of view. That's the deception ... So the answer is?'

'Fifty minutes,' said John. 'You must have been exhausted ... That reminds me. Are we all going up Ben Lawers tomorrow?'

'Provided it's not an early start,' said Betty.

'And we drive half-way up,' said Soraya. 'No heroics.'

They wished one another a Happy New Year and retired.

Chapter 31

John had difficulty in getting to sleep. He could not understand why. Here he was, well fed, thoroughly wined and entertained, with Soraya in the next room and all his friends around him, looking forward to another pleasant day with them after a leisurely start. He was on holiday, for heaven's sake. Maybe that was the problem. Professional people, his father had said, are at their worst on holiday. Nurses off duty are sloppy about making beds. Hairdressers let their hair grow long and untidily. Soldiers don't shave, don't even get out of bed half the time. His father told him of a retired diplomat in Washington D.C. who attended a party at the time of the Vietnam conflict. One of the ladies was dressed expensively in a black pants suit. The retired diplomat recognized her as a member of a Scottish Country Dance group in neighbouring Alexandria.

'You look like one of the Viet Cong,' he said.

So what have I done wrong, John asked himself, to feel so restless ... Careless with that line about the frustration our adversaries must be feeling. Should know by now that triumphalism always backfires. Didn't mean to impune Aisha. Soraya forgave me, bless her. What else? Can't think. Seem to have shut down all faculties. Not listening well. Must make a New Year's resolution: never become so unalert.

With that settled, John drifted off to sleep.

Dougal woke everybody up by barking. Roddy ran down in his pyjamas and found him at the front door, trying to get out. He held Dougal by the collar, unlocked the door and looked out. Two blue vans were driving into the hotel's parking lot. Roddy shut the door and called to John.

'Are you decent, John? We seem to have visitors.'

John came down in his dressing gown as the front door was flung open.

Chapter 32

Kasim al-Zaman lumbered into the hallway, his rifle at the ready, looking like a bear hunter. He hesitated when he saw Dougal. They had not told him to expect a large dog. But the man holding the dog by its collar seemed to have it under control.

'Keep a hold of that dog,' he said, 'or I'll shoot it.'

He walked to the foot of the stairs where John was standing. He thrust the barrel of his rifle against John's throat, forcing John to step backwards up the stairs. As he retreated John kept his eyes on the doorway. A total of nine other men, each armed with a pistol, entered the hotel. They were caucasian, dressed as climbers.

One had a rope wound diagonally over his left shoulder. Eight of these followed John and Kasim al-Zaman up the stairs. The ninth remained in the hallway with Roddy and Dougal. Pointing his revolver at Roddy he cheekily patted Dougal.

'Who's a good boy, then?'

Dougal wagged his tail until Roddy ordered him to sit.

Upstairs there were shouts from the men ordering silence as each bedroom was entered. Nicol thought he recognized accents from Liverpool and Glasgow. Kasim al-Zaman stood on the upstairs landing and addressed everyone through the open bedroom doors.

'Resistance is impossible. Put it out of your minds. All of you, get warmly dressed. Put on your climbing boots.' He still had his rifle barrel against John's throat.

Making eye contact with his captor, John opened his palms pointing outwards in front of his chest and tilted them downwards a couple of inches in a gesture appealing for calmness. Then he gently gripped the rifle barrel with his left hand and moved it off his throat and over his shoulder.

'At least let the ladies have some privacy,' he said. 'They're hardly likely to jump out the windows. Why don't we all go downstairs and talk about this. I'll make breakfast.'

Kasim al-Zaman laughed. He equally gently pulled his rifle out of John's hand. Then he turned it around and whacked John across the face with the butt, drawing blood.

'You will all do exactly as ordered or suffer severe beatings. There will be no breakfast, no discussion. We shall stay outside your rooms but you may not close the doors while dressing. No mobile phone calls. No talking. Five minutes only.'

The man guarding Roddy called up the stairs. 'Do you want him up there too, with his dog?'

'Yes. Send him up ... Put that dog on a lead when you come out.'

Soraya had started dressing as soon as she heard voices downstairs. By the time her bedroom door was opened she was in her underclothes and stepping into trousers. The man entered the room and closed the door behind him.

'Not bad. Not bad at all,' he said.

Soraya looked at him coldly, turned her back and fastened her trousers. Without undue haste she put on a shirt and sweater. The man watched her, a smirk on his face.

'You'll need your boots and a jacket, Lassie. Wouldn't want you getting cold. Now listen to the main man.'

He opened the bedroom door and waited outside her room.

They were marched downstairs, five of the men in front, then the eight friends, and the remaining five last. Roddy had a whispered conversation with John.

'Strategy?'

'Play for time.'

'Tactics?'

'Give Dougal to Soraya. She has the best chance.'

The message was passed on as they walked to the vehicles. Buffy pretended to slip and bent to retie his laces. This earned him a kick from one of the guards. Elspeth kicked the guard in the ankle and was pushed to the ground. Buffy helped her up.

Dougal had never seen such violence. Humans had always been kind. Clearly this new bunch was exceptional. He growled and tried to run at the guard who had pushed Elspeth but Soraya had him on a short lead.

Kasim al-Zaman organized the transport. Roddy was to drive his Laguna, taking Soraya and Dougal and two guards. Buffy was ordered to follow in his Land Rover with Elspeth, John, another guard and Kasim himself. Margaret, Nicol and Betty would be in the lead blue van with two more guards, and the remaining four guards were to bring up the rear in the other blue van.

The village was deserted as they drove through in convoy. In the Laguna the guards forbade Roddy and Soraya to talk. The only sounds were excited whimperings from Dougal, his eyes on the van in front. They passed the Bridge of Lochy Hotel and the Killin Golf Club. There was no one about. It was dreich. The highland cattle at Cruachan Farm looked miserable, hunched in a corner of the field. It was a long four miles before the turn uphill.

The drive up through the woods was eerie and foreboding. Fir foliage met over the middle of the road shutting out what little light had seeped through the clouds. Then they were out of the wood and in bleak moorland. A sign told them they were in the Ben Lawers National Nature Reserve. Soon they were above the snow line at the deserted Visitors' Centre. The guards gestured to continue up the hill. Redundant passing places lined the route as they pressed on towards Glen Lyon. A sign warned that the road was closed beyond the dam.

They came to the Lawers Dam and parked. There were no other vehicles. Evidently the Scottish Hydro employees had been given days off. Soraya was ordered to remain in the parking lot with Dougal and one of the guards. The rest were made to walk towards the crests.

Soraya looked around her. Even on a grey day like this there was no denying the beauty of the place. The only signs of life were wakes from speedboats on the loch. That would be the SBS, too far away to do any good.

She watched the progress of the others. So did Dougal. He strained at the leash, anxious to join the larger group. She held him tightly.

'Soon they'll be over the skyline,' the guard said with a leer. 'Then we'll have the place to ourselves. We'll have to think of some way to keep warm.'

It was the man who had entered her room.

From higher up the mountain John looked back to the parking lot. He waved to Soraya and made a sweeping motion with his arm indicating a route from the Visitors' Centre across the face of the mountain. For this he was punished with another blow to the head. Kasim al-Zaman chose this moment to require that his prisoners rope themselves together. They continued the ascent and were soon over the skyline, out of sight of the parking lot, and heading for the top of the crags.

'Why don't we wait in one of the vehicles?' Soraya asked. 'It's perishing standing out here.'

'Thought you'd never ask.' The guard opened the rear door of one of the blue vans. 'Put the dog in here. You and I will be more comfortable in the Laguna.'

Soraya led Dougal to the van where he jumped in.

'Can you help me get his lead off?'

'Sure. I know just what to do with it, Girlie.'

As the guard leant in to unfasten the lead Soraya slammed the door, catching him on the neck. She heaved him into position for a second crack. He fell to the ground. She released Dougal who sniffed briefly at the unconscious guard and then, encouraged by her gesture, went bounding up the hill, aiming for the point where the others had disappeared. Soraya started to run across the moorland, taking the route which John had indicated.

The top of the crags, which had appeared to be in easy range as the captors and captives set out, now seemed a long way off. For a time they were on a plateau, even pointing slightly downhill, but a steep climb awaited them. There was no sign of life, no footprints in the snow.

Soraya slowed to a fast walk as she joined the steep path from the Visitors' Centre. The guard was still on the ground beside the van. If he recovered and felt like chasing her, so much the better. The more movement on the hill, the greater the chance of attracting help. Soon she would be over a brow and out of sight of civilization below. Help, if there was any, would have to come from above. She pressed on, swinging her arms with determined metronomic action.

Dougal saw them first and started barking. One of the guards took aim but was restrained by Kasim al-Zaman.

'Don't be a fool. The sound of shooting will travel far. Hit it with something when it catches up.'

They reached the top of the crags. Wasting no time, al-Zaman ordered the prisoners towards the edge of the precipice. When they refused he grabbed Elspeth who was on the end, pulled her down the slope causing the others to fall and slide, and hurled her over the edge.

Buffy, roped next to her, frantically tried to pull her back, but this released his hold on the snow and he drifted inexorably towards the edge. The others tried to gain handholds in the snow and ice but it was a losing battle. Buffy went over and dangled above Elspeth. Now there was much more weight pulling them down. John managed to clasp his hands around a submerged rock to halt the slide. Dougal ran straight to Roddy and licked his face. Margaret pretended to bark. The others joined in. This got Dougal barking again as he ran to each person on the slippery slope.

Soraya heard the barking and started to yell herself. Then she began to run again to a mini-summit. From a quarter of a mile away she watched in horror.

Under al-Zaman's instruction guards positioned themselves above each of the five remaining prisoners on the slope. He himself began to kick at John's clasped fingers. Dougal sprang at him, knocking him over, then dodged away as one of the guards tried to kick him. John clung on. But al-Zaman was on his feet again. 'This time,' he said.

Kasim al-Zaman fell past John and the shot that killed him echoed off the mountain. More shots were fired. A dozen soldiers in white camouflage came running. Three other would-be assassins were killed. The rest were quickly subdued while other soldiers grabbed the rope and pulled until first Buffy and then Elspeth could scramble to safety. There were concerned handshakes all round. Major Phillips ordered the dead to be tossed over the cliff to join Kasim al-Zaman.

'Peter Lipscombe asked us to look out for you. We didn't know whether the threat was from drowning in the loch or falling off the mountain. So we split 50/50. Lot of territory.'

Just then Dougal saw Soraya running across and bounded over to meet her. Colin Phillips continued. 'It was this energetic young lady who first attracted our attention. Thank God we made it in time ... Well, let's go down and find the lawman. You can tell me how you want to play it, John.'

Chapter 33

January 2006

John remained in the village with Major Colin Phillips and the soldiers. He sent the others back to the hotel.

'Here is the key in case they slammed the door. Make yourselves a late breakfast or whatever. I'll join you eventually.'

It was 3 p.m. when John finally drove up to the hotel. Soraya ran out to kiss him. Buffy poured him a stiff drink. 'Everything all right, old man?'

'Yes, all's well ... But right now I have to call Peter Lipscombe at his home. If you crowd around me you'll get the whole conversation.' He dialled the number and held out the receiver.

'Nice of you to call, John. Happy New Year. How's Lock Tay? Been in for a dip?'

'Peter, this is not a social call. I have a confession to make.'

There was a brief silence. John continued. 'I was caught napping. They came after us.'

'The Iranians, you mean?'

'In effect. The leader, now dead, was an Iranian I'm sure, but the others were hoodlums from Liverpool and Glasgow we think. Three of them are also dead. We're all OK ... Look, I have to thank you for arranging the protection. We had no idea.'

'Glad it worked. Where did this happen?'

'On Ben Lawers ... They nearly had us over a precipice. All but Soraya. She helped to attract the attention of the soldiers. They arrived just in time ... Major Phillips and I got the local Police Chief out of bed. He's a good man, Inspector Cunningham. Understands the delicacy. He went with the soldiers to collect the bodies. He'll report it as a climbing accident.'

'What about the other members of the gang?'

'He has them locked up, charged with illegal possession. They'll do some time on that lesser charge provided they keep their mouths shut.'

'Good ... Well, John, we'll have to play it by the book from now on. First thing is to get you all down here for a proper debrief and medical. Can you all fly down from Glasgow tomorrow?'

'I don't want to risk having all of us on a plane. Once bitten.'

'C'mon, John, it's over. I think you're being paranoid ... All right. Come any way you like, short of hitch-hiking. My office, 5 p.m., day after tomorrow, the 3rd. That give you enough time? You'll owe me a beer afterwards.'

That evening they relaxed. They told the returning hotel Staff that they had enjoyed walking up Ben Lawers but had heard that another group, proper climbers going up the hard way, had fallen to their deaths. There was no more news. No doubt it would be in the papers tomorrow or the next day.

Over dinner they planned their various routes to London. Recorded messages told them that there were no trains running on New Year's Day and services were patchy on the 2nd. Nicol and Betty opted to spend the night of the 2nd in Glasgow and to take a Virgin train the next day.

'We'll head back with Dougal,' Roddy said, 'put him in a kennel – he's quite used to that – and catch a GNER from Arbroath on the 3rd. It'll be interesting, Nicol, to see which of us gets to London first.'

'Go first class, all of you,' said John. 'You've earned it. Just keep the receipts ... What about you and Elspeth, Buffy?'

'Shall we fly down tomorrow, Elspeth, and spend the night at the house? What about you two?'

'We'll drive,' said John. 'We can drop Nicol and Betty in Glasgow on the way. May stopover in the Lake District. I'd like Soraya to see that.'

'Have a lovely day in Glasgow,' Soraya called out as John and she waved goodbye outside the hotel at Glasgow Central.

Although the hotel was busy Nicol was able to book a room for the night. It would not be available, however, until after 2 p.m. They left their cases at Reception and began to walk along Buchanan Street, looking for a place to have lunch. There were not many people on the streets. Glasgow was evidently convalescing.

'We missed lunch yesterday,' said Nicol. 'A late breakfast doesn't count. Last time that happened to me was in the mid nineteen hundreds.'

'Poor arithmetic: you weren't even born then ... Nicol, we nearly died yesterday.'

'I know. Oh God, Betty, when I saw Elspeth being hurled over the cliff and then Buffy going over and you were next and I could do nothing ...'

'Stop, Nicol. We made it, all of us. We're all OK.' She squeezed his hand and smiled at him.

He did not smile back. 'Betty,' he said, 'will you marry me?'

John turned off the M6 and took the A66 towards Cockermouth. They took rooms in The Ivy House Hotel in Braithwaite. After showering and changing they relaxed by a fire in the sumptuous, red lounge over wine and canapés. In spite of the congenial atmosphere John was unusually quiet. Soraya did her best to cheer him up. Her light conversation was improving by leaps and bounds. But she soon realized that if they were to converse at all it would have to be in a serious vein.

'John, my love, don't heap it all on yourself. We were all taken by surprise.'

'I should have been more careful. Nearly got us all killed.'

'We survived. You clung on, Macho Man ... And now you're back in the saddle. Clever of you to insist we split up going to London, no matter what Peter Lipscombe says.'

Soraya looked at him apprehensively. Had she gone too far? But John simply shrugged. So she kept going. 'We'll be meeting Peter Lipscombe tomorrow, John. Tell me about him.'

John shifted his position in the deep armchair, exhaled, and roused himself. 'Peter is a legend in the Department. When he was our age he was sent to Iran to gather intelligence on the regime. He was captured and interrogated under torture. They cut off one of his fingers. He managed to escape, bringing two colleagues with him. He's probably the cleverest person I know, apart from yourself.'

Finally they were able to smile at each other.

They had an exceptionally good dinner and overnight stay, and continued their journey the next day. It should have been a wonderfully happy time, but John, reverting to critical introspection, was quiet for long periods, and Soraya, matching his silences, was deep in thought.

So it was that the eight friends in moods ranging from elation to sombreness converged two by two on the Foreign and Commonwealth Office at precisely 5 p.m. on the third of January. Peter Lipscombe was in the foyer to greet them.

'We'll do the debriefing formally in the Upper Conference Room, nice and quiet there, and then I'll have Dr Hesquith look you over.'

They were pronounced fit and well apart from cuts and bruises. 'Nothing worse than after a tough game of rugger,' Dr Hesquith said. 'You are an amazingly resilient bunch.'

'This calls for a celebration,' said Peter. 'I know just the place.'

They went in two taxis to a pub close to the London Eye. John bought the round and toasted Peter for arranging the protection that saved their lives.

'Now it's my turn to honour all of you.' Peter held up a leather case. 'I have a couple of bottles of malt whisky, Lochnagar no less, (he exaggerated the heuch) and plenty glasses. What do you say we polish it off on a ride in the Eye?'

As they walked out of the pub Soraya pulled John aside.

'Listen to me, John,' she whispered. Her compelling look gained John's instant attention. 'We are about to enter a confined space, all of us at once. Think the unthinkable. What if Peter is a sleeper or a double agent, turned when he was captured in Iran? What if it's a suicide bomb in that case?'

It took a moment but the monosyllabic answer came out. 'Right.'

John caught up with Peter and tapped him on the shoulder. 'Listen, Peter. The ladies are tired out. I'm sure you understand. We're going to have to take a rain check.'

Peter smiled. He held out his hand. 'Well done, John. I had to be sure the lesson had been learnt. You had some help, I think. Have you noticed that neither you nor Soraya is fully up to speed on your own, but together you are devastating? So do something about it, Chump.' He grinned. 'Now give me some space just in case.'

Disobeying Peter's instruction they all walked closer and huddled around him. Peter opened the case and poured out nine small measures of Scotland's finest which emptied the first bottle.

'Slange,' he said.

They all downed their drams.

'Your accent is improving,' said Roddy.

'It gets even better with the second bottle.'

Betty suggested, 'So ... All for one in the Eye?'

She linked arms with Peter and John and led the way in.

As their gondola slowly ascended to provide panoramic views of the brightly lit city Peter said, 'This calls for a proper toast.' He opened the second bottle and refilled all their glasses. 'To our next adventure.' He raised his glass in the direction of the Foreign and Commonwealth Office.

'Don't drink it,' Soraya screamed. 'It's poison.'

There was a moment of shocked silence as everyone froze. John was the first to recover. 'Soraya, how do you know this?'

'It's not proper proof, just probability. Think about it. For heaven's sake don't drink in case I'm right. Please put your glasses down.'

All of them, except Peter, bent down and placed their glasses on the floor. Elspeth and Buffy looked particularly embarrassed.

'Look here, Soraya,' Buffy said, 'surely you are over-reacting. If Peter had wanted to kill us why did he arrange for our rescue? Why did he send John to the mine and to Afghanistan?'

Peter said nothing. He just looked blankly at Soraya.

'Because,' Soraya said, 'he had to appear to be doing his job and he didn't think John would succeed at the mine. There was always a chance that John and Roddy would be killed in Afghanistan and it did not matter much if they succeeded in that mission.'

'But saving us on Ben Lawers?' Buffy persisted.

'Remember that I was to have survived. Peter saw that as a weakness. This way he could kill us all.'

John said, 'Well there's one quick way to find out if this is true. Care to drink to your toast, Peter?'

'Oh don't,' said Betty. 'Why, Peter, why?'

Peter shrugged. 'Squeamish Betty, you're not cut out to be a spy. You have to have conviction with a capital C ... I see things from their point of view. It would have been ironic if you had all died imbibing whisky. In any case decadence will soon bring your defunct civilisation to an inglorious end.' He put the glass to his lips.

'Just a minute,' said Roddy. 'How could you possibly explain it? Eight dead bodies going round and round in the Eye.'

'Nine,' said Peter. 'I'd have to die too, to remain above suspicion ... The investigation would conclude that some terrorist had sold me a poisoned bottle. It's easy to drain some of the whisky and put the poison in: a couple of holes in the stopper, a piece of label from another bottle and some glue. Did it myself … They'd have put it down to rotten luck that it took out so many of us.' He turned to John. 'You, on the other hand, have a more difficult explanation to perform. How do you explain your revered boss's dead body with no one but yourselves in close proximity? You'll have to think quickly or your credibility will be shot. We'll be down soon.' With that he drained his glass and smiled. 'Lovely taste. You should try it. Or not. Either way, I bid you goodbye.'

The poison had to have been carefully chosen. There were no symptoms for the first minute. Then pain gripped him, his pink face went red, and sweat poured down his cheeks. John and Roddy crossed the cabin to support him as he began to slide to the floor. His breathing had stopped by the time they were three quarters of the way round.

John took charge. 'Soraya and Betty, would you pour the glasses of whisky back into the bottle and repack the case? Bring it with you. Roddy, hang on to Peter's glass. When we reach the bottom we'll all walk off as if nothing major has happened. Don't want to attract a crowd. Walk in groups of two or three. Nicol and I will carry Peter between us with his arms over our shoulders. He's drunk, if anyone asks. Buffy and Elspeth, see if you can commandeer a couple of taxis. We'll go straight back to the Foreign Office.'

'All right,' Roddy said, already having Peter's glass in his hand, 'but what's the story? How do we play this?'

'We insist on a private audience with the Foreign Secretary. We tell her the truth but suggest we make Peter a hero. That's consistent with his reputation. She can decide to play it one of two ways: he died of a heart attack or as soon as he had swallowed he realized the taste was wrong and he warned us not to drink, just in time. I think she'll go for the heart attack.'

They walked off the Eye like any other tourists. Roddy kept close to his two tall friends carrying the shorter man between them.

Evidently older and wiser he pursed his lips and shook his head as he looked alternately at Peter and at the empty glass.

Back at the Foreign Office John immediately asked to see the duty officer. It was a lady whom John knew by sight only. She was in her sixties, grey haired but full of bustle. She pulled up short and turned pale when she saw Peter Lipscombe dangling between John and the other tall man. John suggested that Dr Hesquith should be recalled immediately and that the Foreign Secretary should be informed. Spurred into action, the duty officer quickly regained her composure and followed procedure. Since the records showed that all the friends had signed in earlier that evening she escorted them to the nearest conference room to await the arrival of Dr Hesquith and the Foreign Minister. She watched as John and Nicol gently laid Peter's body on the floor at the far end of the room. Then she left, closing the door behind her.

Margaret said, 'As the lawyer on our side I want to be sure I understand our position, or rather the position we are projecting. I take it we don't want to involve the police, just the Foreign Office.'

'That's right, Margaret,' said John. 'We must try to contain this. We'll tell the truth exactly – so we won't be caught contradicting one another.' He instinctively looked at Soraya, inviting her to speak.

'There's still a loose end, John,' she said. 'We have established that Peter was a sleeper or a double agent. If he was a double agent, active all the time, he must have transmitted information and received instructions frequently. The risk of being intercepted would have been enormous. But if he was a sleeper it would have taken just one signal to switch him on. That is risk free. But who controlled him? Who sent that signal?'

'Does it matter?' asked Buffy.

'I think it might ... Because unless Peter's controller knows he has been eliminated, he, the controller that is, will think he still has an ace up his sleeve and may be unwilling to concede.'

‘I think I see what you mean,’ said Roddy, ‘but aren’t you assuming that Peter’s role was a secret even within the Inner Circle, that just one person over there knew about it ... Has to be the Ayatollah, doesn’t it?’

‘I think so,’ said Soraya. ‘I hope it was not my mother.’

‘Soraya,’ said John, ‘the Ayatollah fits much better and here’s the proof. When the Inner Circle plotted to kill us, you were to be spared. When Peter was switched on, none of us was intended to survive. Your mother had no hand in that. I’m sure of it.’

The others made supportive noises until Soraya gave a weak smile of thanks.

Nicol started to say something but stopped as the door opened and Dr Hesquith came in. He was still wearing the same clothes; probably the call had intercepted him on his way home.

John led him to Peter’s body at the far end of the room.

Dr Hesquith bent down, verified that there was no pulse, and smelt Peter’s face. ‘Where and when did this happen?’ he asked.

‘In a gondola of the London Eye three-quarters of an hour ago.’

‘How was he brought here?’

‘Nicol and I carried him vertically between us,’ said John.

‘Did anyone else touch him ... after he was dead, I mean?’

‘I removed his glass from his hand,’ said Roddy. ‘There it is on the table.’

‘Right. I want a photograph of him taken just as he is. Then I’ll arrange to have him moved to pathology. I suggest the rest of you convene somewhere else while I get this organized.’

They went up to the “bull pen” on the third floor. John put on the lights. He sat at his own desk and invited the others to occupy the seats at desks around him.

‘What I was going to say,’ Nicol began, ‘if I have understood you correctly, is that ideally we want to send two messages. Firstly, we need the Inner Circle to know that their attempt to kill us failed; and secondly and separately we want the Ayatollah to know that Peter is dead.'

'Well the first is easy,' said Betty. 'The newspapers will cover the episode on Ben Lawers as a climbing accident. That information will reach the Inner Circle by, what, the end of tomorrow at the latest?'

'Right,' said John, 'but I think we need to keep the pressure up: make them dismantle the factory. Either Soraya or I should send an email saying we'll fly over in ten days' time to commence technical co-operation.'

'Let's delay the email just a little, John,' Soraya said, 'until we have worked out how to send the message to the Ayatollah that Peter's mission failed and he is dead.'

The Foreign Secretary joined them. They all stood up. She smiled briefly at Roddy and then addressed John. 'We'll do introductions in a moment but first, John, tell me what happened.'

Half an hour later, having absorbed the story and having been introduced to all the friends, the Foreign Secretary took charge. 'You have done exceptionally well.' Her smile embraced them all. 'About communications, the signal from the Ayatollah could have been anything, probably some routine report of the Ayatollah's activities: a visit to a certain place, the text of a sermon, anything at all. It would have been perfectly normal for Lipscombe to keep track of news of the Ayatollah's activities ... Now we have to let the Ayatollah know that he has lost his prize asset. Any ideas?'

'Play it the same way,' said John. 'Report it in the open media. Put Peter's glowing obituary in The Times. Nicol and I could draft it if you want it in tomorrow's paper ... I take it he died of a heart attack brought on by overwork.'

'Yes, that's good. I'll need to approve the text. Bring it to my office when you're ready. And John, look for that diary in Lipscombe's office, but I expect he shredded it.'

'Won't take a moment, Minister.' John forced open the drawer in Peter Lipscombe's desk. It was empty.

'Well, just as well you and Mr McKie read it first.' The Foreign Minister made a face. Then she brightened up. 'You know what this means, all of you. You have finally won this. We are in control. They will destroy the bomb factory.' She held out her hands to Roddy and Margaret. 'Mr and Mrs McKie, I cannot thank you enough. I'm sure we shall meet again but unless you want to stay longer and help with the drafting of the obituary you have just enough time, I think, to catch the night train.'

Roddy and Margaret shook hands with the Foreign Secretary, embraced the others, and departed.

'Now, Lord and Lady Linnhe,' the Foreign Secretary continued, 'while John and Nicol are drafting away, no doubt ably supported by their respective admirers (she smiled at Soraya and Betty), would you please come to my office. I want to hear your impressions on the political situation and how you might be able to help us in future.'

'The main impression,' Buffy said as they sipped tea seated around the Foreign Secretary's desk, 'is that the three members of the Inner Circle whom we have met truly believe that Iran has every right to own nuclear weapons. They think it inevitable that a full-scale war against Israel will break out. They think next time the Arab nations will gain the upper hand. Then they are sure Israel will not hesitate to use nuclear weapons against them unless they have them too.'

The Foreign Secretary smiled ruefully. 'If that were all, we might show some understanding. But I am afraid the temptation to go for a first strike would be too great for them to resist. We cannot trust them to handle détente.'

Elspeth joined in. 'Speaking as the one dangling deepest over the cliff I can tell you that they will not give up. We have stopped them this time – I'm sure John will verify destruction of the bomb factory

– but even while that destruction is happening they will be planning how to get back on track.'

'Well you have confirmed my fears. My difficulty, frankly, will be to persuade the Prime Minister not to gang up with President Bush to destroy all their facilities.'

'Perhaps I can help there,' Buffy said. 'I think you agree, Minister, that although full-scale destruction may be a logical response, it would plunge us headlong into another conflict with lasting and widespread ramifications. Much better for us to help the Iranians with the peaceful development of nuclear energy. Our experts will be able to keep an eye on things. In fact, the more people we can get over there making regular visits for scientific or cultural reasons, the harder it will be for their hardliners to conceal new attempts to develop nuclear weapons ... That is where I may be able to help, with unofficial contacts I mean.'

'Excellent, Lord and Lady Linnhe.' The Foreign Secretary rose and held out her hand. 'I may need your moral support after I have reported to the Prime Minister. I'm sure that in any case he will contact you to express his thanks.'

After having the obituary approved John emailed it with a recent photograph to The Times. He left a copy on the Press Officer's desk. Then at last he was able to relax. The email about technical co-operation could wait.

Nicol and Betty insisted that John and Soraya stay with them. They drove to the flat in Wandsworth.

'I've asked Betty to marry me,' said Nicol ... 'She said yes.'

This brought on embraces all round.

'No ring yet,' said Betty with mock severity.

'No time,' said Nicol ... 'Doing it tomorrow.'

Betty cast her eyes heavenwards. Then she turned to John. 'All right, Fearless Leader. Your turn.'

John looked at Soraya. She smiled back at him. Then she went over to Betty. 'I'm the hold up,' she said. 'I know we will ... We just have to work it out.'

'If anyone can, I'm sure you two will,' said Nicol.

'So cheer up,' said Betty. 'The impossible suddenly happens. Look at us.'

The next morning even the exiled Scots were back at work. John and Soraya were invited to the Foreign Minister's office to scan the newspapers with her.

'This is excellent,' the Foreign Minister said, beaming all over.

All the papers reported the climbing accident. The Sun had a lengthy piece on the dangers of Scottish mountains in winter, cataloguing deaths over the last five years. The dead climbers in this latest incident were named. They were described as experienced and well equipped.

'Well, Soraya and John, we may safely assume that this news will have reached Iran by close of play today. So first thing tomorrow you can email the President, John, offering technical assistance ... Will you need to have Roddy McKie with you?'

John shook his head. 'No. Roddy has explained very clearly what to look for. He's done more than enough already and it will minimize embarrassment if he stays away.'

'All right. Suggest arriving with Soraya on the 15th. That gives them almost two weeks to dismantle. Make sure you witness the destruction of the equipment ... The next time I see the pair of you I want to hear all kinds of good news. Now off you go and enjoy yourselves. Where to this time?'

'California,' they said in unison.

'Aha ... Time to meet the other folks is it? Excellent.'

Chapter 34

While John and Soraya were blissfully involved with John's family in San Diego the atmosphere in Tehran in the President's office could hardly have been more different. The President was apoplectic. There was no way out. He had telephoned the Ayatollah who angrily confirmed the inevitable: the factory inside the storage facility had to be dismantled and destroyed.

'I'll bring in someone competent to supervise it ... Nasher al-Jerad.' He glared first at Aisha with no thought of sensitivity. Then he growled at Saban Kandar. 'You two are finished. Get out of my office.'

A week later Saban Kandar took his Ferrari out for a spin. Tough it out; hope it blows over: that was the only sensible attitude. For old times' sake he headed south towards the beta-spodumene mine. That had so nearly worked. And it had earned him a place in the Inner Circle, not to mention the Ferrari. You can't do much better than that. He thumped the dashboard to reinforce his argument. But he knew it was false. Failure, especially on key events, would not be tolerated.

He wondered how they would engineer his death. A straightforward assassination was not their style. He would not be shot on his way to work. Bad publicity. No, they would make it look like an accident if they had any sense. Give him a good write-up ... That limited their options. It might be possible to elude them if he kept on his toes.

He was half-way to Jilabad when it happened. Ahead of him, on the right hand side of the highway, there was a quarry. He remembered passing it on previous journeys to the beta-spodumene mine. He did not remember seeing the road sign which now warned him to slow down: Vehicles Turning, it said. As he passed the quarry, doing only 60km per hour, he looked inside. There were two large lorries and a police helicopter. Standing in front of the helicopter was his colleague, The Minister for Internal Affairs. The minister did not wave. Instead, he pointedly looked upwards to his right. Kandar looked in the indicated direction. He saw three men with rifles standing on a crest overlooking a short, straight stretch of the road beyond the quarry. One of the lorries pulled out behind him, blocking his retreat.

Disappointingly unsubtle, Kandar thought. He decided to go for it. He accelerated through the gears. He heard the crack of rifle shots but neither heard nor felt any impact on the car. In less than six seconds he had run the gauntlet and was entering a left hand bend at 180km per hour. What a car! What a driver! He started to bang out a cheeky rhythm on the horn. Then he hit the oil slick. So ... Not so dumb after all. As he tried to correct the skid the car began to rotate but could not be made to round the bend. In the milliseconds before the crash into the rocks he tried to dispel fear by focusing happily on the flamboyant spectacle of his exit.

Saban Kandar's death was front page news. He was eulogized as a brilliant and dedicated servant of the State. His kindness to the scientists and engineers following their terrifying experience at the hands of maverick extremists was warmly remembered. A man of style, a loner, he had lived and died in the fast lane. The car crash that killed him had robbed the State of one of its most colourful characters.

Chapter 35

Aisha puts down her newspaper. She knows she does not have long. Well, if you live by the sword you must be ready to face the consequences. Thank Allah, Soraya has come through unscathed. She is safe for the moment. But for how long? She has clearly committed herself to the other side. She will always be in danger. It is up to John Russell to protect her now ... And what of Nasher? He knows what is coming, poor dear. He will be safe, though. They know he's wise enough to keep his own counsel; and they need his competence. Yes, Nasher will surely survive ... What of the cause? It is not totally lost. The equipment will be blown sky high but it can be replaced eventually; and the technical team can be reconstituted. New candidates for the Inner Circle will emerge. The great venture will surely continue.

Nasher and Aisha were at the airport to meet John and Soraya on the 15th. There were no embraces, just polite bows. They were political entities now, determined to keep emotions at bay. As they walked out of the terminal building Soraya looked at John. He was watching her mother. His face was relaxed, expressing a tinge of sadness, not rancour. Soraya could not match his mood. This woman, her own mother, had tried to have John killed. It was unforgivable. Soraya could not look at her. Instead she stole a look at her father. He seemed to have aged ten years. He was thinner, greyer and more haggard. How he must have suffered. She wanted to embrace him but knew that would only make matters worse.

A limousine took them directly to Facility Number One. The snow had left the city but remained on the mountains to a low level. As they walked to the front entrance they inhaled the cold air. They mounted the metal stairs just as Roddy had done and walked through the storage aisles to the balcony. The large central portion below them was empty. All that remained of the factory was a pattern of scratch marks on the polished floor.

John indicated that he was satisfied.

They re-entered the limousine and were driven some miles into the desert. It was a dull day. A fresh breeze lifted the sand in patches. No one spoke on the journey. Nasher had had the equipment laid out as it had been on the factory floor. He accompanied John on a tour of inspection. They had to shield their eyes and turn their backs on the blown sand from time to time. John was thorough. He examined every apparatus. It was all genuine.

They walked back to the others by the limousine. Nasher gave his signal. A series of explosions sent the equipment spectacularly into the air in fragments. As the smoke cleared the total destruction was apparent. They got into the limousine without comment.

On the way back, Aisha, seated beside her husband and facing Soraya and John, spoke for the first time. She had spent the last few days preparing what she would say to them after the explosions when all seemed lost. She would remain dignified and unapologetic. She would defiantly prove to John in particular that his side would lose, that the sovereign state of Iran would inevitably have its way. They just needed a few more years. But as she looked at Soraya and John and saw the quiet determination on their faces she realized that a defiant speech would amount to nothing more than bluster. The truth was that no one could predict whether or not Iran would ultimately succeed in developing nuclear weapons. It was amazing how facing imminent death made one reject unwarranted claims, forced one to focus the mind. The nuclear issue was a mere distraction in the great scheme of things.

'My dear husband and Soraya and John,' she said, 'listen to me. This is what is important. You must resolve the giant anomaly: We Muslims have the most recent truth, and it includes political truth, but yet by every worldly measurement we are, with few exceptions, at the bottom. This perceived injustice produces an unstable situation. Do not dismiss it as driven by mere envy. Our mood is much stronger. It is righteous indignation. Unless the West wants perpetual conflict it must find a way of improving our lot without hurting our pride. If there is hope, it is with people like you. I am too old to change.'

The limousine stops at the al-Jerad's house. There are no tears or embraces, just formal inclinations of the head as John and Soraya get out. They walk a few paces up the driveway and face the house to leave Nasher alone with his wife. After a few moments they hear the door shut. They turn as the limousine departs. They see Aisha, erect in her seat, looking fixedly ahead; and they wait for Nasher as he watches the limousine disappear.

Nasher joins them. There are tears in his eyes. 'We'll never see her again,' he says.

Aisha is driven in solitary grandeur to the President's Office. She reports to her President that the dismantling and destruction have been witnessed and that therefore his order has been satisfactorily completed. She bows, meets his unsmiling eyes briefly, and leaves his office closing the door softly behind her. She returns to the limousine. 'Take me to my office,' she tells the driver. On entering the building she takes a deep breath and walks purposefully up the steps to her office. There is no need to shut the door. Trying to keep her mind blank she takes her revolver from her desk drawer, holds the point against her temple, and pulls the trigger.

Chapter 36

Nasher, Soraya and John are sitting silently in the drawing room, waiting. Eventually the telephone rings in the hall. Nasher goes to answer it. He returns immediately. 'It's over,' he says, 'She's dead. I must go and make arrangements. I'll return as soon as possible.'

Soraya sits motionless trying to fathom the contradiction that was her mother. Her pain is deep and ineluctable. She stirs as John puts his arm around her shoulders. Finally she breaks down. She is shaking. His grip tightens.

'She tried to have you killed.'

'But not you, Soraya.'

'John, you would not have killed her.'

'No, but there's a difference. I was blocking her way. I had to be removed. But I had no reason to kill her unless she had her hand on the nuclear trigger. That stage had not been reached ... Don't judge her, my love. Remember the good things.'

John left her then and walked out of the house towards the centre. He needed to talk privately to Nasher. He was half-way to the Secret Police building when Nasher saw him and stopped his car.

'Get in, John. Is Soraya all right?'

'Yes. She's composing herself as best she can ... I wanted to talk to you, sir. There are so many things ... You know I love Soraya and want to marry her. She is no longer safe in Iran.'

'I know, John. Of course you have my blessing.'

Epilogue

Throughout the funeral Nasher holds John with one hand and Soraya with the other. Later, he leaves them alone in the fruit garden of his house which Aisha had loved so much. Eventually he turns to watch them through the window. He sees John go down on one knee. He turns away again, nodding his head.

John and Soraya embrace. Then they walk through the trees, holding hands and talking. In that quiet place they decide that Aisha's life has not been in vain. They know what to do with any children they might have. They will bring them up themselves, demonstrating and teaching the best of Christianity and Islam. It will be their own tribe, family and friends, living dangerously, going to the root of problems between their peoples.

'The Thirteenth Tribe,' says John, smiling into Soraya's eyes, 'the legacy of Anheim Mossada.'

***

About the author

Top Secret

Also by Ian Ramsay

Grammarwatch UK and Culture Shock: Two short stories *Kindle edition*

A Modern Christian Perspective *Kindle edition*

www.ingramcontent.com/pod-product-compliance
Ingram Content Group UK Ltd.
Pitfield, Milton Keynes, MK11 3LW, UK
UKHW012238230326
469264UK00001B/12

9 798231 384327